ALL OUR YESTERDAYS

Janet Lane Walters

Paranormal Romance

New Concepts

Georgia

Be sure to check out our website for the very best in fiction at fantastic prices!

When you visit our webpage, you can:
* Read excerpts of currently available books
* View cover art of upcoming books and current releases
* Find out more about the talented artists who capture the magic of the writer's imagination on the covers
* Order books from our backlist
* Find out the latest NCP and author news--including any upcoming book signings by your favorite NCP author
* Read author bios and reviews of our books
* Get NCP submission guidelines
* And so much more!

We offer a 20% discount on all new Trade Paperback releases ordered from our website!

Be sure to visit our webpage to find the best deals in e-books and paperbacks! To find out about our new releases as soon as they are available, please be sure to sign up for our newsletter (http://www.newconceptspublishing.com/newsletter.htm) or join our reader group (http://groups.yahoo.com/group/new_concepts_pub/join)!

The newsletter is available by double opt in only and our customer information is *never* shared!

Visit our webpage at:
www.newconceptspublishing.com

New Concepts Publishing, Inc.
5202 Humphreys Rd.
Lake Park, GA 31636

ISBN 1-58608-787-8
2005 © Janet Lane Walters
Cover art (c) copyright 2005 Eliza Black

NCP books are available at special quantity discounts for bulk purchases for sales promotions, premiums, fund raising, or educational use. For details, write, email, or phone New Concepts Publishing, Inc., 5202 Humphreys Rd., Lake Park, GA 31636; Ph. 229-257-0367, Fax 229-219-1097; orders@newconceptspublishing.com.

First NCP Trade Paperback Printing: April 2006

Janet Lane Walters

TABLE OF CONTENTS

EGYPT

In her rush to reach the ringing telephone, Astrid Logan nearly sprawled on the suitcases she'd left in the apartment hallway. She grabbed the receiver on the seventh ring. A deep voice spoke her name and her heart thudded in her chest. "Clive?" Had something happened to her father? Was there a problem at Antiquities?

"Been trying to reach you for hours. Where have you been?"

Astrid sucked in a breath. "Dad knows how to reach me at school." She sank to the floor. "What's wrong with him?"

"He's had a stroke."

"How is he?"

"Doctor believes he'll recover completely, but he'll need time in rehab."

"When did this happen and where?"

"This morning at the gallery. We were discussing the placement of several new pieces. He groaned and collapsed. Ambulance arrived maybe fifteen minutes later."

Astrid frowned. What was he holding back? Her father liked and trusted his younger assistant, but for no reason she could discover, Clive had always made her edgy. "Did they do tests?"

"CAT Scan. Then they gave him some kind of special IV. Guess this will make you change your summer plans."

"Why should it?" Clive had been her father's assistant at the gallery for a year and a half. He knew she spent every summer at Antiquities.

"Then you're really not coming."

"What are you talking about? I had planned to drive down tomorrow." Since she'd turned twelve, she'd spent every summer at the shop with her dad. In sixteen years, she knew as much about the shop as her father.

"Thought your dad said you wouldn't be here. Never mind. It's just ... I was going to move into his apartment."

"Why?"

"To keep an eye on the gallery."

Astrid frowned. That didn't make sense. The thirty-year-old playboy had an expensive co-op on the river. "Isn't there a sophisticated alarm system?"

"Alarms can be by-passed."

"Are there problems?"

"In a way. A few pieces have gone missing and your dad won't hear of calling the police."

"I see." She didn't, but once she was sure her father was recovering, she intended to check.

"When are you coming?"

"As soon as I pack the car."

"Imagine you'll arrive between five and six. I'll close the shop and meet you at the hospital."

"No need. I have keys. After I check on Dad, I'll stop by the gallery." She hung up and started to call the hospital. Why? It would be a futile gesture. They would merely confirm her father was a patient, but they wouldn't disclose the information she wanted.

She made a quick check of the nearly empty apartment. Her furniture was in storage until she found a place closer to the university where she would begin a graduate program in September.

Twenty minutes later, she'd packed the car. On the way out of town, she dropped the keys at the real estate agency and began the four-hour trip to Rockleigh, the Hudson River village where her father lived.

During the drive, she tried not to think about her father. If she didn't dwell on her fears, they wouldn't come true. Think positive, she told herself. She recalled her father's excitement over the changes he and Clive had made at Antiquities and the enthusiasm over a new customer.

What would happen to the gallery if he wasn't there? Though the shop contained some valuable items, expenses for taxes, insurance and new stock often found him strapped for cash. The changes he'd made in the gallery had been expensive. When she'd questioned the wisdom of the move, he'd laughed and said he would manage. Could he now? She gripped the wheel and shifted mental gears.

* * * *

Astrid parked in the hospital lot and stopped at the information desk. With a visitor's pass in hand, she went to the third floor and found her father's room. The odors, the moans and cries, the bustle of activity made her feel as though she'd entered an alien land. Her job as a school nurse held none of these scenes. She paused in the doorway of the semi-private room. One bed was empty. Her father lay in the window bed.

For a moment, she stared. How had he aged so much since the last time she'd seen him? Easter had been just two and a half months ago. During their weekly phone calls, he'd sounded the way he always had. She approached the bed, checked the intravenous site and the rate and looked at the oxygen meter on the wall. Seemed fine.

"Dad."

He opened his eyes and tried to smile. She took his hand. He spoke, but the words were so garbled she couldn't decipher them. Tears threatened. She swallowed against the lump in her throat.

"Don't worry about Antiquities. I'll keep Clive in line. I'll have the records in order by the time you're back."

Her words seemed to give him peace. The lines around his mouth relaxed. Until the urge to cry grew too strong, she remained. "I'm going to the apartment, then the gallery. I'll be back this evening."

He mouthed a word.

"Good?" she asked.

He nodded.

Outside the room, she pulled a tissue from her bag and wiped her eyes. At the nurses' desk, she paused. "I'm Mr. Logan's daughter. How is he?"

A gray-haired woman looked up. "He's stable and responding to treatment. We were able to start things within hours after the stroke."

Astrid cleared her throat. "I'm a nurse." She asked a series of questions about the prognosis and course of treatment.

"You'll have to speak to his doctor."

"Who is?"

The nurse gave Astrid a name and phone number. "Thanks."

After paying the parking fee, she drove to Antiquities and pulled onto the paved area behind the building. As she took two suitcases from the trunk, Mrs. Rayson, her father's tenant and long-time friend, stepped onto the deck. "Astrid. I'm so glad you're here. That Clive said you weren't coming this summer."

"He misunderstood Dad. Probably confused my decision to resign my position at the school and go to grad school with my summer plans. You know how Dad sometimes carries on two discussions at once."

Mrs. Rayson laughed. "How true. What happened to Lloyd this morning was dreadful. I was so scared."

"Were you there?"

The older woman nodded. "Heard him arguing with Clive so I stepped in. Saw Lloyd collapse. Called 911. That Clive just stood and stared."

"Shock." Astrid started up the steps. Would Clive have called an ambulance? She chewed on her lower lip. She couldn't let her distrust of the man color her opinions.

"How is Lloyd? I wanted to visit, but wasn't sure if he was in Intensive Care or a regular room."

"I stopped by on my way here." Astrid sighed. "He looked so old and fragile."

Sarah Rayson hugged Astrid. "He'll be fine."

"Aunt Sarah, I'll take that as a prophecy. Let me unload the car. Then I need to check the gallery."

"Come to dinner. Around six."

"I'd like that. We can go see Dad together."

Astrid opened the door and stepped into the apartment's main room. She turned on the air conditioner. The large picture window showed a view of the river. Breakfast dishes were still on the counter that divided the kitchen from the rest of the room. Stacks of books covered the couch, chairs and coffee table.

A groan escaped. Not only would she have to organize the gallery records, she'd have to make order here. She carried the suitcases to the small bedroom she used when she visited. At least the clutter hadn't invaded her space. After several trips to the car, she stepped into the bathroom and splashed cold water on her face.

What had caused Dad and Clive to quarrel? They seldom disagreed. Would Clive tell her?

* * * *

When she entered Antiquities, she turned a full circle. The usual disorganized appearance had vanished. The enormous room was now broken into small areas. Dividers of wood and glass separated the displays.

"Astrid."

Clive strode toward her. The tall, blond man moved with a predatory grace. He looked like the Viking hero some of her acquaintances had dubbed him. He was handsome, but the coldness of his blue eyes made her wary. "Hello, Clive."

"You made good time. Have you seen your dad?"

"I stopped at the hospital." A sigh escaped. "I can't believe he had a stroke. He's always been so healthy."

Clive clasped her hands. "He's tough. Before long, he'll be back cluttering the place."

"Hope not. You've achieved wonders here." She tried to free her hands. He tugged her closer. "The apartment looks like a magpie's nest."

"Good description." He brushed her lips with his.

Astrid shook her head. She wanted to wipe her mouth. Would he start another pursuit this summer? "Let's stick to business. I like the arrangement of the stock."

"A suggestion from a new customer. Rich playboy type, but he has good taste. Garrett and your dad connected. Act like they've known each other for ages."

She crossed her arms on her chest. "Why were you and Dad arguing?"

He groaned. "Guess you talked to nosy Sarah. Was more like a heated discussion about displaying two new pieces he recently found. Bought this sealed box at a sale. Odd assortment."

"How odd?"

He laughed. "Nothing bad. Mostly a collection of Victorian jewelry and these two pieces. He wanted to research them before they were offered for sale. I wanted to price them immediately. You know how hard it is to date the things we acquire."

She nodded. "So where are they?"

"Most of the jewelry is in the vault and I can't get to them."

"I--" She cut off her response. She knew the code for the vault and would see what he meant in the morning.

He took her arm. "I'll show you the two pieces I kept out and introduce you to Paula Winters. She's photographing a number of our best pieces for a catalogue we're launching."

"Another suggestion from Dad's new friend?"

"In a way." He entered the Egyptian area. "Astrid, Paula Winters. Astrid is Lloyd's daughter. She's here for the summer, then it's back upstate."

Astrid didn't contradict him. Her plans weren't his business.

The woman turned. "Teacher?" She gazed at Clive.

"School nurse." Astrid read admiration in Paula's eyes. Did Clive return the interest? He usually went for petite and curvy. Paula was slim, almost boyish. The blunt cut of her shoulder-length auburn hair reminded Astrid of styles she'd seen on ancient Egyptian women.

Paula's crooked grin warmed Astrid. "Glad to finally meet you. Your dad talks a lot about you."

"Don't believe everything he's said. What are you photographing today?" Astrid asked.

"Starting with the Egyptian collection. The new pieces are stunning. Clive thinks it's a good idea to have a visual record of the things in the shop."

Astrid turned to Clive. "Then there is a problem."

"I told you several pieces were missing."

"Thieves?"

"I hope not, but this has been going on since right after Easter."

Astrid frowned. Why hadn't Dad mentioned the problem? Had he reported the missing pieces to the insurance company? Or had he feared the premiums would increase too greatly? She edged toward the stand where a necklace and crown were displayed on a black velvet cloth. Where had she seen these pieces before? The necklace resembled a wide collar. Semi-circles of a pale gold metal were inlaid with lapis. Carnelians dangled from the last row. The headband of the same metal had flowers of inlaid lapis with carnelian centers.

"Are these the items you and Dad argued about?"

Clive nodded. "He wanted to put them in the vault."

"Why have you displayed them?"

"One, I can't open the vault and two, they're too attractive to hide."

Astrid brushed a finger over one of the dangles. Sadness washed over her. As though under a spell, she lifted the necklace. Waves of dizziness rocked her.

* * * *

Seshat stood at the entrance to her workroom built against the wall of the villa. She stared into the garden. Though chaos ruled the Two Lands, in this house at a distance from Thebes, only echoes of the troubles were heard. How fortunate that her father, Nomarch Sehetep, had distanced himself from the politics of both halves of the divided land.

She heard her younger sister giggle and watched her run toward the workroom. "What have you done now?"

"Spied on Father," Tiy said.

Seshat shook her head. Tiy hovered between childhood and womanhood. She delighted in mischief. Seshat left the doorway and reached for the tallies of the recent harvest.

"Don't you want to know what I heard and what I saw?" Tiy's warm brown eyes sparkled with mischief.

"Tell me."

"We have guests. From Thebes. Oh, Seshat, they are the most handsome men I have ever seen. They seek father's support. One of them wants the Double Crown. Maybe he will choose you as his wife and ignore Nefru."

Seshat sighed. If she were chosen, Nefru, daughter of their father's dead first wife, would be furious. Though Seshat's mother had been a princess of a past dynasty, Nefru denied the claim. Seshat sighed again. Anyone seeking Sehetep's support would choose the oldest daughter. Since no sons had been born to the house, Nefru's spouse would claim the nome when Sehetep left this world.

"We're to eat the evening meal with them," Tiy said. "Nefru stamped her foot when she heard. When these men see you, they won't look at her."

Seshat shook her head. That would bring spiteful attacks from her sister. Besides, Seshat had no desire to leave her father. Wasn't she his right hand and his star to comfort his last days? She lifted a quill and began to record the number of baskets of harvested grain.

Before she finished the tally, Bastet, her aging maidservant, entered. "Come, child. You must make ready for the evening."

Seshat put her quill and papyrus aside and followed Bastet to the bathing room. After washing, her skin was rubbed with scented oil. Bastet combed and braided her hair. Not for Seshat the shaved head and the hot, heavy wig. The maid applied kohl to make Seshat's gray eyes appear more luminous and darker.

"What will you wear?" Bastet asked. "These men have come from Thebes. You don't want to appear a country girl."

Seshat chose a robe of fine linen that covered her body from beneath her breasts to her ankles. The broad straps formed a vee as they crossed her shoulders. For jewelry, she selected the necklace her mother had left her. The electrum semi-circles of the collar were inlaid with lapis. Carnelians dangled above her bare breasts.

"Will you wear the crown?"

Seshat shook her head. She was sure Nefru would wear her finest linen tunic and adorn herself with jewels. Her wig would be ornamented as well. *A subtle touch is best*, Seshat thought.

She and Tiy entered the large hall where their father, sister and the guests waited. Sehetep smiled. "Daughters, come and meet our visitors. Seshat, how like your mother you look. She was the loveliest flower in my garden. You are indeed the star to delight my last days."

Nefru's lips thinned. She glared. Rings glittered on her fingers. Her armbands were studded with gems. The nipples of her heavy breasts had been colored with henna.

Seshat ignored her sister's displeasure. She kept her eyelids lowered as her father drew her toward the guests. "Mermeshu, Commander of the Army, and Intef, his advisor, my daughters, Seshat and Tiy."

Seshat glanced at the men. Both wore kilts and tunics. A jeweled pectoral hung on gold chains about his neck, covered his chest and gleamed against the pale linen of Mermeshu's tunic. The men were taller than her father. Mermeshu had the arms and shoulders of an archer. Though of slighter build, Intef seemed fit. She shuddered. His eyes had the coldness of a serpent.

Mermeshu's dark eyes captured her gaze. As though to see her better, he smiled and stepped back. Her skin felt hot. A throbbing low in her belly brought an urge to touch and be touched by him. Her nipples tightened. His smile broadened.

In that instant, Seshat knew she would desire this man for all eternity. *Hathor, goddess of love, bring him to my side. Fill him with desire for only me. Let him see my beauty and my grace. Bring him to me.*

Nefru clapped her hands. The serving maids set the individual tables before Sehetep's chair and the stools for the others. Since this was the main meal of the day, course followed course. Beef, lamb and goose were served with lentils, carrots and spinach. Wine and beer were lavishly offered. The meal ended with melons, figs and dates. Though Seshat ate, she tasted nothing.

Mermeshu and Intef spoke of the Hyksos who controlled the north and of the troubles in the south. Many men competed for the Double Crown, but only one could wear it. Mermeshu had come to ask for men, supplies and coins. He believed with the army's backing, he could win the crown and drive the usurpers from the land.

Bits of conversation entered Seshat's awareness. For twenty years, the land had been torn asunder by men who wished to be pharaoh. Then came the Hyksos with their chariots and armies. Only a united Egypt could repel them.

Seshat had no care for tales of war or warnings of battles to come. Her body thrummed with a desire she didn't fully understand.

When the meal ended, Nefru signaled the slaves to remove the tables. "Mermeshu and Intef, would you like to stroll in the gardens?"

The men rose to follow her. Seshat paused beside her father's chair. "Do you wish me to play the harp?" Though she wanted to join the others, her first duty was to him.

"Go to the garden." He patted her cheek. "Star of my last days, you have your mother's heart."

Seshat kissed him on the forehead and strolled into the garden. Nefru walked with a hand on each man's arm. Tiy was nowhere to be seen. Had Nefru sent her away? The trio paused beside the pool.

"Alas, my father has no sons or male kindred," Nefru said. "The husband I choose will be fortunate. All this will be his."

"And your sisters?" Mermeshu asked. "Have they no share in your father's wealth?"

Nefru snorted. "Daughters of concubines have no

standing. They will be grateful for what I give them."

Intef laughed. "Don't you mean what your husband gives them?"

Nefru smiled. "He will be so entranced with me, he will do as I wish."

Seshat joined them. Anger sizzled through her veins. "Nefru, you can insult me but not my mother. She was wife to our father, duly witnessed in the temple."

Nefru giggled. "I'd forgotten. She was only second wife and brought nothing of value to the marriage."

"She was a princess."

"So she said."

Seshat bit her lip. Quarreling with Nefru before their guests was in poor taste. She looked up. Mermeshu grinned. Heat seared her core. He stepped away from Nefru and took Seshat's arm.

"Come and enjoy the beauty of the garden," he said. "The night and the company are too lovely for heated words. Your father said the garden was your realm."

"And the fields and herds," Nefru said. "She acts like she's our father's son."

"And for that reason, I must leave," Seshat said. "'Tis harvest time and I have much to do."

Mermeshu leaned toward her. "Pleasant dreams." He lightly caressed her arm.

* * * *

As Seshat walked away, Mermeshu watched the graceful sway of her hips. He had to possess her. Though Intef had spoken of the advantages of a marriage to the nomarch's daughter by his first wife, Mermeshu had no desire for Nefru. He'd seen the courtesy Seshat had shown her father. Unlike Nefru, Seshat had lingered to make sure of her father's comfort. She was sweet and dutiful, yet there was a banked fire in her eyes. He wanted to be the one to stir the embers into flames.

She had none of Nefru's boldness. The way the older sister ogled made him feel like a slave on the block. He believed he could take Nefru in the garden, then watch while Intef enjoyed her lush body.

"The day has been long." He yawned. "I'll see you both in the morning." He strode back to the house. Let Intef have Nefru. His friend had a liking for short women with rounded hips and melon breasts.

* * * *

Mermeshu was awakened by Intef. "My friend, you missed an enlightening time. You'll have no trouble claiming Nefru."

Mermeshu eyed his friend's rumpled kilt. "Seems she prefers you."

Intef laughed. "She likes men. All she spoke of was you."

"And you encouraged her."

"What else can I do?"

"Marry her and try for the Double Crown."

Intef shook his head. "I could, but I'm a practical lam. You have the army behind you. I'll be content to be your vizier."

How often had they discussed this plan? Their schemes were nearing completion, but he no longer desired to see them reach fruition. "I...."

Intef nodded. "Desire the beautiful Seshat. Fear not, you can have them both. Once Nefru gives you a son, you need not spend time with her."

Mermeshu nodded. He wasn't certain he wanted any woman but Seshat.

"Let me think about this new direction. We came for Sehetep's support, not the daughters. We should see what he offers before I go any further with a courtship of Nefru."

Intef clapped Mermeshu's shoulder. "You must do what is best for the Two Lands."

* * * *

When her father led Mermeshu into the room where she kept the tallies, Seshat's breath caught. His fingers brushed her hand and her breasts felt heavy. His eyes caressed her body. Her heart fluttered like the wings of a bird in flight. Heat pooled in her belly.

"Show Mermeshu the tallies for the fields, flocks and herds," Sehetep said. "Intef and I will examine the warriors of the nome."

Once her father left, she wanted to run after him and she wanted to feel Mermeshu's arms around her. Today he wore no tunic. She stared at his tanned muscular chest and wondered if his body was as hard as it appeared. She inhaled his scent, a musky odor that tantalized. She handed him several scrolls. "These are the latest accounts."

He ran a finger over the back of her hand. She sucked in a breath. How could such a light touch make so many exciting changes in her body? He began to read. She walked toward the door.

"Don't go. I may have some questions."

Seshat went to the chest where the papyrus was stored. She studied his broad shoulders and the way his muscles moved as he read.

He finished the last of the tallies and stood. A wave of disappointment swept over her. "Have you no questions?"

He stepped behind her and caressed her shoulders. "I have two." He slid his hands across her shoulders and cupped her breasts. She moaned. "Do you feel what pulses between us?"

"Yes."

"Will you come to the garden after moonrise to meet me?" He moved a hand to stroke her abdomen.

The sensations storming her body stole her breath. She sighed and leaned against him.

"Seshat, be my star tonight."

"I will come."

He pressed her against his groin. She felt his body change. "Oh."

"'Tis my desire you feel. Tonight you will know the power of my love." He brushed his lips over her shoulders. "Tonight."

Seshat sank on her stool. She felt feverish. She hovered at the edge of a discovery that excited and scared her. She gulped water and gathered her wandering wits. As she stored the scrolls, she rubbed the ones he'd touched over her lips. The scent of him lingered and filled her with longing.

Thanks be to Hathor. He wants me. He holds my heart in his warrior hands. She prayed he wouldn't crush it. *May he spend the day with thoughts of me.* Tonight, she thought and returned to her work.

* * * *

When she reached her sleeping room, she found Tiy pacing. "What's wrong, little sister?"

"That Nefru."

"What has she done?"

"Banished me from taking the evening meal in the large

hall. Just because Intef smiled and remarked on my skill with a bow. Since I don't behave like a lady, I must eat in the small hall. Then, when she heard Father had left Mermeshu with you, she spat like an angry cat."

Seshat shook her head. "I fear Nefru desires a life of unhappiness."

Tiy sat on Seshat's sleeping couch. "What did Mermeshu do? What did he say?"

"He examined the harvest tallies." She would keep his words and caresses secret.

"That's all? I saw the hungry look in his eyes last night. He left the garden soon after you. I hid in the bushes and watched Nefru and Intef. She rubbed his body and kissed his man thing. Put it in her mouth. He made funny noises. Then he acted like a babe and suckled her breasts. He pulled her robe up and did things to her private parts. She moaned and cried for Mermeshu."

Seshat grasped Tiy's arms. "You shouldn't spy." She walked to the door. Tiy followed her to the bathing room where they paused in the doorway. "I'll eat the evening meal with you."

"And miss being with the guests?" Tiy asked.

To spend the lengthy meal time in Mermeshu's presence might make her

betray herself. "They have come to see Father. After we eat, I'll help you with the harp." Seshat covered her mouth with her hand for she hadn't seen Nefru.

"Good." Nefru rose from the couch where her maid had oiled her body. "An important decision should be reached this evening." Her sly cat's smile didn't hide the hatred in her eyes. "When Father dies, Seshat, beware your fate. You have no kin to protect you. Tiy will be my handmaiden. You will be my slave." She caressed her breasts. "Mermeshu will be mine. Intef said the Commander of the Army finds me most pleasing."

Seshat turned away. Nefru was clever at finding ways to gain her desires. Would she steal Mermeshu's love?

* * * *

Mermeshu wished the evening meal would end. Dish after dish was offered. Where was Seshat? Would she be at the pool or had she changed her mind? Surely, he hadn't misunderstood her response to his touch. Just thinking about her made his groin tighten and his erection pulse.

Sehetep leaned back in his chair. Tonight, Mermeshu sat in the seat usually taken by the first wife. The nomarch clapped his hands. "Nefru, since Seshat is ailing, play the harp while I discuss what I will give these men and what I expect from them."

The rippling notes formed a background for the discussion. Mermeshu focused his attention on the older man's offer. Though a marriage wasn't mentioned, was this the string attached to such generosity?

When the older man rose, Nefru suggested a garden walk. Mermeshu shook his head. "I have much to consider. I'll see you tomorrow."

She rose. Light from the torches shone through the sheer linen of her dress. Mermeshu tensed. Was Nefru the bait Sehetep dangled? She was too willing to be seduced. As she glided away, her rounded buttocks moved in a sensual dance. He groaned. Slim women were to his taste. He also preferred women who enjoyed being chased and captured, not those who pursued.

Intef followed him to the doorway. "Soon she will be yours. Why not sample her bounty?"

"Since you're so entranced with her charms, make her yours. Keep her amused tonight. Take her to your room."

"She will only toy with me for she wants the Commander of the Army. She wishes to become a pharaoh's wife. Take care. The spite of a rejected woman can be as poisonous as the bite of an asp."

Though Intef was right, Mermeshu only wanted Seshat. Nefru repelled him. He wiped his hands on his kilt. Tonight, he would bind Seshat with cords of love. Once she was enmeshed in the web, if he had to do take Nefru as his wife, a love-caught Seshat would willingly enter his woman's court.

He glanced into the garden and saw the moon had risen. "Go to Nefru. We'll talk in the morning." He strode to his sleeping room and removed his kilt and pectoral. After sponging his body, he strode to the garden.

As he neared the pool, alert for alien noises, he listened to the sounds of the night. He saw Seshat. His erection pulsed against his loin cloth. He wanted to seize and toss her to the ground, then thrust into her woman's passage. He gulped deep breaths. This was not the time for haste. By her presence, he knew she was his.

* * * *

Seshat heard a sound and looked around. Mermeshu stepped into view. Her body hummed with the desires he'd stirred that morning. She plucked one of the lotus blossoms and offered the flower to him.

He took the bloom, kissed each petal and brushed the blossom over her lips. Her gaze locked with his. The soft petals caressed her breasts.

"You are as lovely as the Evening Star," he said. "You have captured my heart."

"You are a hawk of Horus. You warm me like the blazing sun."

He placed the flower on the water and gathered her into his arms. His tongue touched her lips. "You taste of wine and honey. Your scent is sweet and heady. I would feast on your bounty."

She stared into his eyes. "Warrior, your arms are metal bands holding a prisoner who has no desire to escape."

He nibbled on her lips. His tongue explored the seam of her mouth. He grasped her hips and pressed her against his engorged shaft. The hardness of his body made her shiver in anticipation of what was to come and of the passion she had never tasted. Her lips parted. His tongue slid into her mouth and moved with a rhythm her body captured.

She met him thrust for thrust. Her hands moved along his arms and circled his shoulders. Seeking, wanting, she pressed closer. Her nipples brushed the skin of his chest. He inched the skirt of her tunic up. Cool air brushed her legs, then her buttocks. The heat rising from his hands as they caressed her flesh sent flames along her skin.

He drew back. She reached for him. "Don't leave me."

"Not this night. Seshat, my star, we must find a better place. I won't take you on the ground."

She returned to his arms. "Come to my room."

He rained kisses on her face. "What about your sisters and your maid?"

"Bastet sleeps in her wall chamber. My room is far from those of my sisters. Don't you want me? I am new to love or I would have found a better place for us to meet."

He grasped her hand and pressed her fingers against his

loincloth. "Feel how much I desire you."

She stroked his male organ through the cloth and knew what would happen. He would cover her the way the bull covered the cows.

He groaned and the sound delighted her. She raised her head and touched his lips with hers. His arms tightened and she moved. He growled. "Show me to your room before I have you here."

Hand in hand, they returned to the house and made their way to her sleeping chamber. A single lamp cast pale light. He loosened the straps of her tunic and slid the cloth over her hips. His hands stroked her body. His teeth nipped her mouth.

She unfastened his loincloth and touched the head of his engorged penis. She closed her hand over the shaft and stroked his sac. Should she take him into her mouth the way Tiy had seen Nefru take Intef? His breath came in rapid gasps. "Not yet, my star. Let me show you passion."

Mermeshu lifted her. He laid her on the sleeping couch. "Bend your knees so I can kneel between your thighs. When she did, he stroked the inner surface. He leaned forward and ran his lips over her forehead to her mouth. He nibbled on her lips and sucked her tongue.

She reached to draw him closer. As a storm of sensations swept over her, she cried her desire. "Mermeshu, cover me as the bull covers the cow."

He raised his head. "In time, but first, let me worship your body."

His words, the feel of his flesh against hers made her yearn to be one with him. To be loved was wonderful. To be worshipped brought sensations she'd never known and wished would last forever.

His lips moved from her mouth. He nuzzled her neck and ran his tongue over her throat. When he drew one nipple into his mouth, she moved restlessly beneath him. Soft cries poured from her mouth. He took her other breast between his lips. When he suckled, he rolled the other nipple between his fingers.

Something exploded inside her. As exquisite pleasure filled her, she pressed her hand against her mouth to keep from screaming. Somehow, the effort to hold back her cries intensified the moment.

Mermeshu continued his assault on her body. His tongue circled her navel, then flicked inside. He moved closer to the place that pulsed, the place she had rubbed to bring pleasure. She spread her legs wider and raised her head to watch. When his tongue licked, she fell back and allowed the fire to consume her.

She felt his fingers probe. "Please, please," she whispered. She lifted her legs and rested them on his shoulders. He raised her hips, sucked and stroked.

Her body began to move. He lowered her and thrust inside. She gasped. His mouth covered hers and caught her cries. The instant of pain faded. She savored the feeling of fullness. He moved, slowly at first and then with a frenzied tempo. She moved with him.

She felt as though a fountain of steam built inside and was about to tear her body apart. He kept his mouth sealed over hers. She erupted. Her muscles contracted and he spewed his seed. He rolled to his side and pulled her into a tight embrace.

Once her breathing slowed, she kissed his chin, his cheeks, his mouth. "Mermeshu, my warrior, I love you."

"And I love you, my evening star." He stroked her back and drew away. "I would love you again, but 'tis too soon for one newly come to the pleasures. Let me leave before I fall asleep and am discovered here."

"Will you return tomorrow?"

"Yes." He sat on the edge of the couch.

She knelt and put her arms around him. "Tomorrow night let me come to your room. 'Tis a place where we can cry our pleasure without fear of anyone but your friend hearing."

"I'll see he's elsewhere. During the day, Intef and I will be with your father arranging for men and supplies to be sent to Thebes." He rose and pulled her to her feet and into his arms. His kiss made her wish he would stay.

"Until the moon has risen once more and I am in your arms," she said.

Once he left, Seshat returned to the couch. She inhaled the aroma of him and of their lovemaking. When she saw the splotch of blood on the cover, her eyes widened. She couldn't let Bastet see. The maid would know what had happened and she would go to Sehetep. Seshat removed the cloth and buried it in the laundry that awaited the slaves. What she and Mermeshu had done felt so right, but she wanted to hold the secret close. If her father learned, he might be angry and turn against the man she loved.

* * * *

The day seemed endless to Mermeshu. He couldn't believe he'd been trapped by the threads of the web he'd meant to weave around Seshat. Today's events had pleased Intef. Fifty men had been sent to Thebes along with several barges of grain and other foodstuffs. Cattle, sheep and goats were being herded to the city.

Mermeshu reached the large hall and searched for Seshat. Nefru was the only one of Sehetep's daughters present. Mermeshu sensed the jaws of a lion open before him.

Nefru glided toward him. "Will you walk with me tonight?"

He shrugged. "Your father and I have much to discuss."

She turned to Intef. "Will you bury yourself with these boring matters as well?"

Intef grinned. His hand slid along her arm. One finger touched her breast. "I prefer the garden, or perhaps elsewhere. There are things you and I must decide."

She laughed. "So there are."

Mermeshu studied the murals on the wall. Could he avoid Nerfu without causing her to turn her spite on her sister?

Sehetep entered the room. He held a number of scrolls. "Mermeshu, after the meal, I would like to review these with you. Then we will sign our alliance."

"I'm at your service, Nomarch."

Nefru tapped her foot on the floor. "Father, why must you talk business tonight? I want to spend time with our guests. The moon is full and the sky clear."

"We leave in the morning," Mermeshu said. "We have been gone from Thebes long enough for one or more of my rivals to attempt to undermine my standing with the army."

"When you finish your business with my father, I expect you to join us."

The demanding tone of her voice irritated Mermeshu. "I do not take orders kindly."

Her giggle rasped over his skin. Once they finished the meal, Nefru and Intef rose. She paused behind Mermeshu and brushed her nipples against his back. "You will be sorry if you don't join us."

Mermeshu held back an angry response. The lion's jaws were about to snap shut.

Sehetep chuckled. "Nefru needs a strong man, one she can't turn into a house cat."

"A man would be fortunate to take one of your daughters as his wife." Though he wanted to ask for Seshat, the time wasn't right.

"Such a union may be necessary, but enough about my daughters. We will talk strategy. I have long observed the scene in Thebes through my spies. When you return, seek these men." He named several. "They will tell you much."

The moon had risen and moved along its path by the time Mermeshu made his way to his sleeping room. Would Seshat be there? Would she think he wasn't coming? He glanced into Intef's room and saw his friend hadn't returned. Mermeshu smiled and hoped Nefru would entertain his friend all night.

As he stepped into his room, he caught the scent of Seshat's perfume. He whispered her name.

"I am here." She lit another lamp. In the flickering light, he saw she was nude. He started to remove his kilt.

"Beloved, let me serve you." As she lifted the pectoral over his head, she ran her hands over his chest. Then, she bent and teased his nipples with her tongue.

Twin bolts of lightning shot to his groin. He groaned. "Seshat, I must have you now."

She touched her lips to his. He crushed her against his chest and seized her mouth in a fierce kiss. How could he bear to leave her? If only he could take her with him.

She slid her hands between them and unfastened his kilt. When she removed his loincloth, she ran her hands over his thighs and erection. As need threatened to erupt, he shuddered. He stepped back and gulped great breaths of air.

"Sit on the couch so I can remove your sandals. I would worship you as you did me last night."

He wasn't sure he could wait that long before embedding his spear in her sheath. "My evening star, you are my dream of perfection. I desire you with every breath." He pulled her close and stroked her face. "In the morning, I must return to Thebes. Once I have the Double Crown, I'll return and claim you as my wife."

She smiled. "I'll give you strong sons and beautiful daughters. Once we are wed, through my mother's line, you can claim the throne. Let us spend this night affirming our love."

Mermeshu sat on the sleeping mat. Could he believe what she said about her mother or were Nefru's tales the truth? Sehetep had said nothing about the connection to a past dynasty. If her mother had been a princess, why hadn't the nomarch taken the Double Crown?

Seshat knelt and removed his sandals. Her hands slid along his calves. She kissed his knees. Mermeshu leaned back on his elbows. Her hands glided along his inner thighs. The magic of her touch made him harder than before.

She flicked her tongue from one thigh to the other. He clenched his fists to keep from grabbing her. Spears of flame engorged his penis. Her fingers stroked his scrotum. She ran a nail along the length of his erection. When she captured his shaft in her hands and ran her tongue over the head, he growled. The sound rose from his depths.

She leaned over him and rubbed her nipples over the head of his shaft. She pressed his penis between her breasts and moved her body. "Seshat, come to me. Let me take you."

Her answer was to draw him into her mouth. As she licked and sucked, she stroked his abdomen and chest. He fisted his hands against the couch and strained to keep from spilling his seed.

She raised her head and knelt with her knees on either side of his hips. As she leaned forward to lave his chest, he felt her wetness brush his erection. He strained to enter her. Her mouth reached his and as her tongue slid into his mouth, she slowly sheathed his shaft.

He pressed his feet against the floor and grasped her buttocks. He slid one hand between them and stroked. She released his mouth and arched back. She rocked and slid.

"Mermeshu," she cried.

When her sheath convulsed around him, he thrust once and erupted. "Seshat, Seshat." He pulled her down and kissed her. As his tongue thrust and parried with hers, he felt his spear swell. Carefully, he shifted position until she lay beneath him. This time, their lovemaking was slow. After she peaked, he held her in his arms.

As he drifted to sleep, he knew he wanted her beside him for all his days. Once he held the Double Crown, he would ask Sehetep to bless this union.

When he woke, she was gone. He washed and dressed. When he saw one of his pectorals was missing, he frowned. Had Seshat taken it for remembrance? As he and Intef reached the gate, he looked for her. Of the daughters of the household, only Nefru was present. He saw her sly smile and Intef's grin. What did it mean?

* * * *

Seshat spent the next two lunars in a euphoric state. She had found her love and he would return to claim her. As she went about her duties, Mermeshu was ever in her thoughts. The room where she did the accounts and the one where he'd slept became places of refuge and memories. His promise was a constant echo in her thoughts.

The days were well into the third lunar since his departure. Tiy burst into Seshat's sleeping chamber. "You won't believe what Nefru told Father."

"Are you in trouble again?"

"No. She says she carried Mermeshu's child. Father said she must marry him."

Seshat sucked in a breath. Why would Nefru lie? If she was with child, surely, the father was Intef. "When did she say this happened?"

"She claims he came to her room the night before they left."

Seshat sighed with relief. "She lies."

"How would you know?"

"He was with me. We were in his room."

Tiy gasped. "But I heard her call his name. And he shouted hers."

"Are you sure the voice was his? Intef was with her."

"Oh, Seshat, what will you do? She has a cloth with her virgin's blood and one of his pectorals."

Seshat sank on the edge of the couch. She had buried her cover in the laundry. She had taken nothing from his room. How could she prove he'd been with her, not her sister?

"Father sent a message to Thebes. He demands a marriage. He and Nefru are making ready to journey to the city. We're staying here."

Seshat covered her face with her hands. What could she

do? Surely Mermeshu would tell the truth. But he seeks the Double Crown and sees Father's help as necessary. Will Mermeshu speak of what happened and risk losing that support? Will ambition or love win?

* * * *

Mermeshu stared at the words on the papyrus. He turned to Intef. "How can she say I came to her? How can she claim she carries my child?"

"Who?"

"Nefru." Intef's grin angered Mermeshu. "Have you an explanation?"

"Her room was dark. She mistook me for the man she wanted. She cried your name and I didn't correct her. She is lusty and inventive. Three times, she brought me to paradise. You'll have no complaints when you bed her."

"And if she's with child, the babe won't be mine."

"There are ways to rid her of the child."

Mermeshu held his anger inside. "You know where I was on those nights. Why have you betrayed me?"

Intef frowned. "What you see as a betrayal is anything but. To have Seshat, you must first take Nefru as your wife. Nomarch Sehetep wants a strong man for her. I told him you were strong."

"I pledged my heart to Seshat. She is the first woman to capture my love."

"Would you give up the Double Crown?" Intef grasped Mermeshu's arms. "Would you lose Sehetep's support? You can have them both. Take Nefru as your first wife and Seshat as your second. Will you toss our plans aside?"

Mermeshu turned away from his friend. What choice did he have? Of those vying for the Double Crown, he had the best chance of leading the army to defeat the Hyksos. With Sehetep's wealth behind him, he could achieve honor and glory. "I'll leave today to speak to Sehetep."

Intef walked to the door. "No need. He and Nefru are on their way here."

"And Seshat?"

"Her name wasn't mentioned. I'll prepare a feast of welcome and arrange for the priests to bless your union. The eyes of your rivals will gleam with envy."

And what of Seshat's eyes? Would they show anger or hatred?

* * * *

On the morning after her father and sister departed for Thebes, Seshat knew she was with child. She sent a messenger to Mermeshu. Weeks later, her answer came, not from him but from Intef. The priests had blessed the union of Mermeshu and Nefru. Seshat slashed the papyrus to shreds. Her anger was so great she couldn't cry.

During the fifth lunar of her pregnancy, news of her father's death arrived. Seshat screamed and tore at her hair. She ran to the family temple. There, she mourned her father by spending days fasting and praying.

A message arrived. Seshat and Tiy were ordered to journey to Thebes where Seshat would become Mermeshu's second wife. Grief changed to anger.

Intef arrived with a troop of soldiers. He brought a letter from Mermeshu. Seshat went to her room to read her lover's words.

My evening star, I await your presence in Thebes. Though second to Nefru in my house, you are first in my heart. Your sister brought land, money and men to my cause. Without them, I would stand no chance of ruling the Two Lands. Soon my army will move against the Hyksos. Egypt will be free of the usurpers and I will be Pharaoh of a united land.

As she had the first letter, Seshat destroyed this one. She fell on her couch and wept.

Tiy came to her. "You must stop this weeping. We are to leave for Thebes in two days."

Seshat shook her head. "I will not leave this house. I will not take Nefru's leavings. I will not be second wife in Mermeshu's house. I turn my back to him."

Bastet splashed cool water on her mistress's face. "You will make yourself ill. You will lose the babe."

"You do not understand. He has betrayed me." Seshat's tears continued through the night.

In the morning when Intef entered the room, Seshat refused to look at him. Her head shrieked with pain. Fluid had begun to fill her legs and her hands. He summoned a physician.

For days, the physician invoked Amon Re and Hathor, calling on them to protect and heal Seshat. He tried remedy after remedy. Finally, he shook his head. "There is nothing I can do. The gods desire her presence."

Bastet's wails beat against Seshat. "Oh, my child, I have failed your mother. I vowed to keep you from harm."

Tiy spoke. "Send for Mermeshu. Maybe he can keep her anchored to this life."

"I've already dispatched messengers," Intef said. "Why does she disobey? She would be happy in his woman's court."

"Happy? With Nefru taunting and tormenting her? This is his fault. Why didn't he expose Nefru's lie?"

"To do so would have lost your father's support. Nefru was with child."

Seshat turned. "Not Mermeshu's. Yours. Why did you betray us?"

"I did what had to be done for the Two Lands."

She laughed. "No. For yourself. You are strong where Mermeshu is weak. You look only for yourself and not this land for you would rule Mermeshu and see your sons wear the crown you can't."

He raised his hand, then let it drop to his side. "If you love this land and Mermeshu, you would greet him with joy."

Seshat licked her dry and cracked lips. "On the day Mermeshu arrives, I want to be bathed and dressed. Oil my skin. Paint my face. Bring a headrest so I can sit. Adorn me with my mother's necklace and crown. I could have made him pharaoh for I come from a line of rulers."

Tiy held a cup to Seshat's mouth. "All will be as you wish."

Several days later, Bastet summoned slaves to carry her mistress to the bathing room. With gentleness, she washed and oiled Seshat's swollen body. She washed the salty encrustation from Seshat's face. "When he comes, you will get well."

Seshat shook her head. "Not so. I am poisoned and will die."

Tiy gasped. "Nefru? How did she do this? I will see she follows you."

"Do not. She gave me nothing. Her lies have done this. She will never know happiness. Her house and this nome will lie in ruins."

Soon Seshat wore her finest dress. Bastet combed and braided Seshat's hair. When she was on her sleeping couch,

Tiy placed the crown on Seshat's head and the necklace around her neck. Outside, thunder rumbled.

Mermeshu entered and stood beside the couch. "My evening star."

She released a breath. "Bastet, Tiy, leave. What I have to say to this man is for his ears alone."

He knelt beside the couch and ran a hand over her face. "Only tell me you will come to Thebes."

She looked into his eyes and ignored the love she saw there. "You drank deeply of my love. You feasted on my body. You have denied the child you gave me."

"Never. Why do you say these things?"

"You did not come when I wrote and told you about the child. Instead, you took my sister for your wife and left Intef to tell me what you had done."

He clasped her hand. "I did not know about the child until the marriage was made and your father was dead."

"Does that matter when you let Nefru's lies stand? You sent your friend, our betrayer to carry me to Thebes like spoils from a battle. You lied when you said your heart was mine."

"I swear you hold my heart." He opened the small chest he held in one hand. "I bring gifts." He lifted a necklace, arm bands and anklets.

"Give them to your wife. I wear the ones from my mother." She raised a hand to touch the crown. "Look on them and see what you rejected."

"What's done cannot be undone. These jewels are yours. We leave for Thebes in the morning and you will wear them. Our son will be an honored advisor to his brother when the child of my first wife becomes pharaoh."

"Nefru breeds?"

"The child she carried was lost. Of the next, there will be no question of parentage."

Seshat laughed. "Intef's child. Nefru will never give you or any other man a child. Her womb will be closed."

He brought her swollen hand to his mouth and kissed her fingers. "On the way to Thebes, I will hold you in my arms and give you strength."

Seshat's vision blurred. Sharp swords stabbed her head. "None but my ghost will dwell in your house. You let ambition for wealth and power guide your course. You chose these things above love."

"Seshat, no."

She straightened. "Adorn me with your jewels. Wrap me in the finest linens. Carry a dead woman to your house. I curse you. Over the years and into eternity, we will meet. You want a son. He must be mine. Until you know what to value, you will find me only to lose me." She sank onto the headrest.

Mermeshu kissed her. "Seshat, I love you. You do not understand the ways of men. Love is like a sweet to be enjoyed at a meal's ending. Power, wealth and ambition are the meat. In cursing me, you curse yourself. You, too, will seek and lose. Until you learn pride is a fool's weapon, you will never find happiness." He pressed his head to her chest and listened to her breaths until there were no more.

* * * *

Astrid groaned. "What happened?"

Clive shook his head. "You lifted the necklace and collapsed. Good thing I caught you. Are you all right?"

"Shouldn't we call an ambulance?" Paula asked.

Astrid pushed into a sitting position. She knew what had occurred, but she wasn't about to explain. If she did, they would lock her up. As a child when she'd touched any of the artifacts, a glimpse of another time and place had arisen. The pictures she'd described had been historically accurate, but none had been as vivid as this morning's event. She'd never lived another person's life before.

"I'm okay." She smiled. "That'll teach me not to skip breakfast and lunch."

Paula lifted the necklace from the floor. "This is lovely. I recognize the lapis and carnelians. The metal looks like gold, but it's so pale."

"Electrum," Astrid said.

"What's that?" Paula asked.

"A blend of silver and gold."

Paula put the necklace on the velvet cloth. "How old do you think these pieces are?"

"Middle Kingdom." Clive turned to Astrid. "As usual, the office is a mess. I can't find your father's notes."

"Why am I not surprised? I'll start sorting tomorrow."

He clasped her arm. "Why don't I close the shop and take you to dinner?"

"Too late, Aunt Sarah invited me."

"Cancel. We've a lot to discuss."

"We can't solve anything today. Besides, I thought Antiquities stayed open late Friday evenings."

"Usually, but with your father gone, I'll close. We need to hire at least one clerk. I'll have to check sales and attend them."

"Have anyone in mind?"

"A woman who works here occasionally. Not sure she's available."

Astrid thought of Sarah. With her knowledge of history, the older woman would be perfect. "Do you have Dad's keys?"

"I'll get them." He strode to the office.

Paula stared after him. "How well do you know Clive?"

"Well enough. He's worked here for a year and a half."

"Are you two involved?"

"Not on a bet."

Paula arched a brow. "Is there something wrong with him? Something I should know?"

Astrid shook her head. "He's just not my type. Too smooth."

"He is that." Paula grinned. "He's slick enough to slip through the hands of any woman who tries to cling. Have lunch with me tomorrow and I'll fill you in. Say noon at the Village Cafe."

"I'd like that, but if I get involved with the office, how do I let you know I can't make it?"

"If you're not there by twelve fifteen, I'll come here."

"Sounds good."

Clive returned and handed her the keys. "See you tomorrow morning. Don't believe anything Mrs. Rayson tells you."

"What would she say that worries you?"

"She accused me of not doing anything for your dad. I was so shaken, I couldn't think, let alone move."

Astrid smiled. "That's what I told her."

The bell above the door jangled. Astrid sucked in a breath. The man who entered was definitely her type. His rugged features, muscular body and tousled dark hair impacted her senses with sledge hammer blows. Who was he? Her smile faded when she saw the petite blonde who followed him.

Clive sauntered toward the couple. "Duncan, Lorna, I thought you were headed to the shore."

"We heard about Lloyd and wanted to see if there was anything I could do." His deep voice vibrated through Astrid.

The woman glided toward Clive. "I told him to leave Lloyd to the doctors." She ran her tongue over her bottom lip. "But you know Duncan. Thinks he can handle everything."

A picture of a preening cat popped into Astrid's head. The woman's slanted eyes were the same color blue as the eyes of Aunt Sarah's Persian cat. The rings on the blonde's fingers glittered as she reached for Clive's hands.

The man strode toward Astrid. His smile was volcanic. Heat collected low in her abdomen. What fires would his hands raise as they caressed her skin? *Whoa.* She wrenched her gaze away.

"So Antiquities is yours to play with, Clive," the woman crooned. "Now you can show me the goodies in the vault."

Astrid stepped toward the pair. "The gallery isn't Clive's."

The blonde pursed her lips. "And who are you?"

Clive released her hands. "Lloyd's daughter. Lorna Stinit and Duncan Garrett. They're excellent customers."

Lorna Stinit pushed strands of hair from her face. "So you're Lloyd's daughter. Duncan, stop staring and ask about her father. Then we can leave."

Duncan took Astrid's hands between his. "Your father's mentioned you many times. How is he?"

"Responding to treatment." She met his gaze. His hazel eyes held her fast. She wondered if he felt the heat between them. *Stop it. He's taken.*

"Duncan, come see these marvelous Egyptian pieces," Lorna called. "I want them." She held the necklace that had sent Astrid on a wild trip into an ancient land.

Duncan's eyes narrowed. He looked from Lorna to Clive. Tension built. What was going on?

Paula glared at the woman. "You ruined my picture."

"You can always take another. How about with me wearing them?"

"Beautiful, but not for you," Duncan said.

Lorna pouted. "Why not? The lapis would enhance my eyes. I'd change the carnelians for sapphires."

"And ruin the value." Duncan took the collar. "This necklace calls for a tall woman." He turned to Astrid. "Let me show her what I mean."

As he draped the piece around Astrid's neck, his fingers brushed her nape. Her body responded. For a moment, the room shimmered and she feared falling into the past to re-live love and death once more. Duncan's deep voice kept her anchored to the present.

"See what I mean." He removed the necklace. "Clive, I'll buy the set if Astrid agrees to model them at the gala for the local opera company."

"Really, Duncan," Lorna said. "Shouldn't you check with me? Aren't I your co-sponsor?"

Astrid met Lorna's icy glare. "I'll be too involved with Dad to attend. And, the necklace isn't for sale until Dad agrees."

Duncan leaned closer. "I always get what I want."

She met the challenge in his eyes. "And what is that?"

"When I decide, I'll let you know."

His words held a threat to her emotions. "Don't bother."

Lorna laughed. "See, my dear, you can't always have everything."

"We'll see." Duncan arched a brow. "Clive, let's see some of the other new things. The pectoral with the hawk interests me. Same time frame as these?"

Clive shook his head. "Later. We should have some new items next week."

As they moved away, Astrid released her breath. She didn't know what was happening, but she felt on edge. As she left, she thought about her odd adventure. She had been Seshat, a woman betrayed by her lover.

Had the dream been a warning?

* * * *

As Astrid left the shop, Duncan watched the sway of her hips. He'd been blindsided. He wanted to taste her lips, to caress the contours of her body, to thrust inside until they exploded. He wanted to see her gray eyes flare with passion.

The moment he'd seen her, he'd had an erection. He wanted her in ways he didn't understand. Though an attraction so potent couldn't last, he would enjoy the conflagration as they drove each other to burn.

She'd been aware of him. The way she'd met his gaze in answer to his challenge had told him that. When he'd clasped the collar at her nape, he'd felt her body's response.

He sucked in a breath and uncoiled his fisted hands. He liked tall women with dark hair and trim bodies. Astrid was all of his fantasies in one woman. Had Clive and Lorna noticed his reaction? Lorna wouldn't be pleased. She'd been angling for an invitation to his bed since the day six weeks ago when Clive had introduced them. She'd thought this weekend at the beach would give her what she wanted. *Not on a bet. Not now.*

Lorna was Clive's type. When they'd roomed during their undergraduate years, the women his friend had chosen had been petite and curvy. Was Clive interested in Astrid? Would be one way for him to profit from the valuables in the shop. Clive's envy of Duncan's wealth had been one reason they had drifted apart. And now? He wasn't sure why Clive had come into his life again.

Duncan wandered away from the pair and returned to study the necklace and crown. These had to be the ones described in his great-great grandfather's journal. Duncan recalled the day he'd found the diary in the attic. The Egyptian set, along with a number of other artifacts collected by his ancestor during a world tour, had been described in detail. They'd been stolen and his great-great grandfather had believed the woman he loved had taken them,

In our circles, one beds, not weds the daughter of a servant. But Madeline was chaste. Having fled this all-consuming passion for her, I toured the world. During the trip, I purchased various items, mostly jewelry, that seemed to call to me. The desire for these things was so strong a compulsion they seemed to guide my steps.

The journal pages had described eight different purchases. Duncan ran his finger over the necklace. They had to be the ones. Matched every point of the description. Where had Lloyd found the set? Duncan intended to learn. Had the owner of Antiquities found any of the other items described in the diary? Duncan clenched his fists and thought about the other entries. The journal had presented a mystery at the end.

Today I landed in New York. At a welcome home party, hosted by my cousin, Chester, I announced my intention to wed Madeline. Our friend, Bonnie, acted as Chester's hostess. Her eyes followed my every move and she can't believe I've chosen one not of our circle to be my wife. The months abroad had firmed my resolve to have Madeline. After dinner, I showed the three of them my treasures. Chester, whose father had frittered away his share of the family fortune, looked with envy at my purchases. Bonnie expressed a wish to add a gold bracelet from Italy and a jeweled cross to the glitter she loves to wear. Madeline touched one piece and blanched. She said she was going home. I followed her outside and escorted her to the small house where she lives with her father and cousin. They weren't there. The passion I'd held inside erupted and we consummated our love. I gave her the ring I'd purchased in Paris and asked her to meet me in the morning so we could apply for a marriage license.

Duncan pulled himself from his ancestor's story. The marriage hadn't happened. Madeline, her father and cousin had vanished. So had the chest of treasures. Nine months later, a letter had arrived along with an infant and his wet nurse. Duncan's great-great grandfather learned Madeline had died in childbirth. The letter begged his forgiveness. She had fled because her life had been threatened. If she married him, she would die. No mention was made of the items in the chest. Duncan's ancestor had believed Madeline's family had sold the jewelry as a means of support.

Duncan nodded. He was sure some of the stolen items were here. He intended to claim them, no matter by what means. That Astrid was Lloyd's daughter was a complication he wasn't sure he could solve.

Duncan smiled. He would have his great-great grandfather's treasures and he would have Astrid. With this thought, he strode to where Lorna and Clive stood discussing a piece of Victorian jewelry.

"Here." Duncan tossed the keys to the beach house to Lorna. "Something's come up and I'm staying in town. Enjoy the sun and surf."

"What are you talking about?" she asked. "You can't do

this. You promised to go with me."

He braced for an explosion. Clive grabbed Lorna's arm. "The sales I have to attend aren't far from the beach house. Why don't I come by when I'm done, or you could come and watch me work?"

Lorna released a breath. "I just might do that." She turned to Duncan. "You don't know what you're missing."

"You can tell me on Monday." Duncan headed for the door. "See you."

BABYLON

Astrid stepped onto the deck and stared at the sky. Only seven AM and already the humidity rose. She wanted to have her morning run before the temperature soared to match the humidity. She trotted down the steps and began a series of warm-up exercises. As she settled into the familiar routine, her thoughts drifted to her last night's visit to her father with Sarah.

Hope filled her. The intravenous had been removed. He'd been sitting in a chair. His grin, his handclasp had heartened her. Though she'd noticed a slight weakness on the right side, his improvement pleased her. They'd even managed a conversation. His answers had been single words or nods and shakes of his head.

When she'd mentioned how Clive had displayed the Egyptian necklace and crown, he'd scowled. "No."

"Not for sale?" she'd asked.

He had nodded.

"That's what I told Clive's friend, Lorna. Do you want me to store them in the vault?"

"Yes."

She'd wanted to tell him about her strange adventure in the past, but not yet. She refused to add any worries to whatever troubled him. The childhood incidents had rattled him and they'd only been glimpses of another time and place. Her choice of nursing as a career rather than archeology had pleased him.

The blare of a car horn startled her. She nearly rapped her chin on the railing. She turned, frowned and walked to the car. The driver rolled the window down. "Clive, what are you doing here so early?"

He glanced grazed over her legs, her hips, her breasts. She clenched her fists and wished she'd worn something less revealing than biker shorts and a body-hugging tee shirt.

"Figured you were still taking early morning runs." He grinned. "Makes me want to take up the habit. Have to say you're looking … fit."

She gritted her teeth. "What do you want?"

"If I weren't in a hurry, I'd show you."

"Enough."

"Can't fault me for trying."

She fisted her hands on her hips. "I'm sure you didn't come to banter."

"Wanted to let you know I won't be in the shop this weekend."

"Why?"

"Checked your dad's calendar. He starred a sale today and a street fair tomorrow. The sale includes some jade, and you never know what can be found at these fairs. Have to leave you on your own so I can handle the buying."

Astrid nodded. "Better you than me. Do you need checks or money?"

"I'm set. Hope you don't mind being alone both days."

"I won't be. I asked Aunt Sarah if she'd like a few hours work every weekend. She said she'd be delighted. I think she'll be good."

Clive made a face. "I agree, but I don't have to like her."

"Did you reach the other woman?"

He nodded. "She'll come by Tuesday or Wednesday. Be glad to work from noon to four on weekdays."

"Sounds good."

"How is your dad?"

"Much improved. You should stop by to see him."

He nodded. "I will. Have a thing about hospitals. Give me the creeps."

"Bad experience?"

He shrugged. "A little. Also, I thought he might not want to see me. I sort of feel responsible. Maybe the argument triggered the stroke."

She shook her head. "More like poor diet and no exercise."

"Hope he's well enough to discuss real issues soon." He held up a hand. "Don't scowl. I won't say a thing until he's a hundred percent. See you Monday when I drop off anything I buy."

Astrid watched him leave. She returned to the exercises. Once her muscles loosened, she jogged around the building and up the street toward the Hook.

Most of the shops and restaurants along Broadway were closed. She passed a bakery and inhaled the aroma of coffee and fresh bread. She resisted the lure. On the way back, she promised herself. She ran along several blocks where houses were set back from the sidewalk. Green lawns were dotted with beds of flowers and persistent dandelions.

The houses changed from small to large Victorian structures. Just ahead, she saw the wall that hid mansions from view. As she neared the brick barrier, a gate opened and a man stepped onto the walk. To avoid a collision, she veered.

He blocked her path. "Astrid."

"Mr. Garrett, I can't stop now." She edged around him.

"I'll run with you. We can stop for pastry and coffee on the way back."

Astrid gulped a breath. Hopefully, she wouldn't trip over a sidewalk crack and sprawl on the ground. His cut-off shorts and muscle shirt exposed more of his flesh than was good for her. He kept up the pace and matched her stride for stride.

When they reached the Hook, she paused to gaze at the Hudson River. How good to be back in Rockleigh. Wavelets washed against the narrow beach. In the distance, the bridge was framed against the sky.

Duncan rested his hands on her shoulders. Heat infused her. She should move away. Instead, she leaned back. "Thought you were going to the shore."

"I discovered more interesting matters here."

"And your friend?"

Lorna." He chuckled. "She's there. Clive plans to stay at the beach house after the sales. Lorna has ideas about me, but we're not involved and never will be."

He wasn't taken. Her heart beat a staccato rhythm against her chest. Did she want to be involved with him or any man? There were her father's illness and her plans for school to keep her busy. She turned to leave and found herself in his arms.

His mouth seized hers. A shudder swept through her. It was almost as though she knew his scent, his touch, his taste. She fit against his body with perfect alignment. As if entranced, she slid her arms around his neck. He pressed her against his erection. They moved in a synchronous dance.

She opened her mouth to his probing tongue. The kiss continued until she felt lightheaded.

He raised his head, but kept her imprisoned in his arms. "Come with me. To my house."

At first, she couldn't make sense of his words. Her heart thundered and she felt as if she'd run miles through the desert. "What?"

"We can close the gates and finish what we've begun. No one will see us."

With the speed of a snail, sanity returned. "I don't even know you."

"What better way to get acquainted?"

Lord, she was in trouble. She inhaled several deep breaths and nearly succumbed to his heady scent. "I don't think so."

He laughed. "Maybe after we stop at the bakery."

She pulled free. "A rain check on the coffee." As she raced down the street, she glanced over her shoulder. He wasn't following. For that, she was thankful. What had happened back there? She wasn't sure she wanted to know.

* * * *

Duncan waited until Astrid vanished in the distance. He groaned. So much for a subtle seduction. He'd grabbed her like an invader seizing the spoils of a battle. He couldn't believe he'd acted like a boor, but once his mouth had touched hers, the only thought in his head was a frantic desire to possess her completely.

"Now what?"

Apologize, a little voice said. He shook his head. She'd been as involved in the lethal kiss as he had been. She couldn't say she hadn't been willing, or that there hadn't been an explosive connection.

He groaned and started walking. He needed a plan. Except, all his energy remained focused on the part of him he'd always had under control. Even with her gone, his erection throbbed and ached for release.

He opened the gate and stepped into the garden surrounding the large stone house. Moments later, he stood in the shower where a frigid spray failed to wash away his desire for the tall, dark-haired Astrid whose curves had fit his body perfectly.

What did he want from her? He laughed. The answer was evident. Sex. Mind-blowing sex. Would a thousand encounters fill the hunger he felt?

He briskly dried. He'd better decide what else he wanted before he was mired in quicksand. He needed to know more about her before he plunged into the morass. He could ask Clive for information, but his friend had his own agenda concerning Astrid.

Duncan frowned. He had the impression she didn't like Clive. Why? Who would know?

He dressed and, for a second time, headed to the bakery. A plan began to unfold. This afternoon, he would visit Lloyd. If he helped her father, Astrid might be willing to become involved in a lengthy affair.

* * * *

What had she been thinking? The question followed Astrid into the apartment and the shower. She'd never acted or felt the way she had in Duncan's arms. What was she going to do about her heated response to the man? She didn't know him, yet being close to him felt right and the kiss had stirred responses she'd felt in every cell. Could she handle a wild affair? Anything so volcanic was sure to go cold after the eruption occurred.

She pushed these thoughts aside. She had enough on her plate to give her acute indigestion.

Once she'd dressed, she tapped on Sarah's door. The older woman answered. The gray Persian mewed a welcome. Astrid bent and scratched the cat's head. "Portia looks good."

Sarah laughed. "She's getting fat. Come in."

"Can't. I'm on my way to see Dad. Are you available to work in the gallery today and tomorrow? Clive needs to attend the sales Dad had scheduled to take in."

"What time?"

"Between noon and one." Astrid groaned. "I have a luncheon date with Paula. I should cancel, but I don't have her number."

"Maybe it's in your dad's files. She seems nice."

Astrid nodded. "I felt a connection with her. Most of my old friends have moved away so I need to make new ones."

"You will. See you later."

Astrid drove to the hospital and arrived just as an aide delivered the breakfast tray. When she saw what he'd been served, she grinned. "None of the fat-loaded foods you prefer."

He shrugged. "Hungry."

"Then eat and I'll fill you in on what's happening at Antiquities."

Though he spilled some of the cereal, he managed to eat most of the serving. She told him about Clive's decision to attend sales this weekend.

"Good."

"What will he by buying?"

"Maybe nothing."

"Do you mind if I clear the clutter in the apartment?"

His smile, though crooked, brought one from her. When he tried to lift the teacup, his hand shook. She took a straw from beside the water pitcher. "Try this." She bent the straw. "What do you know about Duncan Garrett?"

"Good man. Lost. Treasure. Help him."

Astrid tried to make sense of the string of words. "What treasure?"

"His. Family. Stolen. Long ago. Help find."

"All right, I will." I just won't go to bed with him, she added silently.

"Letters. Read."

"I will. Wish me luck today. Aunt Sarah is helping."

"Good."

She kissed his cheek. As she left the room, a doctor strode down the hall. When the nurse Astrid had spoken to the day of her father's admission greeted her, the doctor paused. "Miss Logan? Dr. Gregori. Your father's my patient."

"He seems improved."

"Better than expected, but that's the beauty of prompt treatment. If he continues to improve, I'd like to arrange a transfer to a rehab facility early next week."

"Wonderful." She asked the questions about his treatment she'd stored since learning about the stroke. The answers reassured her. "Do you think stress was a factor?"

"Possibly, but lifestyle is more probable. Long hours, fatty foods, lack of exercise, age."

Astrid nodded. "Over the summer, I'll work on changing his habits. Thanks." As she hurried to her car, she decided to involve Sarah in the health campaign.

After opening Antiquities, she checked the cash register and the credit card set-up. She hoped she would remember how to use them. When she felt comfortable with the machines, she strode to the Egyptian collection. Using the display cloth, she lifted the necklace and crown and carried them to the office. Once Sarah arrived, Astrid stored them in the vault.

The bell above the door jangled. "Paula, guess you got tired waiting for me."

"Actually, I figured you'd be stuck. Ran into Clive at the bakery." She grinned. "Since he's not here to interfere, I thought I'd get some work done."

"Good idea." Astrid paused. "How about dinner tonight? At the apartment. We can order in."

"Let me do a pickup. How does a veggie pita with heavenly dressing sound? There's a place up town that makes them."

"You're on."

"What time?"

"Say seven. I'd like to pop in on my dad."

Paula pulled a portfolio from her case. "Show him these. He's a great guy."

Before long, the shop was filled with browsers. Several people made purchases. During a lull, Astrid began to sort through the stacks of papers on her father's desk.

At four, Sarah waved her over. "You need to make a deposit. I'll lock up and set the alarms."

"Thanks." Astrid noted the checks and counted the cash, leaving enough to start the next day. After filling the deposit slips, she walked to the bank and left the packet in the night slot. Back at the apartment, she stood in the middle of the main room. Where to begin? She found a stack of index cards to mark the places in the open books.

What was Dad looking for? There were books on many countries, but there seemed to be nothing to tie them together. She stacked them in a corner of the room.

Once the chairs and coffee table were clear, she moved to the couch. Beneath a stack of books, she found a necklace made from a single strand of beads. A cylinder seal carved from onyx hung from the center. Without thinking, she lifted the necklace from the cushions. A wave of dizziness

claimed her. She collapsed on the couch.
* * * *

Istari smoothed the clay on the tablet and once again, checked her observations of the stars. The Assyrian army had been camped outside the city for nearly a week. Soon, they would storm the gates. With a sigh, she shut out the cries of the hungry and frightened people. She could do nothing to soothe their fears and she'd given all the food the temple could spare.

She choked back a cry of despair and raised the stylus to mark her findings. She checked her observations against those provided by the astrologers.

"Alas, poor Babylon. Your night has come. War is a part of life. Countries wax and wane like Sin, the moon. Sleep well, my beloved land until the dawning of your new day."

Though she felt tempted to scrape the tablet, she knew nothing could change the approaching time. During her learning days in the temple of Marduke, she had become a reader of the future and a student of the past. Her own chart showed she would leave the city of her birth as a prisoner. She carried the tablet to the main room of the temple and placed it on the altar before the statue of the god.

Lamaru, the youngest of the priestesses, ran from the entrance to the living quarters. "Istari, Ishtar-ishtaru sent me to find you."

Mardu, priestess and kin to the rulers of Babylon, stormed toward them. "Why does she want to see this one? Does she think she can name one who has no family as her successor?" Her fleshy fingers extended into claws. "Istari, you are not fit to serve Marduke. Who knows what your parents were? You were a foundling."

Istari eyed the other woman. Why hadn't she lost weight the way the other priestesses, priests and servants of Marduke had in the days since the siege began? Mardu's lush curves were a mockery.

"Ishtar-ishtaru is my foster mother. Why wouldn't she want her child's presence at her death?"

"She must choose her successor, yet she remains silent."

"As is her choice."

Mardu glared. "We will see who is named Ishtaru. Before another day passes, I will rule the temple and you will be driven into the streets where you belong." She marched away.

Istari released a sigh. At least Mardu would be gone for hours while she searched for kinsmen to gain their support in her quest for power. Those relatives may have fled the city. Even if they pressured Ishtar-ishtaru to name Mardu as high priestess, the city's fate was written in the stars. The king and his advisors were responsible for the trouble. For months, the astrologers and diviners had given warnings the rulers had ignored.

"Don't listen to her," Lamaru said. "She envies your knowledge and your beauty. She wants to be high priestess so she can command reluctant men to her bed. She's always bringing some new slave to her sleeping chambers, but she really wants those of noble blood as her lovers."

Istari frowned. "If she's not a virgin, how will she perform the Tammuz rite?"

"She whispered to one of the others of the ways to appear untouched."

Istari shook her head. Through Mardu, the corruption of the rulers had tainted the temple. But it mattered not. The day of the city and the temple drew to an end.

She hastened down the hall leading to the sleeping chambers where her foster mother awaited death. She paused in the doorway and struggled to remain calm. Ishtar-ishtaru lay on a low bed. Her skin was ashen. Except for an abdomen swollen in imitation of pregnancy, she appeared skeletal.

Bel-mar-tammuz, her foster father and consort of the high priestess, knelt beside the bed. The illness of his beloved had aged him. His noble face was scored by lines and his dark eyes, heavy with grief.

Istari knelt beside him. "Foster mother, I am here."

"And the stars," Ishtar-ishtaru asked. "What say they of the future?"

"Alas, the dark night comes for Babylon."

"And for you?"

Istari sighed. "My fate is to be a captive and to serve Marduke no more."

"Nay, you will honor him in your heart." The dying woman smiled. "Never have I doubted you or your love. Ah, Bel-mar, remember the small girl you found in the market and brought here to ease my sorrow over my barren state?"

Bel-mar touched her arm. "She became the child of our heart and the joy of our life."

Ishtar-ishtaru sighed. "Remember how her big eyes peered into every corner of the temple. Question after question. Always seeking to know what and why."

"We taught her," Bel-mar said. "She learned to read and write before most boys begin their schooling."

"My child, you have given us laughter and fulfillment," Ishtar-ishtaru said. "Would that we could give you the same, but these days aren't for pleasure. Bel-mar, the necklace."

Istari's eyes widened. For the first time in the years since she'd come to the temple, her foster mother's neck was bare. The symbol of her office was in Bel-mar's hand. The temple seal dangled from the single row of beads strung on a metal wire. "I'm not worthy. No one knows my origins."

"Who better than one of the people to serve Marduke in his final hours in Babylon," Ishtar-ishtaru said. "Bel-mar, fasten the seal for my fingers have no strength."

Istari blinked tears from her eyes. "I will treasure your gift and serve the god with joy. Go soon, mother of my heart. Do not linger to witness the end." She kissed the older woman's cheek and fled the room. In the hall, she leaned against the wall and waited for her tears to stop.

When she reached the main room of the temple, Lamaru saw the necklace. "She chose you."

A group of priests and priestesses gathered around Istari. "Is she gone?" one asked.

"She lives but barely."

"What would you have us do?" one of the priests asked. "This is no time for a gathering of the nobles for the Tammuz ceremony."

Istari nodded. "There will be no rite of passage for me. You've seen the chart and heard the prophecies. I would see everyone depart the temple. Hide in the city. The gates will fall by morning and by evening the invaders will hold the temple. I will face them alone for 'tis written in my stars that I will go into captivity."

Though many protested, Istari exhorted them to leave. As she watched the departures, she wondered if she would see any of her companions again. She knelt before Marduke and sent wishes for their safety on the winds.

"Istari, let me stay." Lamaru knelt at the altar. "I have no one and nowhere to go."

Istari nodded. The young priestess was another foundling. A bond of friendship had grown between them. "If I can, I'll protect you. Come, let us take bread, cheese and beer to Bel-mar and sit with Ishtar-ishtaru."

Throughout the night, they kept a vigil over the dying priestess. Of Mardu, there was no sign. Istari prayed her enemy had found refuge with her kin.

As the first rays of the sun brightened the sky, her foster mother breathed her last. Bel-mar rent his clothes and streaked his face with ashes from the fire.

As the day moved forward, the sounds of fighting drew near. Screams and the clash of metal on metal roused Istari from her silent grief. She rose and walked to the door.

"Where are you going?" Lamaru asked.

Istari turned. "Even on a day as evil as this, duty must be done. I have neglected the god and he must be served." She hurried to the main room of the temple to perform the neglected duties. With care, she drew the curtains around the painted statue of Marduke and knelt at his feet to beg forgiveness.

The shouts grew louder. Screams pierced the air. When she peered around the curtain, her hand flew to her mouth. The Assyrian soldiers were expected, but Mardu's presence in their midst was not. The plump priestess stood between two men in the fore of the invaders. Istari stepped into view.

"That's her," Mardu shouted. "Istari, the false priestess."

One of the men strode toward Istari. The other held Mardu against his side. Istari's breath caught in her throat. The warrior was handsome with well-developed muscles. When he seized her arm, she felt as though lightning pierced her core.

* * * *

Ashur-dagan-shu's heart thudded against his chest with the thundering beat like the hooves of his chariot horses. He'd never seen a woman who matched the beauty of this priestess. Though her dress covered her from neck to ankle, he noticed her narrow waist set off by the short over-skirt. Tall, slender, perfect features. She could be the goddess come to life.

"I am Ashur-dagan-shu, leader of the Assyrians. I claim all that lies within this temple for my king." He pulled her into his arms. "I claim you as mine."

He brought his mouth to hers, felt her shudder, then surrender to the heat flashing between them. Perhaps she had cast a spell on him, but she was his and he would carry her to Nineveh and sequester her in his woman's house. He deepened the kiss and pressed her against his swollen penis. Only the cheers and urgings of his men to take her halted his assault. Not for him a public display of his mastery of her or any other woman.

Trutanu-ilu, his second, strode toward Ashur and the priestess. The woman who had led them here clung to his friend's arm. Ashur felt the heat of her gaze on the place where his erect member thrust against his tunic. He stepped in front of his captive.

Mardu jerked away from Turtanu. "Despoil her. Kill her. That's my price for opening the gate and leading you here." She ran her tongue over her lips. Her dark eyes glittered.

Ashur shook his head. "A traitor's life is reward enough. Turtanu, control your slave."

Turtanu laughed. "Let us share this false priestess. She's responsive to a man's touch. All who serve Ishtar are."

The priestess stepped from behind Ashur. "I am Ishtar-ishtaru. Those who serve in Babylon are not prostitutes who sleep with any man the way your Assyrian temple women do. Until I choose my Tammuz, I lay with no man."

Mardu spat. "You haven't the proper lineage to claim the guise of the goddess who walks among us. I should have been named successor. No noble of Babylon will accept a skinny foundling. How can you expect to find a consort?"

Ashur chuckled. "There is one noble of Assyria who places beauty over birth. I will be your consort."

"Though I am not a noble, only a soldier risen through the ranks, I would be your consort," Turtanu said.

Mardu whirled and spat. "Neither of you will have her." Her voice rose to a piercing scream. She drew a knife and rushed toward Istari.

A priest with gray-streaked hair dashed across the room and acted before Ashur could move. The blade meant for Istari plunged into the old man's chest. His body thudded on the stone floor. Istari dropped to her knees. A wail rose from her lips and she fell across the body.

Ashur grabbed Mardu and shoved her into Turtanu's arms. "Bind and gag her. She is twice a traitor and for this act, she will be punished." He turned to the assembled men. "Remove the statue of their god. Marduke will come to Assyria and bow before our king and our gods."

* * * *

When Bel-mar collapsed, Istari no longer heard the enemies' voices. Her entire being focused on her foster father, the man who had been her rescuer and her teacher. "Bel-mar-tammuz, why did you act? Now I have no parents and no homeland."

"Ishtar-ishtaru," he stretched his hand as though grasping another's fingers. "Beloved." He smiled.

Istari kissed his cheek. Sobs shook her body. She tore her gown and streaked her face with his blood.

Lamaru stroked Istari's arm. "He's at peace. He's a hero. He saved your life."

"Do you think this is what I wanted?" Istari stared at the younger girl. Her earlier numbness vanished. Holding her grief inside brought nausea. She wanted to scream and attack Mardu, but the other priestess was gone. She bent her head. Tears gushed and she keened. "We must carry him to his room so he can lie beside Ishtar-ishtaru in death as he did in life."

Lamaru crouched at Bel-mar's feet. They tried to lift him, but he was too heavy. Istari's body shook with frustration.

The Assyrian leader came to her. "What are you doing? Why have you marked yourself with his blood? Was this old man your lover?"

"Bel-mar was my foster father. I want him to lie beside my foster mother. She died as the sun rose. At least, she escaped the tragedy that has befallen her Tammuz and her beloved land."

He motioned to several of the soldiers. "Do as she bids you and leave the room of the dead untouched. Don't harm either of these priestesses." He pulled Istari to her feet. "Wash the blood from your body, then remain in your room until I come."

"Am I not allowed to mourn my dead?"

He clasped her hands. "In your heart and in your thoughts.

Istari, you are mine and will have a better fate than most of the women in Babylon."

"What of Lamaru?"

"She will remain untouched. She goes to my king."

"Can't she remain here and serve Marduke?"

He laughed. "Your god travels to Nineveh. He returns to his home. You stole your gods and goddesses from Assyria. Go and do as you are bid."

Istari followed Lamaru and the soldiers who carried Belmar to the small sleeping chamber. They washed his body and changed his robe. Istari let her tears flow. "Now they are together."

"What will we do?" Lamaru asked. "I heard the men laugh when their leader kissed you. The soldiers have brought women from the streets into the temple. They violate them before the altar."

"Such are the ways of war. We are prisoners."

Lamaru nodded. "I'm afraid."

"So am I." Istari stroked the faces of her foster parents. "May your spirits soar in death as in life." She rose and held out her hand to the younger girl. "Come. I must bathe and wait. Stay with me for a time."

* * * *

Ashur watched Istari leave. Her body moved with fluid grace. The kiss of conquest had been but a taste to whet his appetite. Was she the embodiment of the goddess? Her face and form were perfection.

The sounds of revelry reached him. The screams of the captive women rose above the deeper voices of the men. Before he sought Istari, he needed to gain control of the men. Though looting and taking unwilling women were part of a victory, he feared the lack of discipline would cause the men to turn on each other. Babylon belonged to Assyria and the men would be better occupied seeking slaves and plunder to take to the king.

"Turtanu," he bellowed his second's name. Ashur strode into the main room of the temple and saw his friend buried to the hilt in the body of the woman who had betrayed her land and people. "Turtanu, attend me."

The second shouted his release and turned from the woman. "You want a turn?"

Ashur glared. He'd been repelled by Mardu when she'd

crept into their camp during the night and offered to show them an entrance into the city. "She was to be bound and gagged."

"I had need of her."

"Obey my orders now. The men are out of control. I wish to seize the loot and slaves and be on our way home before long. We must end these games."

Turtanu smiled. "They but celebrate our victory. About Mardu. Don't you recall what we owe her? Because of her, the city shattered beneath us like an over-ripe melon."

"I haven't forgotten what she did." Ashur grasped his friend's arm. "Come. Form ranks." His booming voice cut through the shouts and screams.

Before long, the men stood in orderly rows. "Place the women under guard in one of the rooms." He indicated several men to act as guards. He turned to Turtanu. "Set the patrols to gathering spoils. Select slaves from the artisans and children. Once this is done, we can return home in triumph."

Mardu moved toward him. "Come, Commander, let me soothe your ill-temper." She stroked her breasts.

Ashur turned away. "Put her with the other women."

She laughed softly. "I know much about pleasing men."

Disgust filled Ashur. "Turtanu, do as I order. Friendship is no reason for disobedience."

Mardu grabbed Ashur's arm. "You go to her. She stole the temple seal. Why should she also have the man who rules our lives? I want you. Come with me."

"You have no right to make demands."

She stamped her foot. "Turtanu, tell him what I have promised. Tell him I know where the treasure of Babylon can be found. I'll give it all to him if he does as I wish."

Turtanu laughed. "Ashur is above bribery." He turned to Ashur. "Will you give the king the beautiful Istari to insure your place at his right hand? Isn't it enough he has promised one of his sisters as your wife?"

Mardu laughed. "Would your king accept one who has been with many men? Istari even lay with her foster father. Every day, she tells Bel-mar of her love. You're a fool."

Ashur walked away. In time, he would learn the truth.

* * * *

Istari scrubbed the blood from her skin. She couldn't halt

the tears spilling from her eyes. All was gone. All she loved. Her foster parents, the temple and her city now lay beneath the sandals of the Assyrians. She fingered the beads of the necklace and traced the markings of the seal. Even the power of the gift had vanished. How could the god have failed to protect her people? She shook her head. Not the god, but the leaders. They hadn't listened to the warnings. Marduke couldn't aid those who would not hear.

She rinsed the soap from her skin and washed her hair. A picture of the Assyrian leader flashed in her thoughts. Ashur-dagan-shu. Tall, handsome, muscular, the very embodiment of a god. Would that he were a man of Babylon. She would gladly have taken him as her consort. She rose from the water and dressed.

Lamaru joined her. "What will we do?"

"I'll go to my room and wait." Istari grasped the girl's hand. "You should run and hide."

Lamaru shook her head. "Where would I go? I have no kin and know no place but the temple. Cast my chart so I may know my fate."

Istari nodded. Doing the calculations would keep her from thinking about what had passed and what was to come. She wiped away the tears trickling down her cheeks. After smoothing clay on a tablet, she used the stylus to mark the surface. She smiled. "You will survive, even prosper. There will be grief but you will find a great love."

Lamaru laughed. "And for you."

"My fate is hazy. Mars lies atop Venus and the Moon passes over my Sun. The warrior will give me a child." She closed her eyes. And more grief will come, she thought.

"What of him?"

"I don't know his birth so I can't chart his stars." She failed to mention how in her own chart Saturn opposed Mars and Venus and Jupiter, her sun.

The guards brought them bread and cheese. Istari felt restless, but she dared not leave the room. Shadows crept across the chamber. The moon rose. When would he come? What would he do?

Footsteps on the stone floor caused her to turn. Ashur stood in the doorway. The intensity of his gaze both thrilled and frightened her. His dark eyes seemed to strip her clothes away. He gestured to Lamaru. "Go with the guards.

They will see you come to no harm."

Once the girl left, he sat on a stool and removed his high-laced sandals. Then he stood and removed his clothes.

Istari watched the play of muscles as his body was revealed. Her mouth felt dry. When she saw his jutting male organ, her eyes widened.

"Look not at my spear, but gaze into my eyes," he commanded. With the gliding movements of a cat stalking prey, he moved toward her. The gleam of sweat on his skin made her want to stroke his flesh. The scent of him grew stronger, until she could smell nothing but his desire. Her heart quickened.

A smile curved his lips. "Am I more man than any you have known?"

She frowned. "I've never had a man come to me unclothed."

He laughed. "Don't think you can fool me. Soon, I'll know the truth. Mardu said you lay with many men, even your foster father."

"She lies. Since I passed from childhood, I never crept into my foster parents' bed. Even when the gods beat their war drums and slash the sky with their swords. When the storms come, I cower in my room."

He crushed her against him. His mouth touched hers. When she gasped, he thrust his tongue inside. His hands roved over her body the way they had in the temple. She felt wetness in her woman's parts and remembered her foster mother's instructions on the ways a woman's body prepared for invasion by the male organ.

Her arms slid around his neck. She tried to move closer, but her clothes kept her from feeling his skin against hers. He released her lips and slid his mouth to her neck. He sucked her flesh, then raised his head. "You're mine for I have marked you." He grasped the neck of her dress and ripped. His hands covered her breasts. The nipples peaked and pressed against his palms. He ran his lips to one and then the other and sucked.

Istari felt hot enough to burn. "Tammuz," she cried. "As I was before, I am yours now."

He tore the rest of her clothes away and carried her to the low bed. "Do not name me the god who is sacrificed." He nudged her legs apart and lay atop her.

"Not so. Tammuz is the one I choose as consort."

He captured her hands in one of his and held her arms above her head. With a single thrust, his spear penetrated her woman's core. She screamed. He put his mouth on hers and stopped her cries. She bucked against the pain that stole her breath.

He raised her head. "She lied." He released her hands and began to slide from her.

She grasped his shoulders. "Ashur-dagan-shu-tammuz, until I receive your seed, the rite isn't complete." She pulled his head down and brushed her tongue along his lips.

"Istari, I fear to hurt you more."

She stroked his face. "What was done cannot be undone. The stars foretold you will give me a child." More than anything, she wanted a child and once again have a family.

He raised himself and drew her into his arms. "Then I will give you my seed." He caressed her back and kissed her, gently at first, then with increasing urgency. He sucked her tongue and nipped her lips. "Though I can't take you as my wife, you will have an honored place in my harem."

Not as a wife. For a moment, she stiffened. Could she live with other women who shared his attention? For a child, she had to try.

He ran his hands over her skin. He cupped her breasts and lowered his head to lave them. She felt a pulsing in her lower abdomen. His organ began to harden. She rubbed against the firm shaft. She raised one leg and slid it over his hips. He pulsed against her woman's parts. One of his hands pressed against her back and he moved his hips, drawing his penis across her sensitive skin.

"Ashur," she cried. "Come into me."

With a quick movement, he rolled and pulled her beneath him. She stroked his hair. He rose so his weight was supported by his hands. Their gazes locked. As she put both legs over his back, he slid into her.

He growled. "So wet, so tight, so hot."

Without knowing why, she squeezed her inner muscles. He groaned and the sound vibrated through her. She pressed her heels against his buttocks to draw him closer. As he moved, waves of heat spiraled. She arched her back.

"Come with me," he whispered.

'Yes, oh, yes."

Istari wanted to soar, to reach beyond the exquisite sensations. She thrust against him until they moved in concert. She pressed her hands against his chest. At the moment of explosion, she pinched his nipples.

He roared her name again and again. "You're mine. Mine." His seed spurted, then gushed. His mouth met hers in a possessive kiss.

"And you are mine," she whispered.

He rolled from her and pulled her against his chest. "I'll never let you go."

She closed her eyes and savored memories of the way he'd made her feel. "Tammuz. My consort."

Soon, the sounds from him told her he slept. She leaned on one elbow and gazed at him. Though she no longer served Marduke, Ashur was her consort for now and all her days. Was there a way to change their fate?

* * * *

Ashur stared at the sleeping woman. He longed to kiss her awake and bring them to fulfillment. A thousand nights wouldn't be enough to sate him. She was so responsive and so heated. Istari was to have his son, and he knew but one way for that to occur. He had to gift her with his seed until one was firmly planted in her nest. He grinned. The act he had to perform was no hardship, only pleasure.

His gaze moved from her belly to her breasts. For an instant, he glimpsed a dark-haired infant nursing. His spear stiffened. In the days to come, he would have her read his stars. Would his reward be the one he sought? The king's sister, a place on the council as advisor to the king's young son, and wealth. He'd already befriended the boy. Once the king died, Ashur believed the friendship would make him the true ruler of Assyria.

What of Istari? Would she continue to accept a lesser place in his life? She'd been trained to rule the temple. Could she be content to dwell in a harem? Why did her wishes matter? She was his captive now and forever.

He slid from the bed. She opened her eyes and reached for him. Desire built. A mere glance acted like a spark on oiled kindling. She rose. "Come to the bath and let me clean the blood of sacrifice from your organ."

"More of the ritual?"

She smiled. "Don't you like to be clean? The water will

soothe my aches and give us a chance to explore each other."

He followed her to a room where the open roof allowed the rays of the sun to warm the water, though at this, the dawning hour, the water was cool. He stepped into the pool and sat with his legs stretched before him. Istari coated her hands with soap and began to lave his chest and abdomen. Her touch roused him. When she touched his spear, desire grew. Her soaped hands slid back and forth on his organ.

Ashur groaned. "I would give you my seed."

She knelt between his spread legs. "I would welcome the gift."

He lifted her onto his legs and slid her onto his engorged penis. He raised his knees and brought her breasts to his mouth. He suckled one, then the other. As he stroked her lower lips, he watched her expression change. With a finger, he found the center of her desire. She arched back and cried her pleasure. He held back his seed for he wasn't ready to relinquish the delight he found when deep inside her.

"What's wrong?" she asked. "Why do you withhold your seed, the bringer of new life?"

"Wrap your legs around me." A picture of Turtanu thrusting into Mardu as she lay on the altar flashed into his thoughts. Istari's face and form replaced those of the other priestess. Not on the altar, he decided, but in the same manner. He rose and carried her to the table used by the servants to massage the aches from sore muscles. He sat her on the edge of the table and withdrew.

"Ashur, why?"

"Lean back so I can admire your beauty." He pressed his lips to her throat and marked her as he had before. His mouth trailed over her breasts and he stroked her nipples with his tongue before sliding them along her abdomen. With his tongue, he explored the folds between her legs and when her juices flowed heavily, he thrust until her tight passage encased his spear,

She moaned and moved. He caressed her breasts until her cries grew frantic. One touch to her pleasure knot and she spasmed. Her sheath tightened around his spear and with a roar, he released his seed.

"Ashur, Ashur, my Tammuz, my love for now and ever."

He gathered her close. "You are my star of love." He carried her back to the pool.

When they returned to her room, they found bread, meat and beer. With laughter, they fed each other. Though he would have liked to linger, he dressed. "I must see to the gathering of spoils and slaves. The guard will keep you safe and bring your young friend to keep you company. Ready your belongings. We leave for Nineveh soon."

"I hear."

He saw tears in her eyes and wished he could stop them. There was no way he could change the past or the future.

* * * *

Ashur cornered his patrol leaders and examined the goods they had selected to carry away. Already, carts containing cloth, metals, jewelry and other wares had left the city. Slaves--men and women who had skills and also children-- had been selected from the pens. He spotted Turtanu and scowled for the priestess, Mardu, stood at his friend's side.

Ashur strode toward the pair. "What is she doing here? You were ordered to see her with the slaves."

Turtanu pointed to a line of scratches on her arm. "The women attacked her. She will be my gift to the temple of Ishtar when we reach Nineveh. Once in the temple, with her skills, she will be given the status she has been denied here."

"How can you trust a woman who has betrayed her people?"

Turtanu laughed. "She only saw to herself and that's the first law of life. Mardu wants the life I've promised. She will obey me. Is she different from you or me? You let ambition rule. So do I."

Ashur frowned. Turtanu had risen as high as possible for one of low birth. How could he expect to become a noble?

"I serve the king," Ashur said. "My ambition is to see Assyria prosper and become powerful."

"There we differ." Turtanu stroked Mardu's arm. "She will obey my commands."

"And when she's chosen to participate in the spring ritual, will you be her consort for the night and then die to insure a good harvest?"

Mardu's eyes narrowed. "Turtanu is safe from that fate. I have another choice, but he can escape if he kills the false priestess and delivers the seal to me."

"I have no desire for you."

She stared at his groin. "Desire can be stirred. Let me touch you and you will beg me to mount you."

"There's more to desire than the body's response." He moved away. "Turtanu, speed the gathering of the spoils. We leave for Nineveh in two days."

* * * *

Istari sank to the chariot floor. The days of travel seemed endless and she wished for sleep. She'd lost track of how much time had passed in the monotony of the journey. Her hand stroked her abdomen where Ashur's seed had taken root.

He helped her to her feet. "Not far now. If we hurry, we can reach the city soon after nightfall." He pointed to a dark line on the horizon. "There are the walls."

She leaned against him. This was her last chance to change their fate. "Must we rush? I am with child and am tired."

He halted the chariot and hailed the captains. "We'll camp now."

Turtanu pulled his chariot beside Ashur's. "We could reach the city tonight."

"Better to arrive during the day so the people can share our triumph." He laughed. "Besides, I've just learned I'm to be a father and would celebrate with Istari this night."

Istari saw Mardu whisper in the other man's ear. Turtanu nodded. "You're right. Tomorrow, you should bear the statue of Marduke in your chariot."

A sense of foreboding filled Istari's thoughts. She was certain the pair schemed against Ashur. The stars moved toward the pattern that meant the death of the man she loved.

Ashur lifted her from the chariot. "I'll have the tent set up and meet with my captains. See that the cook brings our meal when it's done." He strode away.

Mardu grabbed Istari's arm. "The child you carry will never breathe or cry. Give me the seal so I may enter Nineveh as high priestess."

Istari shook her head. "I cannot. The seal is not for you. What evil are you planning?"

"Not evil. Justice. The diviners have spoken. The

astrologers know. Look to the stars and see the truth."

Mardu was right. Istari pulled away. There was a chance for the fate to be changed. She had to convince Ashur to leave and come with her.

When she entered the tent, she found Ashur and his captains discussing their entrance into the city. Ashur leaned forward. "Our making camp has allowed the tribute wagons and slaves to catch up."

Turtanu's smile made Istari stiffen. Hatred flashed in his eyes. "After consideration, I'll take Marduke in my chariot," he said.

"The statue goes with me," Ashur said. "The captive god travels to Nineveh with the leader."

Istari gasped. "No."

Ashur waved his men toward the tent opening. "You're dismissed. I must see to my woman." Once the others had departed, Ashur took Istari into his arms. "Don't fear, my star. Not for you the wagons of the slaves. You will ride with me."

She sank to her knees and grasped his legs. "Ashur, please. What if the god chooses to punish you for what happened in the temple?"

He chuckled. "He should be pleased for he returns to his home."

She swallowed. "I love you. I want to see you hold our child. Don't go to Nineveh. Let us leave this camp and find a place where we can live apart from all strife."

He pulled her to her feet. "I've heard being with child gives a woman strange notions. All will be well."

"Not the child. The stars. I have lost my country, my family. The stars say my grief is not at an end. Heed my warning. Turtanu and Mardu mean to harm you."

He laughed. "Why would my friend want to hurt me?"

"He envies you. He listens to Mardu. She is angry that you chose me and rejected her. She plays on his inner demons."

He pulled her into his arms. "Turtanu has gone as far in the ranks as is possible for his lowly birth. Harming me, his sponsor, makes no sense."

"She has closed his eyes to what is real and feeds him a dream."

His lips brushed hers. "Istari, I love you."

She sucked in a breath. "Then come away with me."

"And throw away my moment of triumph? When I enter Nineveh, the people will cheer. The king will honor me. I will become his son's advisor. My name will be sung in the temples. How can you ask me to walk away?"

She lowered her gaze. "Once again, ambition rules. And if taking me into the city means my death and the end of your hopes for a son?"

He peppered her face with kisses. "Star of my heart, fear not. Once I bring the god and the spoils to the king, I will sit at his right hand. His sister will be my wife and you, my beloved concubine. Your nights will be spent in my arms."

Tears spilled over her cheeks. This choice had been made before. Ambition won over love and they were doomed. She pressed her face against his chest.

"Come, show me the depth of your love." He opened her dress and when she was nude, laved her breasts with his tongue. "Soon, my son will feast here and I will envy him." He laid her on the pillows and stripped off his clothes. He knelt beside her and stroked her abdomen. "Hard to believe my son grows here."

She placed her hands over his. "'Tis too soon for my body to change."

"Your breasts are larger."

She beat back her fears and touched his penis. "As is your spear."

He growled. "Istari, I need you, want you, love you."

"Then come with me for I am yours now, forever, and as I was in the past." To hide a surge of fear and grief, she pulled him closer. He thrust inside and she forgot all but him.

Twice more that night, they made love. At dawn, they broke their fast and dressed. As they walked to the chariot, Istari held Ashur's hand. She felt as though she went to her doom.

The smile on Mardu's face increased Istari's uneasiness. The other woman's eyes glittered with hatred and secrets. A chill slithered along Istari's spine.

The statue of Marduke was lashed to the rear of Ashur's chariot. Instead of two horses, there were four. He lifted Istari into her place. She grasped his shoulders. "If you won't go with me, have the men remove Marduke."

He laughed and leaped beside her. He grasped the driving lines. "Don't be afraid. Think of my triumph. People will cheer and toss flowers. You can gather them to scent our bed this night."

Istari shook her head. "You do not understand. Your ambition rules this time as it did before. So be it."

He snapped the reins. The double pair of horses moved forward. Turtanu's chariot drew abreast. "You're a fool to carry the statue. The extra weight will slow you and allow me to receive the first cheers."

Ashur laughed. "We'll see who is first. You've never bested me in a race." He urged the horses into a gallop. They thundered toward the gates. The statue swayed from side to side. One of the ropes snapped.

"Slow the horses," Istari screamed. A second rope broke. The chariot jerked and bucked. Istari was tossed into the air. The horses screamed.

She slammed into the ground. Pain rocketed through her body. "Ashur," she cried. With slow and excruciating movements, she dragged herself to where Ashur lay beneath the statue. She bathed his face with her tears. "My love."

"Next time, my star." He shuddered. His eyes lost awareness.

She glared at the statue. "You have had your revenge. Why us when Mardu betrayed you?"

"Istari, Istari." Lamaru knelt beside her. Tears rolled down the girl's cheeks.

"The necklace. Take it, Lamaru-ishtaru. Don't let Mardu know you have the seal."

The girl fumbled with the fastening. "Let me help you."

"Too late." Istari rolled on her side and kissed Ashur's cheek. "My love, why didn't you listen?"

* * * *

A rapping on the door pulled Astrid from the vivid trip in the past. She rubbed her arms to erase the chill she'd felt. Another betrayal. What was happening? Was there a message to be found in these dreams? If only she could remember more than love and betrayal, but the images and experience had faded by the time she reached the door.

As she greeted Sarah, the image of the dying priestess flashed in her thoughts. Ishtar-ishtaru, her foster mother in that alien land. "Come in."

"I can't stay. I brought you a check I didn't want to leave in the drawer."

"Must be a large one."

Sarah nodded. "That charming Mr. Garrett dropped by to see you. Bought the pectoral you put on display this morning." She smiled. "Just think how great he'd look in the pectoral and a brief Egyptian kilt. As they say, the man is hot."

Astrid laughed. "Aunt Sarah."

The other woman patted Astrid's hand. "A woman's never too old to admire a well-honed body. Even Clive is easy on the eyes. Bit hard on the head, though." She peered past Astrid. "Looks like you made a good start."

"And was diverted. Any idea what Dad was up to?"

Sarah shook her head. "Research, he said. Had me finding books at the library and in used book stores. No rhyme or reason to his selection." She winked. "Back to Mr. Garrett. He was disappointed to find you'd left."

Astrid stared at the floor. Even the mention of his name made her feel flushed. "Did he say why?"

Sarah chuckled. "When an eligible man asks about an equally eligible woman, there's no need to ask why. You interested?"

"Maybe." Astrid felt a pulsing in her lower abdomen. What was wrong with her? Thinking about him made her want to be in his arms.

"He gives off good vibes," Sarah said.

What he emits is an invitation to sin, Astrid thought. When she recalled how close she'd come to surrender, she hoped she wouldn't see him for years, even decades.

"He mentioned an excellent rehab facility. Said he was visiting your father after he left. I'm heading to the hospital after dinner. See you tomorrow."

Astrid closed the door. She wrapped the necklace in cloth and shoved the packet in a drawer of her father's dresser. After a quick shower, she grabbed the portfolio of photos and drove to the hospital. As she left the car, she saw Duncan emerge from the entrance. She'd hoped to avoid him. Though she wanted to hide, she left the car. She couldn't play chicken.

Duncan strode across the drive. "I wanted to talk to you."

"This morning was a mistake."

His eyes narrowed. "I don't think so. Want me to prove you wrong, here and now?"

Astrid breathed the scent of him and felt blood rush through her veins. "Let's call this a stalemate, Mr. Garrett."

"Only if you call me Duncan. Why don't I hang around until you're finished with your visit? I'll take you to dinner."

"I'm booked." She stepped around him.

He placed his hands on her shoulders. Memories of the kiss flooded her.

"Tomorrow after Antiquities closes?"

She stiffened. "I don't have time to get involved with you."

"We're already involved." His breath brushed her nape sending a message she wanted to accept. Could she spend time with him and not succumb to the desire to taste passion? This time she had to be cautious. *Where did that come from?*

"Will you?"

"Dinner then. Tomorrow."

He turned her to face him. "We'll take the sex slow and easy."

"What?"

He grinned. "I have some ideas about your father's rehab. We'll talk about them over dinner."

"Why are you taking an interest?"

"I like him. From the moment I entered Antiquities, I felt a connection." He shrugged. "I can't explain that any more than I can my craving for you."

She shook her head. "Bury your craving and I'll meet you at any restaurant you choose."

"I'll stop by the shop tomorrow and let you know." He leaned closer. "Sex will be incandescent."

Astrid strode into the hospital. He was right, but she wasn't sure she wanted to play the game.

* * * *

Duncan started the sports car. Instead of going home, he headed to the Thruway north and hit the gas. Thoughts of seduction pulsed with the hard rock blaring from the speakers. He grinned. She'd agreed to dinner. He felt like a teenager who'd just been accepted by the most popular girl in school.

Dinner. He knew the perfect place--soft music, candlelight, great food. He owned a piece of the restaurant and the private booth in the rear corner was his whenever he asked.

For a moment, he could almost feel her skin beneath his hands. He sucked in a breath. He couldn't remember a time when he'd been this obsessed with any woman. Even his teenage passions hadn't kept him in a state of constant arousal.

This afternoon when he'd stopped at Antiquities, he'd bought a pectoral. The item hadn't been displayed before. The desire to own it had been almost as strong as his desire for Astrid. A picture of a nude woman lifting the piece of jewelry over a man's head had flashed into his thoughts. Had the incident been real or the product of a vivid imagination?

At the last exit before the toll, he left the Thruway, did a U-turn and drove back to town. Time for another cold shower and to make arrangements for tomorrow's dinner.

* * * *

Astrid left the hospital and hurried home. As she started up the steps, Paula called her name. Astrid waited. "Good timing."

"I try."

Astrid led the way and opened the door. Paula put her package on the bar and walked to the large picture window. "What a great view. I envy you."

"Just mine for the summer. Do you live in town?"

"My small house isn't far from the hospital. Part of a divorce settlement. Next time, I'll have you there."

Astrid took a bottle of white wine from the refrigerator. "Will you join me?"

Paula nodded. She took two wrapped packets and two containers from the bag. "Dessert. White chocolate soufflé with raspberry sauce served in a chocolate fudge shell."

"Calories."

Paula laughed. "We'll make up for the ones we don't consume with the pitas. How's your dad?"

Astrid poured two glasses of wine. "Improving. He loved the pictures." Another moment of her visit to the hospital intruded and she sighed.

"Problems?"

"Maybe. What do you know about Duncan Garrett?"

"A bit. Why?"

"He invited me to dinner tomorrow evening. Seems he has plans for Dad's rehab."

Paula raised her glass. "Go. Enjoy. He's all male and gorgeous. Would love to do a nude study of him."

Astrid laughed. "Aunt Sarah wants to see him wearing a pectoral and an Egyptian kilt."

"He's definitely drool material."

"That's not what I meant."

"Just dreaming of the impossible. His family has been here forever. Probably own half of town with an interest in any number of local businesses. He runs them."

Astrid frowned. Did he own part of Antiquities? Dad had never mentioned a partner, silent or otherwise.

Paula carried the pitas and dressing to the table. "Garrett's kind of a Renaissance man. Black belt in some martial art. Skis, sails, swims, and drives a killer car. Published two action/adventure novels. Supports the local art community."

Astrid grinned. "Sounds like a Jack of all."

"And master of most. Only child. Parents died when he was five or six. Raised by his grandfather. Never divorced, engaged or married. Any woman involved with him shouldn't think long-term."

Astrid looked away. "I'm not going there ... wonder why I never met him. After my mother died, I came here to live with my father, went to the local high school."

Paula refilled her glass. "No mystery there. He attended a private school across the river. Go to dinner and enjoy. Just keep him at arm's length."

Could she? Astrid picked up her pita. After the kiss and her reaction to him this afternoon, she wasn't sure she could.

CHINA

Astrid shoved the last sales slip in the appropriate folder and leaned back in the chair. Five folders lay on the desk. Tomorrow when the shop was closed, she would enter the data into the records and Antiquities' books would be up-to-date. Then the inventory would be the last of her summer chores.

She heard Sarah's laughter, followed by a deep chuckle. What had amused the older woman? Before Astrid had a chance to investigate, Duncan appeared in the doorway. The impact of his presence sent blood rushing from her head to settle low in her abdomen. She sucked in a breath. If she reacted this strongly when he was across a room, how was she going to sit across a restaurant table without revealing how much she wanted him?

"Duncan." Her mouth felt dry and a need for flight surfaced. She wanted to moisten her lips with her tongue. Wrong move. She knew the message that gesture would telegraph. Not a lie, but unwise.

He smiled. "I missed you this morning. Never run on Sundays?"

"Took a different route--down River Road."

He arched a brow. "Afraid of another ambush?"

She shook her head. "Just re-acquainting myself with the area."

He placed his hands on the desk and leaned toward her. "Tomorrow?"

"Maybe, or I might head to the lake. The path around there is one of my favorites."

He laughed. "If I promise not to attack, will you come my way tomorrow?"

"Can you?"

"With the right incentive."

She switched on the computer. "Bantering is fun, but I've work to do."

"Wouldn't want to keep you. About tonight. Emilio's at

seven. I'll swing by at quarter to."

"I'll walk and meet you there. Wasn't that the agreement?"

He nodded. "What if it rains?"

"Not much chance of bad weather, but come rain and I'll drive."

He ran a finger over the back of her hand. "See you then."

His touch left her skin tingling. Why did she feel this connection to a man who was a stranger?

* * * *

After leaving the gallery, Astrid drove to the hospital. She found her father standing at the door, gripping a walker. "Coming or going?"

"Waiting. Walk. Lounge."

"Then let's go." In the lounge, she helped him settle on a chair. "How are you feeling?"

"Frus-- frus-- know what ... mean."

"You don't like to feel helpless." She reached for his hand. "Actually, you're making great strides. By the end of summer, I'll have you running to the Hook with me."

"No."

She grinned. "We'll see."

"Sarah said walk."

"Then, I'll let her take charge." A short time later, she helped him back to bed and kissed his cheek. "I need to go. Having dinner with Duncan."

"En ... joy."

"I hope so."

"Like him."

"He told me you're friends."

"Con ... con ... nect past."

She frowned. What kind of connection did he mean? She walked to the door. "See you tomorrow. Sarah will be here later."

"Have fun."

Astrid hurried to her car. When she reached the apartment, she dashed up the steps. Inside, she paused at her closet. She chose a cotton dress with large buttons down the front.

After dressing, she stared at her reflection. Excitement shone in her eyes. The raspberry color of the dress brought a glow to her skin. She clipped her hair at the nape.

As she left the bedroom, she considered her feelings. She had to remember what Paula had said about Duncan and long-term relationships. Not his style. Hers either. She had no time for more than casual, but the strength of the attraction ruled out anything casual.

When Astrid stepped onto the deck, Sarah emerged from her apartment. "Thought you were having dinner with Mr. Garrett," the older woman said.

"I'm meeting him."

"Good idea on a first date." Sarah tapped her purse. "I'm on my way to beat your dad at Gin Rummy."

"Enjoy."

By the time Astrid reached the restaurant, the town clock chimed seven times. Duncan waited near the entrance. "Not only prompt, but beautiful."

"Flatterer." The heat in his gaze threatened to dissolve her determination to avoid further encounters. They followed the maitre d' to a booth in the far corner. When she saw the only seating was a padded bench big enough for two, she nearly bolted. She'd expected flirtation, not togetherness.

Duncan ushered her in and sat next to her. "I took the liberty of ordering."

"What if you've chosen things I detest?"

"I talked to Sarah and your dad about your preferences."

"You're too much."

He covered her hand with his. "I'm betting I'm just enough."

She sucked in a breath and regretted the action. The air was laden with his soap, aftershave and a trace of the passion they'd discovered at the Hook. She was rapidly losing the battle to remain aloof. Heat from his touch spiraled along her nerves and brought a pulsing throb of need.

"About your dad."

Astrid pulled herself from the erotic miasma. "Yes."

"I know an excellent rehab facility. I was there after a skiing accident. I'll drop brochures with your dad so you can study them. When does he expect to be discharged?"

"Maybe Wednesday. I'm meeting with his doctor tomorrow." She slid her hand away. "I know you want to help, but I'm sure this place of yours is expensive."

He shrugged. "Guess so. Don't worry about the cost."

But she did and she would. Deftly, she changed the subject to Rockleigh and Antiquities. The heavy tension between them lessened. The first course arrived. Astrid tasted the salad and puff pastry.

"Do you like?" Duncan asked.

She nodded. "Great chef. Dressing is perfect."

"I'll let him know."

"I suppose you know him."

He nodded. "Dragged him here from the city." He captured her gaze. "Maybe you'll stay here when summer ends."

"That's a given. I start grad school in September. Once I have the Antiquities' books in order, I'll start looking for my own apartment."

He grinned. "I could use a housemate."

"I don't think so."

He leaned closer and put his mouth against her ear. "I intend to work toward that goal."

The arrival of the waiter with the main course gave Astrid a chance to regain her equilibrium. They talked of books, movies and music. By the time dessert arrived, Astrid felt comfortable with the place and the man. She tasted the raspberry torte and sighed. "Wonderful. I'll have to do ten miles tomorrow to burn off the calories."

He looked at her over the rim of his coffee cup. "If exercise is on your agenda, I'm up for some."

She nearly choked. "You're impossible."

"Never. Astrid, I'm entirely possible."

She finished the dessert and coffee. "Thanks for dinner. I've a busy day tomorrow." She rose.

"I'll walk you home."

Astrid sighed. She didn't want to be alone with him, but she couldn't think of a way to avoid his company. He would only follow. Maybe Sarah would be sitting on the deck. Maybe goodbye could be said at the foot of the steps. Maybe … no other escape route arose.

He signaled for the check. As they left, several people greeted him. Two women gave her a quick appraisal. Duncan kept her hand in his. They stepped into a sultry night. The moon rode low in a star-filled sky. Astrid couldn't think of anything to say. She was too busy trying to order her body into a denial of desire for him.

When they reached the apartment door, he plucked the key from her hand. He slipped it into the lock, then turned her to face him. This time, the kiss wasn't the demanding one of the Hook. He kissed the corner of her mouth, then as though tasting every centimeter, he slid his lips over hers. He pulled her closer. Through her skirt, she felt his erection swell and pulse. An answering throb beat along her vulva. What was she going to do? She craved him, wanted him to thrust into her depths.

By the time the kiss ended, they were both panting for breath. "Let me come in," he said. "I'll go as far as you want."

She pressed her forehead against his shoulder. "We're rushing. I know so little about you."

"A problem easily remedied."

She wished she could tell him to go and never come back, but she couldn't force herself to speak.

He brought her hands to his mouth and kissed each palm. "Ask me in for coffee. We can share our pasts and maybe a few kisses. What I know is I want you more than I've ever wanted a woman before."

Astrid sighed. "I can't deny I'm strongly attracted to you."

"Then let's talk and make-out a bit." He turned the key and opened the door. "Your call. When you tell me to go, I'm out of here."

Could she believe him? After deciding to take a chance, she stepped inside and he followed. While she started coffee, he stood at the large picture window. He turned. "Come here."

Astrid took a deep breath and crossed the room. He drew her into his arms. Lips fused and tongues tangled. A fierce desire to feel his skin overwhelmed her. She found the buttons on his shirt. Once they were opened, she stroked his chest, curled her fingers in his chest hairs. "What's happening to us?"

"Madness. Delightful madness."

Their bodies swayed. She pushed his shirt from his shoulders. His tongue laved her mouth. He opened the buttons of her dress. He ran his tongue over her throat and along the edge of her bra. Slowly, he backed to the couch, sat and pulled her onto his lap.

As he slid her dress from her shoulders, he drew a nipple into his mouth. A jolt of pure pleasure shot through Astrid. She was lost in a euphoric bath of sensations. His assault continued and though she should cry a halt, she inched the zipper of his trousers down and slid her fingers into the opening.

"Oh, yes," he said.

A sound intruded. For a moment, Astrid couldn't think. The phone. She jerked away and grabbed the receiver. Had something happened to her dad? "Hello ... Clive?"

"Did I catch you outside? You sound out of breath."

"Something like that. Did you have a problem at the sales?"

"Absolutely not. Just wanted to make sure you'll be at the shop tomorrow. I've something for the vault. Would make my life easier if you'd give me the combination."

"Ask Dad. I'll definitely be there in the morning."

"I should arrive around noon."

Duncan reached for the receiver. Astrid shook her head. "Bye." She hung up. "Just what were you planning?"

"To tell him his timing was off."

She buttoned her dress. "I think ours is. I had no intention of going as far as we did."

He clasped her hand. "Be honest."

She lowered her gaze. "When we kiss, I can't think. That's not good."

"Are you telling me it's time to go?"

She nodded. "We can't let this attraction blaze out of control."

"You're right." He straightened his clothes. "Next time, we'll have a plan."

"Next time?"

He placed his fingers on her lips. "There will be one."

Astrid sighed. He was right, but she wasn't about to tell him. "We'll see."

"I'll stop by tomorrow."

She needed time to think, to discover why she felt this way and if the visits to the past were involved. If only she could remember more. "Give me some time."

"A week?"

"Yes."

"About your dad. Think about the place I suggested." He

strode to the door. "Night."

When the door closed behind him, Astrid slumped on the couch. Being in his arms had seemed so right, but so had calling a halt. She felt battered, but she had a week to think. Would she have her head straight by then?

* * * *

Duncan bounded down the steps. What was going on? He'd planned a subtle seduction. Instead, the moment he'd kissed her, he'd leaped. She'd been right to send him away. If they continued at the speed they were traveling, they would burn to cinders. Since slow and easy wasn't an option, he had to learn how to handle warp speed. Could he do that in a week?

As he strode up the street toward his house, he thought of Lloyd. He really wanted to help the older man recover. His gut reaction told him Lloyd's health was important. Duncan had no idea why he felt this way, but he was compelled to aid him to a full recovery and quick return to Antiquities. In the morning, he intended to call Lloyd's doctor and offer to help with the cost of the rehab center. During their many discussions, Duncan had learned Lloyd's assets were invested in the shop. With the intensive program, Lloyd would be back in Rockleigh within weeks.

At the house, Duncan strode through the foyer where his footsteps echoed. An empty house built for a large family that hadn't been produced in any Garrett generation. Two children in the first and second, then a single son in the next four. Sometimes, he wondered why he clung to the place, but this was home.

As he entered the study of the master suite, the blinking light of the answering machine caught his attention. He pressed the play button. Lorna's husky voice crooned his name.

"Duncan, just arrived and already, I miss you. Clear up whatever business is keeping you in town. This place is made for lovers. I want you, not Clive."

The second message from her was shorter and a hint of anger colored her voice.

He shook his head. He had no intention of becoming her lover. Since the day Clive had introduced them, she'd been as persistent as a gnat. He believed if he accepted her less that subtle invitation to an affair, he'd be stuck like a bug on flypaper. The only reason he'd cultivated her was for the hints she'd tossed out. Did she really know something about the items stolen all those years ago?

The third message wheedled. He let the fourth play. "Clive's here. Says you're on the prowl. If you think you're tossing me aside, think again. Remember, I have information you want. Stay away from Lloyd's daughter before someone gets hurt."

Duncan stabbed the erase button. No way was he listening to her threats. He would find the missing treasures without her help.

* * * *

When Astrid heard the shop bell, she glanced at her watch. It had to be Clive. Well after one. At least he had arrived before her three o'clock appointment to discuss rehab facilities with her father's doctor.

Clive strode into the office. Astrid frowned. Why had he brought Lorna? The blonde woman troubled Astrid in a way she couldn't define. Though they'd just met, the antipathy made Astrid feel they'd been enemies for years.

Clive placed three boxes on the desk. "You're looking good. Guess the weekend went fine."

Astrid wanted to roll her eyes but refrained. "We were busy. Made deposits both days. The Victorian and Art Nouveau pieces sold well. We'll need to re-stock, but not today. How was your weekend?"

"Fruitful." He tapped the boxes. "Victorian. Art Nouveau. Jade. Should go in the vault until I have time to price them."

"Will do."

"As I've said before, you could give me the combination and save yourself trouble."

"Not my place to do. Talk to Dad."

"I will. Could we have dinner tonight?"

Before Astrid could answer, Lorna stormed into the office. "Where are my necklace and crown? Did you sell them to Duncan?"

"What are you talking about?" Astrid asked.

"The Egyptian set. I have first dibs on them."

Astrid stared at the other woman. All her prettiness had vanished beneath her angry scowl. "They weren't yours and they're not for sale. I don't know where you got the idea you were entitled to them."

"Clive told me I could have them." As Lorna smiled at the blonde man, her features mutated. "Tell her?"

He shrugged. "I said you could make an offer."

"I'll top any amount he offers. Name a figure."

"Why do you want them?" Astrid asked.

"They belonged to a relative. She had to sell them to live and that was how she made the fortune I inherited."

Astrid rose. "Do you have proof?"

"My word is enough."

Astrid looked away. "Just remember, Clive doesn't have the authority to give or sell them to you."

"Then where are they?"

"In the vault until my father returns."

Lorna's hands rested on her hips. "And if I accuse your father of receiving stolen property, he'll be in trouble."

"How? Didn't you say your relative sold them?" Or stole them, Astrid thought.

Lorna turned to Clive. "Take me home."

Astrid watched the pair until they left the shop. Her father had mentioned articles stolen from Duncan's ancestor years ago. Were the crown and necklace among the missing things? She needed answers, but she couldn't question her dad until she was sure he was able to handle the puzzle of her visits to the past.

She locked the outer door and opened the vault. She put two of the boxes on the shelves in the long narrow room. Driven by a need to see the jade, she opened the box. She stroked the back of a horse and admired the intricate carved fish. Several pendants caught her eye. She sat at the desk and lifted a chain carved from ivory and stared at the pendant.

* * * *

Xing-Xing could hardly contain her excitement. Today her silk merchant father, Huang Yu, returned from his travels. Two days ago, his messenger had arrived. Since then, the women and servants of the household had prepared for his home-coming. The house had been cleaned and her father's favorite dishes prepared.

She hurried to the garden to gather flowers. What gift would he bring his lowly daughter? He always found something special for her.

She had another reason for eager anticipation. Her oldest brother had taken Chu Hua, the youngest daughter of a city merchant, as his wife. The bride was Xing-Xing's age and she hoped they could be friends. For all her life, her days had been bound by noisy brothers who had no interest in the things she liked. Of the household women, only Ah Lam, youngest of the concubines, matched Xing-Xing's age. Between them lay an animosity that had no reason to exist.

Xing-Xing straightened. Her second brother, Huang Hsia, slipped through the garden. His furtive glances caught her attention. He ran into the mulberry grove. Where once he'd been a happy and fun companion, since the departure of their father and elder brother, he had turned secretive and surly.

Before she had a chance to follow, Ah Lam crept from the house and hurried toward the trees.

As silently as possible, Xing-Xing followed. She moved from tree to tree until she heard their voices. Then, she edged closer and peered around a trunk. With a hand, she muffled a gasp.

Ah Lam grasped Huang Hsia's arms. "You must come to me as you have every night this lunar. My lotus craves your jade stem. How can you desert me? I need your vigor."

Huang Hsia jerked away. "Ah Lam, I love you. I want to be with you, but I can't. Father returns today. I must regain my honor."

"He is old. He is fat. His stem is a withered reed. Give me a child and he will leave me alone."

Huang Hsia evaded her grasping hands. "I will ask him to give you to me."

She scratched his face. "He won't. If he was dead--"

"Then my elder brother would rule the house. I cannot do what you ask. All I can do is ask my father for you."

"He will punish me. Would you see me beaten and cast out? Don't you desire me? What happened to your eagerness for my lotus? Even now your jade stem strains to pleasure me." She turned away. "I will find another man, one who is young and handsome, to pleasure me."

Xing-Xing heard the gate gong. She turned to run. Her brother grabbed her arm. "What are you doing here?"

His voice menaced. His gaze threatened. "Walking."

"If you say a word to anyone, I'll make you sorry."

She looked at him. "Why Ah Lam? There are women in the village."

"None so eager and as skilled."

"She belongs to father."

He nodded. "He gave her to me for one night so I could learn the ways of love. That wasn't enough. My heart yearns for her and hers for me."

Xing-Xing shook her head. "You may love Ah Lam, but she seeks to make mischief."

"You don't understand. You're only a girl."

She shook her head. "I'm a woman. Father seeks a husband for me." She broke free, ran to the garden for the basket of flowers she had picked. She reached the gate in time to see the procession. First came the palanquin bearing her elder brother and his bride. Her father rode in the second with a stranger. Xing-Xing sucked in a breath. Was the young and handsome man to be her husband?

Her father's wives and concubines gathered around him. Xing-Xing glanced at the women. Ah Lam stared at the stranger. A cat's smile bowed her lips. Xing-Xing wanted to slap the concubine.

After her father greeted the women, he called Xing-Xing to his side. "Star of my future happiness, I have a gift for you."

Her heart thudded. She kept her head bowed. Instead of presenting his companion, he drew a carved jade pendant from its silk wrappings. The chain was ivory, each link intertwined with the next. She couldn't see how they'd been joined.

"This unworthy girl thanks you. Such beauty brightens the day made radiant by your return."

She looked up. Her gaze locked with the stranger's. His heated stare stole her breath, her thoughts, her heart. He was no older than her eldest brother. Surely, he would be hers.

Her father grasped her arm. "Come and bid your Chu Hua welcome. Take her to the rooms prepared for them so she can see to her belongings."

Xing-Xing bowed. "I will gladly do this."

As they walked away, she felt the stranger's heated gaze on her back. She hugged the knowledge inside. He desired her, not Ah Lam. Why hadn't her father named him? Was the man observing her before he asked for her as his bride?

She took Chu Hua to the rooms on the other side of the sprawling compound. The other woman had a merry smile. When she entered the room, her eyes sparkled with delight. "How fortunate you are not to live in the city. My honored father's house there is crowded and our garden small."

Xing-Xing smiled. "The house and land came to my father when he married my mother. She was the only child of her house. The mulberry groves and silk worms were part of her dowry."

"Have you sisters?"

"Seven brothers. Fortunate is my father for he has many sons to care for his bones and venerate him when he dies."

"How fortunate you are. I have two brothers and four sisters. I'm but the second daughter to find a husband." Chu Hua pulled up her sleeve to reveal a line of scratches. "One of my sisters did this when she learned the honorable Huang Yu chose me for his son. What are the household's women like?"

"My mother is strict, but kind. All of the women except Ah Lam, my father's youngest concubine, are nice. She's greedy. Steals the presents my honorable father brings me and says I gave them to her. Stares at all the men like a cat sizing a mouse."

"I will watch for her."

"She hasn't given my father a son. The herb woman says Ah Lam knows ways to rid herself of an unwanted child."

Chu Hua nodded. "I have heard there are ways. How can she deny your father a son?" She smiled. "I think I'm with child. Your brother is a lusty lover. He comes to me every night, sometimes twice."

"Does it hurt?"

"One time. Then it's all pleasure."

Servants carried boxes into the room. Xing-Xing's oldest brother followed. He embraced Chu Hua and caressed her back. Xing-Xing hurried away. Would a man ever touch her with fire and tenderness? An odd feeling throbbed in her lotus. She closed her eyes and imagined the stranger's hands moving on her body.

"Xing-Xing, come. Time to serve the meal," her mother said. "There is no time for dreaming."

"Yes, Mother." Xing-Xing followed the maid who carried the soup tureen into the room where the men and boys had gathered at the large table. She ladled soup into the bowls. Other women brought the many dishes of food and heaping bowls of rice. Her brother and Chu Hua arrived. Her flushed cheeks brought teasing remarks from the women.

Xing-Xing barely ate. The stranger held her attention. How wonderful his scent. How melodious his voice.

"Wu Ping, do you think you can make scholars of these rowdy boys?" Huang Yu asked.

"I can but try. Not all boys have the knack of learning, but they can master enough skills to make them assets for the house of Huang."

Xing-Xing hid her disappointment. Not her husband-to-be. Only a tutor. Yet his clothes were fine and he looked more like a soldier than a scholar.

"Xing-Xing, would you show the teacher to his rooms," Huang Yu said. "See that he has all he needs."

* * * *

Wu Ping followed the girl from the house. She was the loveliest of the household women. How fortunate Huang Yu was to have such a lovely blossom in his garden. This Xing-Xing must be special. The necklace the merchant had given her was costly. Why had his patron sent her as his escort instead of one of the older women? Was this a test? To bring a young stranger into the house was a risk. Wu Ping prayed for the strength to resist.

He clenched his hands. He had to take care. Huang Yu was a wealthy man who had influence at the emperor's court. To anger a current patron would bring nothing but grief. The merchant's generosity could gain Wu Ping entrance to the court to spread the teachings of Lao Tze throughout the land.

Still, the swaying hips of the young concubine and her subtle scent captured Wu Ping's attention. Watching her move filled him with desire. Would her lotus blossom hold his jade stem? A rush of heat stiffened his organ.

The girl opened the door of a small house just beyond the flower garden. "Here is the tutor's place. The classroom, a sleeping and sitting rooms. You will take your meals with the family."

She backed up and collided with him. He put his arms

around her waist to keep them from falling. She trembled. "I won't hurt you," he whispered. Her scent surrounded him. Though he should release her, he couldn't move. Finally, he let his arms drop to his sides. To do the things he wished would cause him to lose his position and maybe his life.

She turned. "You are most handsome."

He looked away. "Go before I do something I will regret."

She peered from beneath lowered lashes. "What?"

Drawn by an urgency he didn't understand, he pressed his lips against hers. The desire to carry her to the sleeping room grew strong. Abruptly, he ended the kiss. "That and more, but you belong to Huang Yu and I dare not touch you unless he gives me leave."

She smiled. "He is my honored father. I will ask his permission to return to the classroom so I can have lessons with my brothers."

Wu Ping stepped away. "Girls do not belong in school. Their place is with their mothers learning womanly arts." If she came every day, he would be tempted to take what he desired.

"I know those things and I have had lessons in reading and writing." Xing-Xing glanced from beneath her lowered lashes.

Wu Ping stepped back. "Go and trouble me no more with your beauty."

She brushed past him. As he watched her graceful flight, he groaned. Why had he kissed her? Only trouble would arise from that action.

"Wu Ping, have you a need for a woman?"

The sudden appearance of the plump concubine startled him. Her blatant appraisal of his groin troubled him. "No." He stepped inside and closed the door. Though no innocent like Xing-Xing, this woman was also forbidden. Unless the patron offered her services, he must avoid the concubine and only dream of the daughter.

* * * *

Xing-Xing ran her tongue along her lips. The taste of him had been better than summer melons. His scent had also intoxicated and his touch had been like silk. She moved swiftly through the women's quarters to her room. She glanced at the gathering of wives and concubines in the sitting room. Where was Ah Lam? Was the concubine with Father or had she been sent to Wu Ping? She was often loaned to guests.

Xing-Xing's hands formed fists. Wu Ping was hers. The moment their gazes had met, she had known they belonged together. His kiss had roused a need she didn't know how to ease.

She entered her room. As the only daughter, she didn't have to share. She stood at the window and stared into the garden. The scents of the flowers failed to mask her memories of Wu Ping's aroma. She lit a lantern and sat at the table where her ink and brushes waited. She would show the tutor how learned she was. She would write a poem for him.

She closed her eyes and recalled the man. Though his hair wasn't flat and smooth, she liked the rumpled look. He was taller and more muscular than her older brothers. Holding his image in her thoughts, she dipped the brush in.

Stranger, teacher, you stand tall
Tease my thoughts with words of need.
The owl spreads wings in my heart
Fans my desire in passing.

When the ink dried, she rolled the rice paper and tied it with a ribbon. She slipped from her room and ran along the garden paths. In the classroom, she paused. Only the soft sounds of sleep came from the inner rooms. She placed the scroll at his place and ran back to the house. Would he reply?

* * * *

On his way to the house to break his fast, Wu Ping found the poem. He smelled the ribbon and savored Xing-Xing's scent. The faint aroma brought a memory of the kiss and a promise of the passion he craved. What should he do?

The wisest course would be to leave and seek another patron. He wanted Xing-Xing as he'd never wanted a woman before. His fingers touched his erection. Hot, hard, ready. He shook his head. He would tell Huang Yu he must continue his journey. But the wealthy merchant had the influence to gain the emperor's ear.

Wu Ping groaned. Choices must be made. He wished to be an influence in the land. He wanted the teachings of the man whose philosophy he admired to be on every man's lips. Could he have the patronage and the woman he wanted beyond all wisdom?

He felt he'd known her before. Had loved and lost her. Had been betrayed by someone he'd trusted.

After the morning meal, he should have prepared lessons for his students. Instead, he spent the morning composing his answer. The students' morning chores gave him this time to take a most improper step.

> *My silent star, far you seem*
> *Beyond the reach of my heart.*
> *I wish to face your presence*
> *A feast to my starving soul.*
> *Oh, come to me, my star, come.*
> *I will stroke you with my voice*
> *And caress you with my eyes.*

He left the poem in his room and waited for his students. How would he find a way to slip the poem to her?

By late afternoon, he felt exhausted. The boys ran from the classroom. Wu Ping stood in the doorway. Xing-Xing and Chu Hua stood in the garden. He hurried to his sleeping room for the poem and entered one of the paths among the flower beds. Xing-Xing held a basket while Chu Hua selected blossoms. He slipped the poem into the basket and returned to the tutor's house. Would she like the poem? Would she come to him?

He opened the door and gasped. Ah Lam stood at the door to his sleeping room. Her tunic was open far enough for him to see her large breasts. "What are you doing here?"

"Waiting for you." She glided toward him. "Why do you look where you dare not touch?"

"Did Huang Yu send you?"

She laughed. "He ignores me. I have needs his withered reed cannot ease."

"He will be angry to find you here."

"I care not. Unhappy is my life in this house. I am despised because I don't bear a child. I want you, not an old man with a weak stem. Give me a child and I will give you pleasure."

"Leave or I will go to Huang Yu."

Her lips thinned. "Walk with care, Wu Ping." As she left, she fastened her tunic.

He sank on a cushion. This house holds too many

dangers. In the morning, he would leave.
* * * *

Xing-Xing's heart fluttered. He had answered. Chu Hua pulled Xing-Xing into the shade of a tree. "He is very handsome. What did he give you?"

"A poem. I wrote one for him." She opened the rolled paper and read the words. He wanted her to come. She smiled. This very night, she would go to him.

Chu Hua giggled. "I saw the way he looked at you. His eyes are heated the way my honored husband's are when he comes to me. You must be careful."

Xing-Xing nodded. She prayed she could trust her new friend, but she had to tell someone. "My father seeks a husband for me, one to increase the prestige of the house. I want Wu Ping. I feel I've known him forever."

"Tell your father of your feelings."

"Not until I know how deeply Wu Ping cares for me."

Chu Hua nodded. "Wise thought. Confusing the hunger of the body for one of the heart can happen."

"How can one be sure?"

"When I first looked on your brother, I admired his face and his form. When we touched, was like my body was seared with flames. We looked into each other's eyes and I knew I wanted him to give me children and to spend the rest of my life seeing to his needs."

"I will think on what you have said."

"You must speak to Wu Ping." Chu Hua patted Xing-Xing's arm. "If your father agrees, you and Wu Ping can live here and I won't lose the friend I've just made."

"I feel we have known each other before."

"Maybe we have."

After the flowers had been arranged, Xing-Xing helped serve the evening meal. She sat at the table and kept her gaze on the bowl. To look at Wu Ping would be to betray her feelings. When the meal ended, she followed the women and went to her room. There, she stripped and washed her body. Though she wanted to don one of her elaborate robes, she dare not be caught in her finery. Once dressed, she sat on her sleeping mat and waited for the household to settle for the night.

The moon was a pale crescent. She scurried through the garden to the tutor's house. She slipped inside and made her way to the sleeping room. Wu Ping lay on his mat. For a moment, she studied his face. His tousled hair called for smoothing. In sleep, he looked young. Her gaze slid from his face to his chest. One hand covered her mouth. He slept nude. Curiosity pulled her attention down. His jade stem was nothing like the ones she'd seen on her younger brothers when she'd helped with their care. His was longer and thicker, but it didn't look hard.

"Who?"

The harsh whisper made her jump. She drew in a deep breath. "Xing-Xing. I would gaze on your face and caress you with my eyes." Her mouth gaped. His jade stem grew larger. Would such a big thing fit into her lotus? Her body felt warm and she wanted to strip off her clothes so the night air would cool her heated flesh.

Wu Ping rose. "Why have you come?"

"You have stirred me in ways I don't understand. I wish to know if what I feel is love of the body or the soul."

He smiled. "Without a meeting of the bodies, there can be no meeting of the souls. Star of my night, shine for me alone." He touched her lips with his fingers.

She lowered her gaze. One finger touched his swollen member. "It's hot. Hard, yet soft. A jade stem, yet alive. Will you pierce my lotus and bring gentle rain?"

He placed his hands on her shoulders. He touched his nose to hers. "I will do all those things and the rain will be a torrent. First, I must prepare you for what is to come." He held her close and stroked her back. "Don't fear." His mouth closed over hers.

The sensations his kiss had raised the day of his arrival returned. She pressed closer to him.

He stepped back. As he unfastened her tunic, he pushed the cloth from her shoulders. The tunic fell on the floor. She wanted to cover her breasts, but his eyes darkened and held her still. He caressed her shoulders and ran his hands over her breasts. The nipples tightened.

"Wu Ping, I feel hot ... different."

"I know. Your body is crying for mine." He untied her trousers and ran his hand along her abdomen.

She threw her arms around him. She felt afraid and excited. His jade stem touched her and she gasped. He led her to the sleeping mat. She turned. "What should I do?"

"Lie down and I will show you."

"Can I touch you?"

He lay beside her. "I would like that."

She rose to her knees. With her hands, she explored his face. When he sucked on one of her fingers, her lotus pulsed. She ran her hands over the smooth skin of his chest and touched his nipples. They tightened the way hers had. Her explorations continued. His abdomen was flat. She touched the top of his jade stem. A drop of fluid wet her finger. She placed her hand around the shaft.

He groaned. "My body is prepared, but yours is not." He pushed her back and cupped her breasts. "I prepare the garden for the rain."

His mouth touched one of her breasts. Xing-Xing placed her hands against the mat. She wanted to move, to cry.

When his hands reached her abdomen, he nudged her legs apart. He stroked her lotus and she moaned. Then, he touched a place that sent heat through her body. "What do you do?"

"This is your pearl, your hidden treasure."

He continued to stroke the spot. Soft moans poured from her depths. She moved restlessly. "Wu Ping, Wu Ping."

He spread his hands beneath her hips and lifted them slightly. "Xing-Xing, look at me." She opened her eyes. "Your lotus gathers dew to welcome me."

She felt a stretching. As he slid into her, her lotus blossomed. He slid his jade stem in and out. She pressed her feet on the mat and strained to reach a summit. Her body burned. She felt ready to shatter. He thrust harder.

He growled. "My star, seek the heavenly palace with me."

Within her, heat roared. She pressed her hands against her mouth. Surely, she would scream for the pleasure was exquisite. He thrust again and again. Her lotus convulsed and tightened around his jade stem. As she cried his name, she felt the rain, not gentle, but like a violent thunderstorm.

He collapsed atop her and was still for a time. Then, he rolled to his side and embraced her.

"Wu Ping, you have captured my soul."

He traced her lips with a finger. "As you have mine."

"I would be with you forever."

"You can't stay."

"I will speak to my father. I will tell him I love you and

want you for my husband."

He silenced her with a kiss. "When the time is right, I will speak to him." He rose and pulled her to her feet. "You must dress and return to the house."

"I will come tomorrow when the moon rises."

* * * *

After Xing-Xing left, Wu Ping cleansed the blood of her maidenhood from his jade stem. What had he done? He should have sent her away, but the words of dismissal had frozen on his tongue. He'd needed her and he wasn't sure why. How could he place love above the desire to change his world? If Huang Yu agreed to a marriage, life would change.

Wu Ping groaned. A place in the merchant's house would be found for the husband of an only daughter, a man who had little more than the clothes on his back and a dream. Could he give his desire to spread the ways of his mentor into the hands of other men?

He should leave, but having once tasted Xing-Xing's sweetness, he couldn't leave her behind. Where could they go if her father said no? He had no house or land. Was there a place where the merchant couldn't pursue them? He couldn't allow Xing-Xing to become a beggar and be prey to any man who would seize her.

When morning came, he hadn't made a decision. That night and every night until the moon was once more a rising sliver Xing-Xing came. And he hadn't found the courage to face her father. Every day, he watched Huang Hsia's glares and Ah Lam's sly glances. He felt certain the pair plotted. Did they work together or separately?

* * * *

Xing-Xing yawned and wished she could return to sleep. Lately, she'd been exhausted. The tension inside her, the nights with Wu Ping, the waiting for him to speak to her father had enervated her.

"Come, Daughter. Dress. Your father desires your presence." Xing-Xing's mother shook her shoulder.

Xing-Xing washed her face. Her stomach felt unsettled. She swallowed a rush of fluid that threatened to spill out. Last evening, a messenger had arrived with several chests and spoken to her father. Though the women had chattered and speculated, not even her mother knew what the message had contained.

Once dressed, she followed her mother to where her father waited. Xing-Xing bowed. "Honorable Father, why have you called this lowly girl into your esteemed presence?"

"To tell you of the great honor bestowed on this house. Our magnificent emperor has offered a marriage between his exalted house and our humble one. You will be first wife of his youngest son. The young man was taken by the drawing the artist made of you and impressed by the poems you wrote. He will honor this house with his presence and arrive at the end of this lunar. The messenger brought gifts for you. My sweet and obedient daughter, you have brought great honor to the house of Huang."

Xing-Xing's legs trembled. Nausea assaulted her. What could she do? She had to tell Wu Ping. They had to find a way to be together. "I am unworthy of this honor." She nearly choked on the words.

Her father laughed. "Go, my dutiful daughter. See what value he has placed on you."

Servants carried a pair of chests, one large and one small, to her room. The household's women gathered around her and watched as she removed lengths of silk, gems, gold and silver, jade carvings. She lifted a large jade pendant on a silver chain. Depictions of the four corners of the earth had been carved into the surface. She decided to give the pendant to Wu Ping. Why hadn't he gone to her father? Why hadn't she spoken of her love for the tutor? Would her father have welcomed him into the family?

She glanced up. Ah Lam's eyes glittered with greed and envy. The concubine ran her hands over the silk. She sidled to Xing-Xing's side and spoke in a low voice. "I want some of the jewels."

"What?"

"You heard me or you will regret." Ah Lam moved away.

Does she know? Xing-Xing shuddered. Who would believe a concubine?

Chu Hua sighed. "I wish you could be here to share my joy. Before I had hope, but now I know I'm with child."

"How do you know?"

"My woman's time hasn't come. My breasts are tender and in the morning, I'm ill."

Xing-Xing bowed her head to keep her friend from seeing the panic in her eyes. Her woman's time hadn't come either. She must tell Wu Ping.

Once she was alone, she hurried through the garden to the tutor's house. Wu Ping caught her in his arms. "I heard the news. What can we do?"

"I am with child. We must flee."

"Where can we go? I have little money and I sold my father's land."

"I have the jewels my father gave me." She dropped a pouch in his hand and leaned against him. "Make me forget the things that have happened this day. I would pledge myself to you."

* * * *

A child. Xing-Xing would have his son. Until she told him, he hadn't realized how much he wanted a son. He nuzzled her neck. "We must tell your father about the child."

She shook her head. "It's too late. He will be angry for he has great ambitions for the house. We must leave."

He nodded. "Tomorrow night. I must look at the maps and plan our route. We'll meet at moonrise in the mulberry grove. Go now."

"Not until we make our pledge."

He kissed her fingers. "I pledge myself to you. Hear what you mean to me."

Five virtues have you and you.
Kindness in warmth and luster.
Goodness seen inside from out.
Wisdom in voice heard tranquil.
Bravery to break and not bend.
Purity of sharp edges.
All the virtues of jade--you.

Xing-Xing hung the jade pendant around his neck. "These words and this gift say how I feel now and forever."

You, four corners of my earth.
Dragon of the east you come,
In spring, rouse me from deep sleep.
Causing me to bud and leaf
As trees take life in season.

Phoenix from the south you are.

Filling me with summer fire.
Full of love and passion nights.

Tiger from the west, I see.
Rich harvest you bring to me.
Reap me with your eager hands.
Gently store me in your strength.

Tortoise and snake from the north.
Dark warrior of the winter.
I am cold when you appear
And I wait for dragon spring.

She gazed into his eyes. "Forever, I am yours." She removed her clothes.

Wu Ping untied his trousers. As though pulled by strings, he walked to her. He caught her in his arms. The tips of her breasts brushed his chest. As their tongues tangled, he slipped a hand between them and stroked her lotus. He released her lips and bent to suckle one breast, while continuing to rub her pearl.

Her soft sighs and moans filled him with desire, yet he wished to prolong this time. He trailed his lips over her skin and moved to his knees. She knelt. Wu Ping groaned. Though he wanted to penetrate her lotus, he wished to savor every moment.

"As was in the past will be again," Xing-Xing whispered.

Though her words puzzled him, they seemed right. He leaned forward and lapped her breasts. She bent back and straightened her legs until she sat on the sleeping mat. Slowly, she lowered her body.

Wu Ping supported his weight on his arms and thrust into her. "My jade stem enters your lotus."

"Bring your rain."

He began to move, slow strokes at first. The tightness of her lotus brought exquisite pleasure. He entered and withdrew. She captured his rhythm and moved with him. Faster and faster, they moved. He arched his back. She tightened around him.

She cried his name and he called hers. He erupted with such force they slid along the mat. Once he caught his breath, he rained kisses on her face. "For now and ever, you are mine."

"Until death parts us and beyond," she said.

A chill wind slid along his spine. "Speak not of death, but think of the new life you carry." A sound startled him. He released Xing-Xing and walked to the door.

"What's wrong?" she asked.

"I thought I heard noises."

She pulled on her clothes. "I must go."

He kissed her brow. "Walk with care."

Until she vanished, Wu Ping remained in the doorway. He thought he saw a movement in the shadows. He stared into the gloom. Nothing. Must have been the trees swaying in the breeze.

* * * *

Waves of sadness washed over Xing-Xing. She slipped from the house to meet Wu Ping. For him, she would cast away duty and honor. There'd been no other way to keep her love and the child. She wanted to throw herself at her father's feet and beg forgiveness, but that act wouldn't change his ambition. He would find a way to use her as a pawn. Wu Ping had set aside his desire to spread his teacher's words. She could do no less.

Would they succeed this time?

She frowned. This time? What did that mean?

She reached the mulberry grove and made her way to the clearing where Wu Ping waited. Moonlight illuminated him. She ran into his embrace. "We must go."

"See!" A shrill scream sounded. "See, Huang Yu, I told you I met no man here. I told you it was your daughter."

Wu Ping thrust Xing-Xing behind him. She peered around his body, saw her father, the concubine and Huang Hsia step into view.

"Xing-Xing, come here," her father commanded. "I will hear what you have done and why you dishonor our house."

"I have given my pledge to Wu Ping and he has pledged to me. I love him and would be with him."

"Come, Daughter." Her mother stepped from among the trees. "We will repair the damage you have done."

Xing-Xing clung to Wu Ping. "I stay with him."

Her father stepped toward them. "Your bridegroom arrives at lunar's end and you will make him welcome."

"No. I love Wu Ping."

"Daughter, love has no meaning in a woman's life," her mother said. "A woman must do as her father commands and harden her heart against love."

"Go," Wu Ping said. "I will not see you harmed. Though I love you, I will learn to live without you."

"What of our child?"

"I don't know." He embraced her.

Her brother shouted. Wu Ping staggered and knocked her to the ground. He fell beside her.

Xing-Xing stared at the knife protruding from Wu Ping's back. She stroked his face. "Huang Hsia, why have you done this? You have ruined my life." Tears flowed over her cheeks.

"What I have done is for the honor of the house."

Xing-Xing rose. She pulled the knife from Wu Ping's body. "You lie. Not for the honor of the house but to muddy your own actions. While Father was away, you spent every night in Ah Lam's arms. She has bewitched you."

Ah Lam laughed. She grasped Huang Yu's arm. "She seeks to turn your anger from herself. Huang Hsia is a callow youth sniffing at my lotus."

Huang Hsia plucked the knife from Xing-Xing's hand. "Go, my sister."

Huang Yu thrust the concubine away. He grabbed Xing-Xing and dragged her toward the house. Ah Lam's scream shattered the silence of the night.

"Mother, Father, what will you do with me?"

"You go to the herb woman for a purging so you may keep the honor of the house," Huang Yu said.

Her mother patted her hair. "A woman's lot is hard, my daughter."

Xing-Xing looked from her father to her mother. She wiped her tears on her sleeve. "How can there be honor when there is no love? I will harden my heart, Mother. My heart is jade."

* * * *

Astrid's body shook. Tears wet her face. Why did she slip into these other lives? She gulped deep breaths and sought to remember more of the past. She'd been in Egypt, Babylon, and now China. Her father had been Huang Yu. But that man had been unlike her father. He'd been cold and cruel. The harder she burrowed for details, the more shadowed they became.

She looked at the clock. If she didn't hurry, she would be late for the appointment with her father's doctor. She wondered if he could recommend a good psychiatrist. A wry smile arose. What would one make of her strange adventures? She took the box of jade to the vault, grabbed her purse and left.

She arrived at the hospital before the doctor. Her father pointed to a pamphlet. "Duncan. This morning."

She kissed his cheek and looked at the brochure. "Looks nice."

"You tired?"

She couldn't tell him about her strange visits to the past yet. "Just a bit of eye strain from sorting the bills and sales slips. You need to be more organized."

His lopsided grin made her shake her head. She lifted the pamphlet and read the contents. The rehab center seemed wonderful, but she was sure the price was out of range. Though her savings were earmarked to carry her through the two years of grad school, she could use them. She wasn't sure there was enough. She was sure she could find a nursing job, but she'd been away from the hospital since she'd graduated.

Her father tapped the brochure. "You like?"

"Yes, but--"

The doctor stepped into the room. "I see Mr. Garrett was here. I highly recommend his choice. What do you think?"

"Good," Lloyd said.

"Expensive," Astrid said. "I don't think the place suits Dad's budget and I doubt his insurance will cover the total cost."

"With Mr. Garrett's help, there shouldn't be a problem," Dr. Gregori said. "He called this morning to let me know." The doctor's knowing glance made Astrid want to scream. She and Duncan Garrett weren't involved--yet. "I don't think we should accept."

"No strings," Lloyd said. "Help him. Help me. Read letters."

"I don't understand."

"You will."

"I'll make the arrangements for Wednesday morning," the

doctor said.

Lloyd nodded. "Yes."

Astrid rolled her eyes. While she didn't like the idea of being in debt to Duncan, she wanted her father to have the best care. "Then, I guess we'll go with this one. I need directions. I'll be by to take Dad there."

"No need for that." Dr. Gregorio walked to the door. "Someone from the center will want to talk to Lloyd's caregivers and do an assessment. They also provide transportation."

After the doctor left, Astrid sat beside her father. "I hope this is the right decision."

"Is."

"Want to walk to the lounge?"

Before he answered, Clive and Duncan entered the room. Astrid felt her heart rate accelerate. She swallowed. "Hi."

Duncan winked. "Clive was afraid to come alone."

Clive made a face. "Don't give my secret phobias away."

Astrid kissed her father's cheek. She had to go before she forgot the week she'd made Duncan promise to give her. "Since you have company, I'll come back this evening."

When she reached the door, she glanced back. Duncan and Clive glared at each other. What was that about? Some kind of male rivalry? Not over her, she hoped. She had no intention of being caught between two men. Especially when she was wary of one.

* * * *

Duncan listened to Clive tell Lloyd about Antiquities. His friend seemed on edge.

"I need the combination to the safe," Clive said. "I can't always ask Astrid to open it."

"Sure." Lloyd recited the numbers.

Duncan stiffened. This was something he didn't need to hear, but the numbers filled his thoughts. He wished he hadn't run into Clive in town. His friend had been edgy and there'd been anger beneath his smile and hearty greeting. Had Astrid noticed? Was that why she'd left? A bit more of her company would have been nice and stressful.

After they left the hospital, Duncan turned to jog down the hill to his house. Clive put a hand on his shoulder. "We need to talk."

"Sounds serious."

"It is."

"Come on. I've got beer on ice."

Clive shook his head. "The Steak Place. That mansion of yours makes me uncomfortable."

"Fine. The Steak Place it is."

A short time later, Duncan slid into one of the booths across from the bar. He ordered nachos to go with the beer. Clive paused to speak to Paula, then slid into the booth.

"What's on your mind?" Duncan asked.

"Astrid. Lorna."

Duncan shrugged. "My business."

"Not when you're hurting a friend. Lorna's torn up about the way you dropped her."

"Did I?"

"Spent the entire weekend listening to her cry." Clive hoisted his beer. "I think you did."

"No matter what she says, I never gave her any ideas about us being a couple. She's not my type. A bit pushy and she makes threats I don't like."

"And Astrid is your type?"

"Absolutely."

Clive leaned forward. "Why do you want ice when you can have fire?"

Duncan thought about Astrid's response to his kisses. Definitely not ice. "Look, Clive, let's drop this."

"Then take this as a heads up. I want Antiquities. Astrid's the owner's daughter. Therefore, she's mine."

"Doesn't she have a vote?"

"Won't matter."

Duncan grasped Clive's forearm. "Why not talk to Lloyd about a partnership. I'm good for a loan."

"No way. You think money's the answer to everything." Clive slammed his mug on the table. "I heard the same tale in college when you paid for our fun. I don't want to be obligated to your generosity."

"Suit yourself."

"I will and one of these days, I'll match you dollar for dollar."

Duncan shrugged. "I wish you luck. Just remember this. I'm not walking away from Astrid."

Clive rose. "You've always had things easy. Not this time." He strode away.

Duncan leaned back. What was with Clive? *Just because I didn't fall into Lorna's lap. Why is he shoving her in my face?*

Paula slid into the seat Clive had left. "What was that about?"

"I won't play the cards from the stacked deck he handed me."

"Be careful. He and Lorna Stinit are up to something. Saw them with their heads together when I was at Antiquities taking photos."

Duncan arched a brow. "Clive's an old friend. We've fallen out and gotten together several times."

"Are you sure he's a friend?" Paula leaned forward. "I like him, but I don't trust him."

"Look, things get tense when two men are after the same woman."

Paula shrugged. "Just be careful."

"Always." Duncan finished his beer. He'd keep his eyes open, but he wasn't giving up his pursuit of Astrid.

* * * *

Astrid closed the vault and tucked the three items she'd taken in a bag. She wanted to study them and read the letters she'd found in the desk. She started to the door. Clive entered. "What brings you back?" she asked.

"You."

She shook her head. "Not interested."

"Why don't you give me a chance? I could show you a better time than someone I won't mention." He smiled.

She supposed his smile charmed most women, but she saw the calculation in his eyes. "Give it up."

"Actually, we need to talk about Antiquities. Do you really think your dad will be back?"

"Why not?"

He shrugged. "He might want to retire."

"His choice. Have you talked to him about his plans?"

"He clams up."

"Then you'll have to wait until he's ready to talk. The gallery is his. I've no say in anything that happens here."

He stepped toward her. "About Duncan. You're too nice to let him hurt you. And he will. Look what he did to Lorna. I thought they were about to set a wedding date and he dropped her cold."

Astrid edged past him. "What Duncan and I do is between us."

"Just a warning. I've known him for years and Lorna even longer. She wants Duncan and she always gets what she wants. She won't play fair."

Astrid opened the door. "Warning noted. Don't forget to lock up and set the alarm." As she headed to the apartment, she wondered what Clive was planning. She wished she could talk to her dad about him. She held the bag at her side. What would Clive think if he knew she'd taken these things?

POMPEII

On Wednesday morning, Astrid followed the ambulance taking her father to the rehab center an hour's drive from Rockleigh. The distance meant she couldn't pop in for visits several times a day. She wished she could have talked him out of the move, but her father thought Duncan's offer meant no strings. She had her doubts.

As she parked in the visitor's lot, she studied the setting. A screen of trees sheltered the facility from the road. Gardens with wide, paved paths surrounded the sprawling one story building. Benches had been placed in shaded spots and she noticed a number of tables. She left the car and walked to the entrance where a young woman waited.

"Ms. Logan, I'm Pam. While your father's settling in, I'll give you a tour and discuss his schedule of daily activities."

"Thanks." As they toured the building, Astrid peered into various therapy rooms. At the end of the corridor, her guide handed her a copy of her father's schedule. Astrid chuckled. The list included classes on proper diet and exercise.

"I'm impressed." Astrid looked into the dining room where most of the patients took their meals.

"We're proud of our success rate."

Finally, she was escorted to her father's private room. She paused in the doorway. A large picture window showed a view of the garden. Her father sat in a recliner facing a large screen television. The fully automatic bed could be hidden by a bright curtain. One door led to a bathroom with a shower designed to accommodate a wheelchair. The other opened into a closet.

He grinned. "Com ... comforts. Home."

She laughed. "After seeing your therapy schedule, you'll need this luxury."

"Good of Dun ... can."

She nodded. "Though I wish we hadn't accepted his offer to cover what your insurance doesn't."

He patted her hand. "Help him. Find treasure. Read letters."

"Not yet. They're in the apartment with the Egyptian pieces, two jade pendants and a cylinder seal."

"Why not vault?"

She shrugged. "I'm not sure, but Lorna Stinit wants the Egyptian set and I think Clive will give them to her."

"Not her, Duncan."

"But she's also Duncan's friend."

"Not."

"Enough gossip. Why don't I bring Aunt Sarah for a visit this evening?"

"Yes." He paused. "En ... en ... velope. Drawer."

Astrid frowned. "Which drawer?" He pointed to the bedside stand. She crossed the room and brought the envelope to him.

"For you. Gala. Go."

"You want me to attend?"

"You. Sarah."

Astrid wasn't sure she wanted to be near Duncan. He'd promised to stay away for a week and the time ended Sunday evening. If she went, she would be tempted to explore the heat between them. One misstep and she could be hurt. Falling in love with him was too easy. All the things she'd heard about him said he had no intention of making a commitment to any woman.

"Go. En ... joy."

"I'll talk to Aunt Sarah. If she wants to go, I'll go with her."

He smiled. "Good."

After Astrid unpacked her father's bags, they talked about Antiquities.

A woman appeared in a green uniform and tapped on the door. "Mr. Logan, I'll show you to the dining room." She turned to Astrid. "Will you join him?"

"Not today. See you this evening." She kissed her father's cheek.

When she reached Antiquities, she found Sarah and a woman at the cash register. Sarah was explaining the system for filing sales slips in the various folders. Sarah looked up. "Do you know Bobbie Sue? She worked here during last year's Christmas rush."

Astrid smiled. "Guess I missed her. Remember, I didn't arrive until Christmas Eve. I'm glad you could help out."

"Since my kids are in day camp, the chance to make some extra money is great. Sure was sorry to hear about Mr. Logan. He's a nice man."

"Speaking of Lloyd," Sarah said. "How is he and what's the center like?"

"He's fine. In for a tough schedule. The center is beautiful and luxurious. You'll see this evening since I told Dad we'd come."

Sarah nodded. "After dinner. Oh, I invited Paula."

"If she wants, she can come with us."

"Good idea. She's nearly finished with the photographs. Has a number to show him."

"I'm sure he'll enjoy." Astrid left them and entered the office where she finished the spreadsheet and paid several bills. Then she began to inventory the stock, checking last year's list along with sales and purchase slips.

At five, she locked the door and set the alarms. She frowned. Where was Clive? Not that she missed him, but it seemed odd he hadn't been in.

She ran up to the apartment, showered and changed. Before long, she knocked on Sarah's door.

Paula answered. "She's in the kitchen doing marvelous things to chicken. You hungry?"

Astrid bent to pet the cat that wove a path around her legs. "Starved since I didn't stop for lunch."

"You're not phasing out on me again."

"I'll remain in the present."

Paula arched a brow. "That's an odd way to speak of a faint."

You don't know how appropriate, Astrid thought. She followed Paula into the large front room. "Aunt Sarah, something smells wonderful."

"Chicken mole. Let me get the wrappers from the microwave and we're ready to eat."

After Astrid ate several bites, she sighed. "I want the recipe."

"I'll get it to you."

"Me, too," Paula said. "I might take up cooking."

Astrid looked from one woman to the other. "Dad handed me a small problem I need to solve. There are three tickets for the Saturday night gala at the Garrett house."

Sarah nodded. "Lloyd mentioned them. He planned for the three of us to go."

Astrid turned to Paula. "Would you like the third ticket?"

"Would I ever. Only a limited number were sold and they were too dear for me." She grinned. "I have just the dress. I'm sure the affair is formal."

"Definitely," Sarah said. "Always wanted a look behind that wall."

"I'll drive," Astrid said. One way to evade temptation.

"Let us finish dinner and go see Lloyd," Sarah said.

* * * *

Early Saturday evening, Duncan stood at the head of the spiral staircase and watched the arrival of the caterers. So far, everything was on schedule for tonight's affair. Men wheeled carts toward the kitchen. Another set the buffet in the large dining room. He was sure the bar and buffet on the patio were in order. Fortunately, the good weather had held with no rain forecast for the remainder of the long weekend.

A man in a brown uniform appeared at the open door. Duncan bounded down the stairs. "Can I help you?"

"Package for Mr. Garrett. Sign here."

Duncan scribbled his name. He carried the package upstairs to his study and opened the outer wrapping. A note was taped to the top of a lacquered box.

Thought you might like to see this. Perhaps the bracelet is part of the collection you seek. Play your cards right and the rest will be yours.

Lorna, he thought. Though the note was unsigned and there was no return address, she was one of the few people who knew of his quest. He opened the box and studied the contents.

Duncan lifted a gold bracelet with a double row of hemispheres connected by links. He pulled the pin from the clasp and held the bracelet to his wrist. Not a man's ornament. A picture of a slender, dark-haired woman flowed into his thoughts. Astrid, and yet not. How was she connected to this piece of jewelry?

He glanced at the clock. He'd better move. After placing the bracelet in the safe, he went to check the remainder of the preparations. The scent of cut flowers added a subtle sweetness to the air. He stepped outside. When lit, the strings of tiny lights threaded on the trees and bushes lining the walk would provide a romantic atmosphere.

After seeing all was in order, he dashed to the master suite, showered, shaved and donned his tuxedo. As he fastened the shirt studs, he wondered if Astrid would attend. Before the stroke, Lloyd had purchased four tickets. He'd given one to Clive.

Duncan grinned. As far as he was concerned, the week he'd promised Astrid ended at midnight. He groaned. Even thinking about her raised his expectations, not to mention an aching erection.

* * * *

Astrid checked herself in the mirror. From the front, the emerald gown looked demure. The halter-top clung to her breasts and waist, then flared from the hips. A deep plunge left most of her back bare. She reached for her evening bag and walked to the deck. There, she knocked on Sarah's door.

The older woman wore a pale green lace gown. Her eyes sparkled. "What a deceptive and stunning gown."

Astrid laughed. "Thanks. You're positively elegant. Let's get Paula and make a grand entrance. Have your ticket?"

"In my bag."

Paula waited on the porch of her small Cape Cod. Her dark green slip gown shimmered with iridescent shades. She chuckled. "Cool. Without discussion, we're coordinated."

Astrid found a parking place on the street not far from Duncan's house. At the gate, a pair of uniformed men took their tickets. Paula led the way down the flagstone walk. Beyond the trees, Astrid saw beds of summer flowers. The full moon and the tiny lights cast pools of brightness and shadows.

Astrid frowned. She'd never been beyond the wall, yet she sensed a haunting familiarity. She drew a deep breath and followed Paula and Sarah toward the large stone house.

Several people greeted Paula. "What, no camera?" one man asked.

"I'm a guest tonight." She sighed. "Almost wish I'd brought one. Look at the play of light on the flowers and the glittering guests."

Sarah stopped next to a couple. She waved Paula and Astrid on. "I'll catch up with you when it's time to leave."

Paula plucked two glasses of champagne from the tray of a passing waiter. She handed one to Astrid and sipped the other. "Lovely. Let's see what's on the buffet."

Astrid saw Duncan beside the long table. Lorna clung to his arm. She swallowed. The man looked good in cut-offs, great in slacks and magnificent in a tuxedo. She turned to Paula. "Should we greet our host and hostess?"

"You can. I'll wait." Paula grinned. "Don't want to be blinded by her glitter. Rings on her fingers, ice around her neck and her dress. Wouldn't need a flash to take her picture."

Astrid chuckled. Lorna's white, strapless form-fitting gown dripped with sparkles. "She could light the entire garden."

"We're being catty."

"And truthful."

"If you want to play dutiful guest, go ahead. I see Clive and I'm going to drag him into a dark corner."

Astrid shook her head. "Do that, but take care. Don't trust him."

"Never."

Astrid stepped onto the patio. Duncan waved and shook off Lorna's hand. In six steps, he reached Astrid. "Glad you decided to come. How's your dad? Hope to get up there soon."

"He's doing great." She smiled. "The gardens are lovely and the house looks impressive."

"Want a private tour?"

"Aren't you the host?"

"I am, but I need to socialize with the guests. Come help me."

Astrid put her empty glass on a tray. Duncan took her hand. Her body hummed with a desire to be in his arms. She couldn't blame the champagne. His presence was enough to intoxicate her.

They entered the foyer where white marble covered the floor and warm chestnut paneled the lower third of the high walls. Astrid paused and stared at the portrait of a woman. She gasped. Who was she? The woman reminded her of her grandmother.

"She's lovely."

"My great-great grandmother. One of the family's scandals. Her picture was painted from a sketch. The day she and my great-great grandfather planned to set a wedding date, she disappeared. Almost a year later, my great grandfather and his wet nurse arrived. Madelaine was never found."

Astrid moved closer. Her father had mentioned a connection between her family and Duncan's. Could this woman have been one of her ancestors? "An interesting story."

"I'll tell you more but not tonight."

She peered into one of the parlors where several older people sat. Duncan paused to speak to them. When he turned back to Astrid, she smiled. "How do you keep this place up?"

"A cleaning service. I seldom use the first floor, except the kitchen and occasionally the dining room. Mainly, I camp in the master suite upstairs. Bedroom, sitting room and study."

She saw loneliness in his eyes and touched his hand. "No other family?"

"Probably some distant cousins. There was a rift in the family ages ago. If there are cousins, I've never met them."

They entered a formal dining room. A group of people drew Duncan aside. Astrid sampled several of the canapés. The lilting melody of a waltz pulled her into the hall. She paused in the doorway of the ballroom and watched a dozen couples move to the music.

"Sorry about the interruption," Duncan said.

"A host must see to his duties."

"Especially when he's soliciting donations." He pulled her into his arms and swept her into the dance. "I sent them to find Lorna. She's handling the gifts."

"How did she become your hostess?" The moment the words emerged, she wished she hadn't spoken.

"In her usual pushy manner." He pulled her closer. "She happened to be at the restaurant with Clive and me when a board member of the opera company asked for my help. Let us table Lorna and enjoy ourselves."

Though Astrid had never waltzed, she found Duncan easy to follow. *Had they danced like this before?* What a strange thought. They whirled around the room and through a set of doors onto a moonlit terrace with a view of the river.

Duncan held her in a light embrace. His lips brushed her forehead. When his mouth covered hers, she succumbed to the warmth infusing her body. He raised his head. Their gazes meshed.

"Stay here tonight," he said.

"You promised me a week."

He nodded. "Week ends at midnight."

"More like tomorrow evening."

"Don't be so literal. Don't you feel the heat between us?"

She couldn't deny her feelings, but she wanted to know why she felt they'd known each other before. "I can't. I drove Paula and Sarah. Have to take them home."

"Give one of them your keys."

She shook her head. "We're moving too fast. Something tells me that's wrong."

He released her and strode to the balustrade. "You can't fight the attraction forever."

She nodded. "True, but I need to understand what's happening." She considered telling him about her experiences in the dreams. Would he understand? What if they were the couple doomed to love, to betray and be betrayed?

* * * *

"So there you are." Lorna's husky voice stopped Duncan from following and asking Astrid to explain. The blonde sauntered toward them, "Some host you are."

"Is there a problem? Unhappy guests? Someone drunk and disorderly? Not enough food or champagne?"

"You know very well everything is perfect. People are wondering why you're not with me."

"People or you? Most of the guests have been here before and they know how I run these affairs. I don't hover."

She tapped her foot on the flagstones. "I'm your hostess. Your place is at my side."

Duncan shook his head. "I see no reason to dance attendance on you."

Anger glinted in her eyes. "Did you receive a package today?"

"Yes."

"And you read the note. Perhaps there are more items

where that one was. Don't you want to recover all that was lost? I can give or destroy them."

Astrid had nearly reached the ballroom door. Duncan strode past Lorna. "Do what you want. I won't play your game and I won't be bullied."

She grabbed his arm. "You'll be sorry. You and I could be the ones to learn the true story of what happened to Madelaine."

Duncan continued toward the ballroom. He caught Astrid at the door. "Don't run away. That won't solve a thing."

She turned to him. "She's out to make trouble."

"I don't frighten easily. Do you?" He clasped her hand. "I'd like to show you what she was talking about."

"Not interested."

He laughed. "There's a bracelet that arrived today. I wish your dad could see it. He might have some idea of its history." He slid his hand along her arm and led her up the back stairs. "We won't be long. Then, if you wish, you can collect your friends and leave. I won't stop you."

"So your invitation was a joke?"

"Not for a moment. Just premature. Don't worry. I'll be on your doorstep tomorrow evening." He pressed a code on his study door and led her into his office. There, he opened the safe and removed the bracelet. "Here." He clasped it around her wrist.

"Duncan, no."

She staggered. He caught her in his arms and carried her to the couch. Had she had some kind of seizure? "Astrid." He felt for a pulse and found a steady beat. "Astrid, wake up."

When there was no response, he headed to the door. He had to find Paula or Sarah. Would one of them know what to do?

* * * *

Estella watched the last of the funeral guests leave. Why did Caten have to die? Though much older than her, he'd been in good health until he'd collapsed while he'd toured the estates she'd inherited from her father. His body had been brought to his home in Rome for the burial. She was again alone, except for her distant cousin.

Blandon strode across the reception room and put his hands on her shoulders. She fought the urge to shudder. She had to hide her dislike of the man who now oversaw her estates.

"Dear cousin, take heart. I'll be your protector."

She drew away. "I wish to be alone to mourn my spouse."

He snorted. "Why mourn a man who surely bedded you but once? Or did he have vigor for more?"

She gulped a breath. Did he suspect? Her servant, Austina, was the only one who knew Estella had been a bride, but never a wife. "You speak of things you have no right to know."

He laughed. "Anger adds color to your face and makes your eyes sparkle. Daughter of an old man and wife of another. Let me show you passion."

"Leave it be. Be content to manage the estates and fill your coffers with coins. I doubt I will wed again."

He ran his hand along her arm. "A woman with your beauty and wealth won't be alone forever." Like a hound after a bone, he pulled her into an embrace and ground his mouth against hers. His tongue probed her lips. She jerked free.

"Estella, don't you see how passion overwhelms me?"

She retreated to the atrium and signaled one of the household guards. "Blandon, leave me. Send your reports and I will read them."

He smiled. "I'll leave, but I will return. Your lovely body will soon crave the attentions of a man."

She sank on a padded bench. His touch and his taste had made her ill. What would she do when he returned? Years ago, he had asked her father for her hand in marriage. Only her pleas had kept her father from agreeing to a betrothal. Her father had spoken to his good friend who had offered an alliance with his house. Caten had married her to protect her from Blandon's greed. Now his protection was gone.

* * * *

The days seemed endless to Estella. She could have gone to one of the estates, but little would have changed. She sat in the peristole and gazed at the garden. The crisp days of autumn had arrived. Soon the flowers would be gone. She felt alone and a bit fearful of the future.

Footsteps sounded on the tiles. She rose and hugged her visitor.

"Gratia, how good to see you. I didn't know you had

returned."

"Just two days ago. Weren't you lonely staying in the city for the summer?"

Estella shook her head. "In these days of mourning, I live a quiet life."

Gratia nodded. "But the end of those days is near. What will you do now?"

"I don't know."

"My grandfather sends his greetings. Sadness rides his shoulders. He is the last of three who were friends from childhood."

"Give him my regards." Estella rose. "Come and walk in the garden with me."

Gratia smiled. "Do you still grub in the soil?"

"How else would my garden be a work of art? If I let another have the joy of bringing the flowers to life, I wouldn't feel fulfilled."

Gratia paused beside the fountain. "Blandon's in town. Does he stay here?"

Estella scowled. "He's not welcome in this house."

"Why not? He is handsome, cultured and of good birth, though of little fortune. I would gladly marry him if my father desired an alliance with your noble family."

Estella turned away. "He offered to end my loneliness."

Gratia sighed. "Why did you refuse him?"

"He didn't offer marriage."

Gratia gasped. "How dare he dishonor you?"

"He wants what he feels was denied him. With me as his lover, he could use all my assets to gain the political power he desires. Then he could find a suitable virginal bride from a family of power. My life would be of little value once he was in charge. But I know him and won't be fooled by his words."

"I see."

"Austina, I know she's here and will want to see me." The husky voice of another woman reached them.

"Calpurnia," Estella said.

Gratia rolled her eyes. "What does she want?"

"Be still. She was once our friend."

"Before she chose that crowd that is now her inner circle." Gratia's voice was low.

Estella walked to the garden entrance. "Calpurnia, how

nice of you to come."

The plump young woman kissed the air near Estella's cheek. "I would have come sooner, but I've been busy setting the town house in order. Florio stayed in the country with the twins. He doesn't think the air in Rome is healthy for them. Older men have such strange notions, as I'm sure you know. Fortunately, they permit their second wives more freedom." She turned. "Gratia, I didn't know you were in town."

"We only recently arrived." Gratia smiled. "I'll tell Austina to bring refreshments."

Estella walked beside Calpurnia to the receiving room. "You hardly look like a woman who recently gave birth to twins."

"Not that recently. They're four months old." She sat on one of the benches. "My new lover has helped me recover. He's a lusty man and oh, the things he does to me." She ran her tongue along her lips. "I could share him with you. He has enough vigor to satisfy several women."

"Calpurnia!"

Her friend laughed. "Last night, he bound my arms and legs like I was his captive. Then he ravished me."

Estella looked away. "I will hear no more of your tales." Her face felt flushed.

Calpurnia caught Estella's arm. "Aren't you lonely? Your husband is gone. If you're breeding, it doesn't show. Doesn't your body crave the touch of a man?"

"You're outrageous. Why did you come?"

"I'm having a small dinner party this evening. There's a Praetorian I have my eyes on." She smiled and a sly look came into her eyes. "He thinks Florio will be there. Estella, he is so muscular and handsome. He makes my heart beat faster." She turned to look at Gratia. "Come to dinner, too."

Gratia shook her head. "I will take no man outside the marriage bed and I will be a loyal and faithful wife."

"How boring." Calpurnia waved away the wine a servant offered. "Estella, please come. You're too young to hide yourself in the house." She rose. "I pray I'll see you this evening."

Estella saw her friend across the atrium. When she returned, she grabbed a cup of wine from the tray and sank on a bench. Did Calpurnia know how the thought of finally knowing what occurred between a man and a woman tempted?

She shook her head. She couldn't take the chance. Should Blandon learn her marriage had been a farce, he would renew his attentions. All thoughts of his touch made her ill.

Gratia sat beside her. "Will you go?"

"I think not."

"Wise decision. I've heard much about what happens in her home."

"Surely the rumors are exaggerated."

After Gratia left, Estella was lost in thought. Austina appeared in the doorway. "My child, come and eat. You are too thin."

Estella looked at the older woman who was the only mother she'd known. "I'm not hungry."

Austina sighed. "If there was hope of a child, you would have a good appetite."

"How can there be a child?"

Austina patted her hand. "Come, at least try."

Estella entered the atrium. "Estella." She froze. What was he doing here? Had he heard what had been said?

"Blandon, you know I don't want you here?"

He clasped her hands. "I have much to report about the estates." He traced circles on her hand with his thumb. "I also came to see if your grieving had ended and if you are ready for the attention of a man who greatly desires you."

She pulled free. "Go. Do I have to send for the guards to escort you out?"

"You can't continue pushing me away. I'll stay to dinner."

She made an instant and impetuous decision she hoped she wouldn't regret. "Then you'll eat alone. I've accepted an invitation." She turned to Austina. "Order the guards and litter bearers to be ready to leave after I rest and dress."

Blandon smiled. "I'll give up my evening plans to escort you."

She slipped past him. "I will not bring an uninvited guest to a friend's home."

He shrugged. "Perhaps tomorrow. It is unnatural for a woman to live without a man to see to her protection and her other needs. You will blossom beneath my hands and mouth. What other man could desire you as much as I do?"

She shivered. His voice was coated with honey, but his eyes held the glow of ice. She hurried to her room. What had she done? She had to go to Calpurnia's. Blandon would know if she remained at home.

After a brief nap, she bathed in the private bath Caten had installed, knowing how she hated the public ones. She dressed for her first public appearance since her husband's death. The pale blue stola was banded with a darker color and the shoulder clasps were set with blue gems. A narrow band of gold adorned her hair. Austina gathered the curls at her nape with a ribbon.

"My child, you look lovely," the older woman said.

Estella sighed. "I pray this is the right choice."

"Perhaps you will find a man who will protect you from Blandon."

"Perhaps." She lifted a darker blue palla and with a deep breath walked to the litter.

The hint of cold in the brisk breeze made Estella thankful Calpurnia's house wasn't far. At the entrance to the passage into the walled house, Estella turned to her guards. "Return in two hours and announce your presence to the man at the gate. Austina will remind you when it's time."

As they left, she drew in a breath. Though she hadn't wanted to come to dinner, being here was better than fending off Blandon's unwanted attentions. She nodded to the servant who guarded the passage and walked into the atrium. She halted abruptly.

A couple stood near the impluvium. Their bodies were reflected in the still water. One clasp of the woman's stola was open and the man's mouth was pressed to her breast.

Estella gasped. Blandon. What was he doing here? She turned to leave. Perhaps she could call her men before they were too far away.

Blandon straightened. Estella sought an escape.

"My love, don't stop," Calpurnia purred.

"I believe a late arrival is here." Blandon released Calpurnia and strolled toward Estella. "My dear, why didn't you say you were joining us? I would have been delighted to act as your escort."

Calpurnia made no attempt to cover her bare breast. "Estella, are you surprised to learn the name of my new lover?"

Estella couldn't speak. She nodded. How could she remain when he was here?

Calpurnia smiled. "Blue becomes you. You can join the guests in one of the rooms, or perhaps you'd like to share with me."

Blandon laughed. He stood behind Calpurnia and cupped her breasts. "My love, let me first see to your needs, then Estella and I will talk about hers."

"We could be a threesome." Calpurnia turned and put her arms around his neck.

"An intriguing thought, but I fear it's too soon for Estella to enter such a coupling." He swept her into his arms and headed for one of the sleeping rooms.

Estella looked for an escape. Why had she come? She couldn't leave until her men returned. A woman alone, especially one richly dressed and jeweled wasn't safe on the streets. Perhaps she could hide in the garden until she could safely depart.

As she moved toward the receiving room, she glanced into the triclinium and gasped. A number of guests lay on the couches before the table where platters of food had been placed. One woman held a bunch of grapes in her teeth while the man beside her nibbled on them. The woman's hands were beneath the man's toga.

Estella ran into the receiving room. The scene was worse. Several of the male guests were unclothed and the women caressed their bodies.

As she ran across the atrium, she feared Calpurnia and Blandon would find her. She paused in the doorway of an empty room, entered and sank on a low couch. She would stay here until her escort arrived and pray no one found her.

* * * *

Marius heard a sound and half-rose from his seat in a dark corner of the room. He'd accepted the invitation to dinner in hopes of pleasing one of his three patrons. When his term of service in the Praetorian Guard ended, he planned to become one of Rome's leaders. His attendance tonight presented a problem, for his host wasn't here. The dinner had been arranged by Florio's beautiful, lusty wife and her ambitious lover.

Blandon, a man he'd known in the past, one who'd been his friend until their paths had forked. These days, they shared not a single interest, other than ambition.

A vision in blue entered the room and slumped on the low couch beside the door. At first, he thought she'd been sent to him. Then he noticed her harried appearance. "Are you all right?"

She gasped. "I thought this room was empty and I could hide here until my guards arrive."

"I'm also in hiding." He studied her more closely. She didn't seem the type to attend one of Calpurnia's affairs.

"Why are you hiding?" She pressed her hand over her mouth. "My pardon. I have no right to pry."

"I thought my patron had arranged the dinner and since he asks little of me, I came. And you?"

She studied her hands. "Calpurnia is a friend. I'd decided not to come, but an unwelcome visitor arrived at my door. I sent him away, but he was here. I fear when he and Calpurnia find me, they will badger me to do what they want." Her voice rose. "What if I'm discovered?"

"By your husband?"

She shook her head. "He's dead. Two months ago."

"You have my sympathy." He motioned to her. "Come and use my chair. It's in the shadows."

"Thank you." She crossed the room.

As she drew nearer, he saw she was more beautiful than he'd first thought. Something about her seemed familiar and he couldn't imagine where he'd seen her before. "I'll wait with you. I'm Marius of the Praetorians." He crouched beside the chair.

"Estella." Her hand brushed his arm as she sat.

A short time later, a nearly nude couple staggered into the room and fell on the narrow couch. Estella grasped Marius' arm.

He rose. "They don't see us. Come, I'll find a litter and escort you to your home."

"Will they not miss you?"

"Does it matter?" When they reached the door, he shielded her from the writhing couple.

Marius held his envy of the man at bay. He'd been without a woman for several months since his favorite courtesan had left Rome. The sensations raised by Estella's fingers on his arm brought urgent desire. He fought the urge to take her in his arms. Though she was a widow, there was an innocence about her and he'd never been one to seduce widows or wives.

They entered the atrium and walked toward the passage. Clouds darkened the sky. Marius paused. "I'll send a servant for a litter."

She shook her head. "The evening is mild and the distance to my house is short. I fear what Calpurnia will say if she learns I've fled. She's known for her tantrums and she had plans for you."

"I bow to your knowledge of the lady." He glanced at the dark clouds. "We must hurry. A storm approaches."

She placed her hand on his arm. "This way."

He felt heat flow from her fingers, a fire that swirled along his skin and settled in his groin bringing an erection to life. He ached to mold her body to his and savor her taste, her scent, her touch. He ached to thrust his sword into her sheath until she cried his name. He sucked in a breath. It was not to be. Estella was a lady, not a woman bent on seduction like her friend.

As they hurried along the street, the wind gathered force. Thunder rumbled and lightning flashed. They passed several houses with shops built into the front walls. "How far?" he asked.

"The next passage."

Just as they reached the atrium of her home, rain poured from the sky. The wind blew in chilling gusts. She tugged him toward the open doorway of the receiving room. "Come inside and wait out this storm. The servants will find you something of my husband's to wear while your clothes are being dried."

Because of the desire that pulsed, he should leave. The sight of the way her soaked stola clung to her body inflamed him. The cloth molded her breasts. Her nipples were erect. He fought the desire to take one into his mouth.

An older woman with graying hair bustled into the room. "Estella, my child, why did you come home so soon and in such a state?"

"The company wasn't to my liking." Estella turned. "You won't believe what went on. I couldn't wait for the men to return. The Praetorian, Marius, was kind enough to escort me."

"I've heard tales of the goings on at Calpurnia's." The

older woman turned to Marius. "I'm glad you were there."

"My pleasure."

"Find some of Caten's clothes for him and see his tunica and toga are dried. Bring food and wine to the small receiving room. I fear we left without dinner."

Austina eyed Marius and smiled. "Come with me. The master was a broad man and I fear his tunicas will be a bit short."

"They'll do." He followed her to a room on the second floor of the house.

The older woman took a tunica and toga from a chest. "Take care with Estella. In many ways, she's still a girl."

Marius stripped off his wet clothes and rubbed himself with the rough cloth she handed him. What did she mean? Estella was sweet and desirable, but he was in no position to take a wife. Not until the remaining five years of his term were served. No woman as beautiful as Estella would wait that long.

He donned the tunica and laughed. Broad enough across the shoulders and chest, but in length, the garment ended well above his knees. At least the toga would cover more of his body, not that he felt embarrassed. His uniforms bared his legs and thighs, but Estella might find the sight not to her liking.

When the older woman returned, she chuckled. "Tall and built like one of the old gods. Come, I'll show you where to wait for Estella. She will join you soon."

* * * *

Estella stripped off her wet gown. Though her skin was chilled, she felt flushed and edgy. What was wrong? Caten's touch had never heated her woman's parts. He'd never kissed her other than on the forehead or cheek. Why would she yearn to feel Marius' lips on hers when Blandon's rough assault on her mouth had repulsed her? She thought of the firmness of Marius' flesh beneath her fingers. The memory raised a fiery need to explore, to touch and taste.

Could she do something to make him desire her? She couldn't act with abandon the way Calpurnia had. Surely there were other ways to capture a man's interest.

Estella dried herself and reached for a vial of perfume. She daubed her throat and wrists with the floral scent. Her breasts felt achy. She stroked them. The nipples formed tight buds. How would she feel if those hands belonged to Marius? Her breath quickened. A pulse throbbed low in her abdomen. She donned a clean stola and left the room.

When she entered the small reception room next to the dining room, she saw him and stared. Marius brushed his fingers over the floral mural painted on the pale yellow stucco wall. For an instant, she felt his touch on her skin. A smile curved her lips. Caten's toga was much too short.

He turned and his gaze met hers. His smile reflected humor. "At least it's dry." He held out a hand.

She felt compelled to go to him. "Come sit." She led him to a low couch. Her heart pounded. What should she do now?

Austina and two servants carried platters of meat, cheese, bread, dates and figs into the room. Austina put a ewer of wine beside the plates. "Call if you need more."

"We will." Estella poured two goblets of wine and handed one to Marius. "My apologies for the simple fare."

He covered her hand with his. "Simple is fine. Sit beside me."

Would he like to seduce me, she wondered. How can I let him know I'm willing? Her mouth felt dry. She sipped the watered wine and began to eat. Once she'd finished her share, she lifted a honeyed date and turned to Marius. "Try this."

Instead of taking the offering, he bent his head and ate from her fingers. Then one by one, he drew each one into his mouth. Estella sighed and turned to him.

He gazed into her eyes. His darkened and drew her closer. Something in their depths sent thrills along her skin. He brushed her lips with his. The scent of him filled her. Her hands slid along his arms and rested on his shoulders.

"Estella, you enchant me."

She smiled. "I'm the enchanted one."

He lifted her onto his lap. She turned and met his mouth with hers. When he caressed her breasts, she felt as though thunder rolled along her spine. Her mouth opened and his tongue slid inside and tangled with hers. Her body ached and throbbed for a thing she didn't know. Her arms circled his neck. "Marius, I feel magic in your touch."

"Nay, you are the magician. I would show you more, but

not here where anyone can intrude."

Estella thought of the man and woman who had invaded the room at Calpurnia's. Did he mean to do those things to her? Her woman's parts felt engorged. If they disrobed, would his touch on her skin take the ache away or make the sensations stronger?

She raised her head and looked at him. What she saw in his eyes thrilled her. He wanted her. He needed her and she needed him.

"Estella, enchantress, be mine."

The rich timbre of his voice added fuel to the fires burning low in her belly. She rose. "Come to my room. No one will bother us there."

He captured her in an embrace. His mouth opened over hers. She leaned into him. He cupped her rear and held her close. As the kiss deepened, she felt a part of him grow hard.

She drew back to catch her breath. "This way."

He kept his arm at her waist. "You are as the evening star. I desire you with every fiber of my body."

She paused on the threshold of her sleeping room. "You are the first man to enter here."

He released his hold on her waist. "You mean your husband never came to you."

She nodded. "He marked the sheets so no one could say we weren't wed. He had no desire for a woman, but he sought to protect me from a distant cousin who coveted my riches."

He turned her to face him. "Are you sure you want to do this?"

"From the moment I saw you, I felt I had known you before. I want your touch, taste and your scent. I would like you to show me what happens between a man and a woman."

"Then all I have is yours." He followed her into the room.

With widened eyes, Estella watched while he removed the toga and tunica. His shoulders were broad, his arms and chest muscular. A line of hair ran down his chest and over his abdomen. As the tunica fell to the floor, she saw his male organ jutting from a bush of hair.

He winked. "Have no fear. My sword is made to fit into your sheath." He moved toward her and opened the clasps of her stola. As he drew the fabric over her breasts, she shivered. "Estella, look at me. In this, I am as near a novice as you are. I have heard there's pain but one time and not for all women, if a man takes care. Let me pleasure you before I take mine."

Estella kept her gaze on his face. "You make me feel strange, different." He caressed her shoulders and the calluses on his fingers raised exquisite sensations along her skin.

He took her hand and led her to the bed. He lay beside her, then turned on his side. "You are beautiful." After raising on one elbow, he ran a finger over her lips. As he had tasted her fingers, she drew his inside.

His mouth replaced his fingers. One hand caressed her breasts. When he teased her nipples, she felt fluid gather between her nether lips. His mouth moved from hers, nuzzled her neck and rained kisses along her collarbone. She tried to slow the rapid beat of her heart. He pressed his mouth to her breast, then drew the nipple into the heat of his mouth. She moved restlessly.

"Marius, let me touch you."

"As you will." He leaned back.

She ran her hands over his chest. The hair tickled her palms. She felt twin bumps like miniatures of her nipples and wondered if they would react as hers did. She ran her tongue over one and felt it tighten. He groaned. "Does it hurt?" she asked.

"Only in the best way."

As she continued her exploration of his chest and taut abdomen, she felt his hands sliding along her thighs. Her legs parted. He touched the throbbing center of her and explored the cleft between her legs. Myriad sensations stormed her body. She grasped his organ and moved her hands restlessly along its length. He leaned forward and kissed her.

As though alive, his sword moved. With a finger, she traced the length and touched the tip. A drop of fluid arose.

He raised his head. "Like this." He placed his hands over hers and moved them up and down on his shaft.

"Hard, yet soft." She found the sac at the base and cupped it with her hand.

"Cease before I spill."

He rose to his knees and knelt between her legs. His mouth slid along her skin. He suckled her breasts. Her sighs became moans. "Marius, what's happening to me?"

"Your sheath is prepared for me. Be still and let me love you as I have before."

His strange words sounded right. She felt a stretching in her woman's parts. He slid his hands beneath her hips and rocked forward.

"Oh." She tensed.

He stopped moving and gazed into her eyes. "You are mine now and forever."

The burning sensation faded. In his eyes, she saw love and desire. "You fill me."

He smiled. "As was meant to be. Wrap your legs around me and together, we'll soar."

Though she was afraid the pain would return, she slowly did as he asked. When he began to move, Estella tensed, then relaxed. There was no pain, only heat flowing through her body. As his movements became harder and faster, she tensed in a different way. Fire spread through her body. She felt ready to explode.

"Please, please," she cried.

"Soon, my love. Come with me."

Their bodies moved in frenzied action. She grasped his shoulders. Her nails dug into his skin. A cry rose from her depths and joined his triumphant roar. Fluid gushed inside her. "My love, my love."

He kissed her forehead, her eyelids, the tip of her nose, then found her mouth. "For now and forever." He rolled on his side and brought her with him. She nestled against his chest and drifted in a euphoric fog. His breathing slowed into the sounds of sleep. She yawned and followed him into dreams of the present and flashes of a strange past.

* * * *

Marius woke to the gray light of pre-dawn. He eased away from Estella. She reached for him. "Must you go?"

"I stand duty today, but I will come this night. My clothes?"

"I'll get them." She wrapped the toga he'd worn around herself and slipped from the room.

Marius shook his head. He ached to possess her again. There wasn't time for a leisurely love-making. He felt sure she was too sore for a quick encounter. He had to bathe and dress and his uniforms were in his room in the barracks.

Estella returned. "You can't go to the baths with my virgin's blood on you. Caten knew how I hated the public ones so he had a heated pool built here. You can bathe there."

"Will you join me?" At least they would have a few more moments.

She pulled his head down and kissed him. "It will soothe my aches."

"Was I too rough?"

She shook her head. "Before I married Caten, Austina told me that the first time leaves aches and some pain."

They left the sleeping room and hurried along the covered way to one of the windowless rooms at the front of the house. Many householders rented this space to shopkeepers, but not this house.

He followed her into the bath. Steam rose from the pool. Estella placed his clothes on a bench and carried a sponge and soap to the pool. He stepped into the water and sat on one of the ledges.

She knelt behind him and washed his back. Her touch raised his desire. "Come to me," he whispered.

She entered the pool. He drew her onto his lap. She leaned forward. "I feel your sword."

He kissed her lightly. "Would that I had time for all I'd like to do."

She slid closer and reached to guide his throbbing shaft along her cleft. "I would love you."

He groaned and thrust into her. He laved her mouth with his tongue. He clasped her hips and rocked her. She wrapped her legs around his waist. As he moved, the water churned. Marius threw back his head and spilled his seed. He held her close. "A promise of what we'll share tonight."

She rested her head against his shoulder. "I'll be waiting for your return."

Reluctantly, he released her. "Until tonight." He left the bath and dressed.

When he returned at dusk, he gave her a gold bracelet he'd purchased years before. As he fastened it on her wrist, she smiled. "I'll wear this every day."

* * * *

Autumn turned to winter. Blandon had left Rome to tour the estates. Estella spent her nights with Marius and her days dreaming of him. Her only worry was the number of years he had to remain with the Praetorian Guards. In the early days of winter, a grim Marius arrived.

"What's wrong?" she asked.

He drew her into his arms. "I'm being sent with a cohort to the Gulf of Naples to work with the Plineys. I leave in the morning."

"Will you be gone long?"

He nodded. "Until summer or longer unless there are messages to be sent to Rome." He pulled her closer. "I will miss our nights."

"There is a way for us to be together and a reason for me to absent myself from Rome."

"How and why?"

"I have a villa in Pompeii. We could meet there."

He opened the stola clasps and kissed her. As he ran his hands over her breasts, he froze. "Estella, are you with child?"

She nodded. "Austina frets people will discover and suspect the child isn't Caten's."

He groaned. "That would be a disaster since I'm not free to marry you."

"If I have the baby in Pompeii and remain there for a time, the baby could be passed off as Caten's or I could adopt a child. If a widow needs an heir, she can adopt."

He bent and kissed her abdomen. "Does anyone else know?"

"Gratia, but she will keep our secret. The adoption was her idea and she will speak to her father and grandfather to see the matter done properly."

He enfolded her in his arms. "A son."

She looked into his eyes. "Or a daughter."

He laughed. "Either will be fine." He carried her to the bed and thrust inside. "We must make the most of this night and store memories for the nights when we're apart."

She grasped his shoulders and caught his rhythm. "I will join you soon, but it will seem an eternity."

* * * *

Just as the sun set, the ship carrying Estella and Austina reached Pompeii. Estella stared at the docks. Her heart filled with joy when she saw Marius waited. Before long, she was swept into his arms. "I feel the swell of your belly where my child grows."

She brushed his lips with a fleeting kiss. "Our child."

He laughed. "As you say. Come, I'll find a litter to carry you to the house."

She shook her head. "Let us walk. The voyage seemed endless and I would stretch my legs."

"A walk began this adventure."

"Any regrets?"

"Only that I'm not free to marry."

Austina signaled that the baggage porters were ready. Hand in hand, Marius and Estella strode through the market. Groups of people gathered around the stalls. Some sat at tables and ate or drank. They passed the baths and reached the walled villa. Once inside the gates, Marius lifted her into his arms and carried her to the house. He entered one of the bedrooms and eased her to her feet. He fumbled to unfasten the clasps of her pella and her stola.

"Marius, let me bathe. I'm sweaty and haven't done more than sponge since I left Rome." He continued undressing her. She saw the way his engorged member thrust against his kilt. "At least remove your clothes." She stroked his thighs.

He laughed and quickly followed her suggestion. While he undressed, she quickly sponged herself.

He moved behind her and cupped her breasts. "Would you deny a starving man the meal he craves?"

She touched his face. "Did you read the slogan above the gate? Lovers, like bees, need a life of honey."

"Your honey is my nectar." He knelt and ran his tongue over her nether lips.

"Marius, come to me."

His laughter ignited her. He carried her to the bed and thrust inside, then paused. He caressed her breasts. "Soon our son will feed here and I will envy him." He moved his hands over her belly. While gazing into her eyes, he began to thrust and withdraw.

Estella surrendered to the raging sensations he raised. "Now, oh, now." She heard his roar of pleasure and felt the gush of his seed.

"My love, this time we will succeed."

What did he mean? She clung to him. "Never leave me."

He stroked her sweat-drenched skin. "Estella, I'm not a free man and may be sent away for a time. Always, I will return, for you are my life and my home."

* * * *

Winter became spring and the days moved toward summer. One morning, Marius arrived in a surprise visit. He held Estella close and kissed her long and hard.

She stroked his cheek. "You are a greedy bee."

"Who has no time to feast. I take a ship for Rome. I hate to leave so near to the birthing."

"I'll be fine. Gratia arrives today. She brings a wet nurse and will stay until you return."

"Wait here for me."

"I promise."

He kissed her again. "Until I see you again. Then we will feast for days." As he strode to the gate, he turned and waved.

* * * *

Gratia arrived at sunset for she'd been staying at her family's villa in the hills above the town. Soon after her arrival, Estella's labor began and lasted throughout the night. The rising sun accompanied the first cries of her son.

Three days later, the wet nurse took over the babe's feeding. Estella's milk was thin and the baby's cries lusty. She regretted the loss of closeness, but the move was right and would make the adoption seem more logical. Through Gratia, petitions were sent to Rome.

The ides of August arrived. Austina returned from the market that morning. "We must leave at once. There's a boat for Rome in port."

"Why?" Estella asked.

"I met Calpurnia's maid in the market. She and Blandon are staying at Florio's villa in Herculinium and intend to visit you."

Estella rubbed her forehead. "I promised Marius I would wait for him here. Gratia, take the baby and nurse to Rome. Find a safe place for them. When I return, I will claim him."

Gratia nodded. "I will keep them at our house and my father will act as his protector. Why don't you come with us?"

"And have Blandon and Calpurnia think I'm running from them. I'm sure Blandon has heard and will attempt to prevent the adoption. If he finds the babe here and sees how much like Marius he appears, he will know. I won't lose my child to his greed. Austina, help Gratia's maid pack."

Until time to go to the ship, Estella held and loved her baby. She carried him to the docks and surrendered him to the nurse. "Stay safe, my son. Grow strong. I will miss you." She tucked the bracelet Marius had given her in his belongings and told Gratia to keep it for him and Marius.

As the boat sailed, she blinked tears from her eyes. Keep him safe, she prayed. She walked home and wept, but she knew she'd done the right thing. As soon as Marius returned, she would depart for Rome and claim her child.

* * * *

On the twentieth of August, a breathless Austina returned from the market. Her face was ashen. "What has happened?" Estella asked. Had the ship to Rome found trouble? Had something happened to Marius?

"I'm fearful," Austina said. "The omens are bad. Waves in the harbor leap high against the shore yet there is no sign of a storm. We must leave."

"I promised Marius I would stay."

Austina stared at the sky. "Look, the birds flee. Listen to the squeals of the horses. They have more sense than you. Come, I will pack and we will go."

Estella shook her head. "Take the maids and the guards. I will stay."

The older woman put her arms around Estella. "I nursed you. I walked the floor when you were sick. You are my child. If you stay, so will I."

The next morning when Estella woke, she heard birdsong. The sky was bright and cloudless. She carried her morning meal to the pool in the atrium. The bell at the entrance to the villa rang. Moments later, Calpurnia and Blandon arrived.

Estella rose. "Greetings."

"Why have you hidden yourself here?" Calpurnia eyed Estella as though searching for something. "They say you seldom venture from the house."

Estella shrugged. "I suffered a chill and the cough lingered. As well, I needed quiet to grieve. The house in

Rome was too filled with memories of my life with Caten."

Blandon's gaze strafed her. "You seem fit now. Perhaps you had another reason to hide away. I've heard rumors you intend to adopt a child. Why would a healthy young woman who is sure to marry do that?"

Estella tensed. He knew and she didn't know how he had learned. The air felt heavy. Was the change because of the company or for some other cause?

"We'll spend a few days with you," Blandon said. "I would see this child."

Estella smiled. "I've sent him and his mother away. There have been ill omens of late." She took her seat. What if Marius came while they were here?

A loud cracking sound made her jump. The sky darkened. A bird fell at her feet. Calpurnia screamed and ran. Austina charged from the house and grasped Estella's arm. The stench of rotten eggs filled the air. Flames spouted from the mountain. Black dust rained on them.

Austina tugged on Estella's arm. "We must flee."

Blandon gripped her other arm and dragged her toward the gate. He tripped over Calpurnia and fell. Estella tried to jerk back, but Austina fell against her.

"You're mine," Blandon said.

"No," Estella cried. "Marius!"

* * * *

"No! No!" Astrid struggled against the hands that restrained her. She had to run. She had to escape.

"It's all right." The man's voice was deep and strangely familiar. What had caused the edge of panic she heard in his words? He was--was--who?

"The bracelet. Take it off." The woman spoke in sharp clipped tones. "The same thing happened when she held the Egyptian necklace. She fainted. When it fell from her hand, she woke."

The weight on her wrist vanished. Astrid opened her eyes. She blinked to focus. Duncan held her in his arms. For an instant, another face flashed in her thoughts. She shivered. He was evil and … Clive.

Paula knelt beside the couch. "You with us?"

Astrid nodded. "I'm fine."

"Let me find a doctor," Duncan said. "There are several among the guests."

Astrid shook her head. How could she explain her strange blackouts? She didn't think any doctor would understand and she would end up in some hospital undergoing a battery of tests. "No need. I'm okay."

"What happened?" Paula asked.

Astrid closed her eyes, but even the vague memories were gone. Except--Pompeii. She'd been there. She shook her head. "I ... I don't think I can explain. Maybe once I make some sense of some vague memories, I'll know."

"And will you tell me?" Duncan asked. "I'm still not convinced this isn't some kind of illness."

Astrid sat up. "This has happened several times recently." She didn't mention the times no one had witnessed. "I'd better go home."

"Are you sure you should drive?" Duncan asked.

"Whatever happened is over. I feel fine now."

"There are guest rooms here."

"And you're hosting a benefit." Astrid clasped his hand. "Thanks for worrying, but don't."

Paula walked to the door. "I'll find Sarah."

Astrid got to her feet and turned to Duncan. "See. No dizziness. No weakness."

He brushed her lips with a light kiss. "I hope you're ready to talk soon. Seems to be more going on than I can imagine."

You have no idea how much, she thought. She nodded. "When I know more, I'll tell you." She held his hand and they walked down the spiral staircase. Paula and Sarah waited at the bottom.

Duncan kissed her. "See you tomorrow." He turned toward the dining room.

Astrid followed Sarah and Paula outside. Lorna grabbed her arm. "I don't know what kind of game you're playing, but leave Duncan alone. He's mine."

Astrid pursed her lips. "He doesn't seem to think that way."

Lorna scowled. "What he thinks doesn't matter. We were meant to be together. When he's mine, wrongs done in the past will be made right. Step aside and you won't be hurt."

"Are you threatening me?"

"Just telling you how it is."

Astrid moved past the blonde. "Time and time again,

you've betrayed us. Not this time."

"You're crazy," Lorna said.

As Astrid strode up the walk, she frowned. Was Lorna part of what had happened in the past? If only the memories of those trips to ancient times were more than fragments that melted under scrutiny.

Paula waited at the gate. "This has been an interesting evening. Could you tell me what's going on?"

Astrid shook her head. "I'm not sure."

Sarah waited beside the car. "What happened to you? Paula says you fainted."

"We'll leave it at that," Astrid said. How could she explain when she didn't understand?

"I'm worried about you," Paula said.

Astrid nodded. "So am I, but I don't know why this is happening."

Sarah patted her hand. "When you're ready to talk, I'll listen."

Astrid started the car. "I wish I could discover why Dad collected all those books."

"Talk to him."

Astrid nodded. "I plan to." She drove to Paula's.

Paula left the car. "I'll stop by the shop tomorrow. Maybe you'll know something then."

"See you."

A short time later, Astrid parked behind Antiquities. She followed Sarah up the steps. "Why don't I have a look at those books? After all, I was a history teacher."

"Not tonight."

"Definitely not tonight." Sarah laughed. "Socializing is tiring."

Astrid opened the apartment door. If only she could remember more from the strange interludes. She walked to the bedroom and changed into a sleep shirt. Though she was tired, she didn't think she could sleep. Might be a good time to look at some of those letters.

* * * *

Duncan spent the remainder of the evening socializing with the guests and avoiding Lorna's attentions. By midnight, the last few strolled up the walk. He smiled. The evening had been successful and the opera company was assured of another season.

Lorna grabbed his arm. "I want my bracelet now."

"Where did you lose it?"

"I didn't. You know the one. The ancient gold one."

He arched a brow. "You mean the anonymous gift I received."

"You know it's mine."

Duncan laughed. "How? Do you have proof of purchase?"

She glared. "That bracelet was a legacy. I want it."

"How interesting since it matches the one stolen from this house." He looked away. He needed to learn about her background and maybe learn what had happened all those years ago. He knew just the man to call. "Possession is nine tenths."

"You'll be sorry." She wheeled. "Clive, take me home."

Duncan watched the pair until they reached the house. The members of the small orchestra filed past. "Thanks," he called.

One of the caterers wheeled a cart past. "We put most of the leftovers in the fridge, along with a selection of desserts."

"Any shrimp?"

The man nodded. "A few and some crab."

Once they left, Duncan locked the doors and set the alarms. He stood at the French doors in the ballroom and stared toward the river. If Lorna hadn't interrupted, would he have persuaded Astrid to stay? He grinned. That would really have set Lorna off.

He recalled Astrid's reaction to the bracelet. Why had she fainted? She had protested when he'd clasped the bracelet on her wrist, but it had been too late to prevent what had happened. Was she all right? He dashed upstairs and changed into slacks and a knit shirt. He needed to make sure of her safety. He grabbed his car keys and went to the garage.

BRITAIN

The sound of the doorbell startled Astrid. She rubbed her eyes. Was it morning? A glance at the window showed night still darkened the sky. The stack of letters she'd been sorting slid to the floor. The peal sounded again. She rose. Had something happened at Antiquities? If there was a problem with her father, the phone would have roused her. She went to the door and peered through the spy hole. Duncan? She opened the door. "What are you doing here?"

"Checking on you. I was worried, especially when I saw the lights were still on."

She leaned against the wall. "I'm fine. What time is it?"

"Nearly two. Can I come in?"

She frowned. "Why?"

His smile made her want to melt at her feet. "I had to be sure you were okay. I need to hold you. I want to kiss you."

She grinned. "Another seduction ploy?"

"I could say no, but whatever works. You'd enjoy it."

She knew she would become like potter's clay to be molded by his hands. "I'm all right. You can go home now."

He shook his head. "I need to know what happened to you this evening. I'll behave."

"Sure you will." She couldn't keep the disbelief out of her voice.

"You can call the shots." He pushed the door open. She expected to be swept into his arms and possessed by one of his mind-shattering kisses. Instead, he clasped her hands. "You look better than you did when you left. Why are you still awake?"

She laughed. "Ever consider you and the doorbell might be at fault?"

"Was I?"

"Sort of. I was sorting some letters Dad wants me to read and I drifted off. The bell woke me. Is the Gala over so early?"

"Midnight. Didn't you read your ticket? Eight until midnight."

"Guess not."

"Once the caterers and orchestra left, I had to see you. Make sure you were okay." He walked to the recliner. "Come here."

"You know where that will lead."

"We'll just talk."

"About?"

"The bracelet. What happened to you? Lorna says it's hers. If so, how did she get one that looks like the one my great-great grandfather described?"

Astrid frowned. "I don't know. As I was leaving, she warned me to stay away from you." Thoughts of her strange response to the other woman occurred and she wondered what she had meant.

"She's not my type." Duncan sank into the chair.

"She said you have no choice." Astrid gathered the scattered letters and dropped them on the coffee table. "How did you become involved with her?"

"Clive. He said he's known her forever. There's something about their relationship that puzzles me. I wonder why he never mentioned her when we were college roommates."

"You've known him for a long time. I have a feeling he doesn't like you." She sat on the arm of the chair.

Duncan clasped her arm and pulled her toward him. "Could be, but I can't figure why. You're not the first person to warn me about him."

"Who else?"

"Paula."

He ran his hand along her arm. She tried to ignore the sensations gathering low in her belly. "So, will you listen?"

"You women don't understand guys. Yeah, he and I are rivals, but we're friends." He tugged on her arm. "I want you. So does he. We're competing for your favor. That's all."

She shook her head. "You're wrong. He envies you. He's angry. He might even hate you."

He grasped her waist. She slid onto his lap. "Clive thinks you're his ticket to a partnership in Antiquities."

She laughed. "Then he's a fool."

"Agreed. He doesn't know Lloyd."

Astrid started to move away, but he pulled her against his chest. His scent and the feel of his muscular body made her sigh. She wanted him. Had desired him before she knew his name. She wished she could remember his role in those dreams from the past.

He brushed his hand over her hair. "You smell good."

"You wanted to talk."

"We have. Now I want to make love." He blew air across her neck.

She groaned. "Why are you trying to find the things someone stole all those years ago?"

"It's time." His tongue flicked her nape.

She straightened. "Talk, Duncan."

He told her about the mystery of Madelaine's disappearance and of his ancestor's search for her. "He never found a trace of her, her father or her cousin. He mourned. Even after the baby arrived, his grief continued. The bracelet was his. So were a number of other things." He began to name the places his great-great grandfather had visited.

Astrid's forehead wrinkled. Some of the pieces in the vault, the ones that had catapulted her into the past, fit the description of the things he named. Should she show them to him now? She pursed her lips. She had to speak to her father first. "Could you show me this journal?"

"Now?"

"Tomorrow." She straightened. "If Lorna says the bracelet is hers and it's also the one from the collection, how did she gain possession?"

"Good question. She says she inherited it. I plan to hire someone to look into her background."

"And Clive's."

"Why?"

"Maybe he's been planning this for years. Isn't it possible he saw the journal years ago? Maybe he read it. He introduced Lorna to you. How and where did they meet?"

Duncan rolled his eyes. "A lot of maybes. For you, I'll set my man looking into that." He hugged her. "Lorna and Clive live in the same building."

"Same apartment, maybe."

He shook his head. "With your imagination, you should

take up writing fiction. Now, tell me what happened with the bracelet."

Astrid sighed. "Something that happened several times when I was a child. This was more intense. I need to talk to Dad and see if there's a connection. All I can say is that I dreamed of the past."

"What past?"

"Eons ago."

"Next time, tell me what you see."

"Maybe there won't be a next time." She started to stand. "You're welcome to come with me when I visit Dad."

"Wish I could. In the AM, there's a cleaning crew coming. My afternoon will be spent at the employees' picnic. I wanted you to come with me."

"Another time. Since you have an early start, don't you think you should head home?"

He nodded and grasped her hand. "A proper good night kiss would be welcome."

His mouth covered hers. His tongue slid along her lips. With a sigh, she succumbed to the heady sensations stirred by the thrust of his tongue.

She raised her head. "Duncan."

"I know. I want you so much I'm always half-aroused."

"Doesn't feel like half to me." She stepped back. "This has happened between us before."

"What do you mean?"

"I'm not sure."

He pulled her into his arms. "Are you sure you want me to leave?" He slid his hands beneath her sleep shirt and explored her thighs and buttocks.

She slid her arms around his neck. When his tongue swept into her mouth, she ran hers over his. One day, she and Duncan would explore these passionate responses. Why not now? Her body throbbed with desire. She sucked in a breath. "Tonight."

He nodded, then groaned.

"What's wrong?"

"No protection. Have you?"

She shook her head. "No and I'm not on birth control. That creates a problem. Pregnancy isn't on my agenda."

He rested his forehead against hers. "I've nothing against children someday, but I don't want one to be a reason for marriage."

She gazed into his eyes. "Makes two of us."

Her answer evoked another groan. He had to leave before he gave into temptation. Though he tried to release her, the silk of her skin and the musky aroma of arousal shredded his will power. "There are ways."

"Dare we take a chance?"

"I want to feel my hands on you."

She sighed. "When we kiss, I want to lose control and feel you deep inside."

"Then no more kisses. Let me love you. I promise not to go too far." She smiled and he wished he could read her thoughts.

"A kiss or two won't hurt, but let me be the one to cry halt."

The look in her eyes made him throb. "You've got the reins."

She touched his lips with her fingers. "Come with me."

As they walked to the bedroom, he kept her pressed against his side. She turned and eased his shirt up to his shoulders. "Did I tell you how great you looked tonight?" She pulled the knit shirt over his head.

"Guess not."

"You did, but you're looking better now." She skimmed her hands over his chest.

He sucked in a breath. Fire shot directly to his groin. She opened the waistband of his shorts. He kicked off his shoes.

As she skimmed the cut-offs over his hips, she grinned. "Black silk briefs." She stroked the cloth.

Duncan felt a rumble in his chest. Good lord, he was purring like a big old tomcat. "Careful, I might burst."

"We can't have that." She pushed him to the bed. "I do like the way those briefs cover you."

Duncan propped himself on the pillows. Astrid pulled her sleep shirt up. The sight of the green thong made him straighten. Slowly, she revealed bare breasts, just the right size for his hands. His mouth went dry. "If I'd known what was beneath your dress, I'd have dragged you to my bed."

She laughed and approached the foot of the bed. "I might have let you." She paused to remove his socks, then massaged his feet. He groaned. "You're driving me crazy. Come here."

She glided along the side of the bed and bent to kiss him. She caressed his chest, gliding her hands in sensuous circles. She touched her tongue to his and then sucked and thrust. Then, she raised her head and inched her hands over his abdomen.

"Astrid," he growled.

"Don't move. I intend to disarm you." She knelt between his legs and feathered her hands over his thighs. I have you where I want you." She ran her finger around the edges of his briefs. "These are so sexy." She leaned over and ran her lips over the silk. He reached for her. "Patience." She looked up and smiled, then inched his briefs toward his legs.

The smoldering heat in her eyes brought guttural sounds from his mouth. "Woman."

"That I am."

His penis sprang free. She traced the length, then cupped his scrotum. When she stroked along the base, Duncan thought he would explode.

She grasped his shaft. His hands fisted. When she brushed her nipples across the head, he nearly shot from the bed. She began to pump, slowly, then with increasing pressure and speed. Duncan grasped the sheet. His hips thrust and retreated. As he erupted, she varied the pressure and speed. He thought he would never stop. He groaned, then shouted her name. He collapsed against the pillows. "I may never recover." Waves of exhaustion swept over him. "I owe you one."

"You'd better be prepared, for I intend to collect."

He tried to open his eyes, but they felt as though they were weighted by boulders. "Now?"

She laughed. "We'll save the next step for a time when you're prepared. Go to sleep."

Duncan obeyed.

* * * *

Bright sunlight woke Astrid. She rolled on her side to check the clock and met an obstacle. Memories flooded her thoughts. Duncan's arrival. Love-making. She whispered his name. Before she could climb over, his arms circled her. His mouth touched hers. His body responded and her desire kindled. Making love wasn't on the morning list of musts. She pressed her hands against his chest and freed her mouth. "Duncan. Protection."

He groaned. "Reflex."

"We'll test them later." She glanced at the clock. "It's after seven. When is the cleaning crew due?"

"Uh. Eight. There's time."

She shook her head. "I intend to collect, but not this morning."

"Got you." He sat on the edge of the bed and grabbed his clothes. At the bathroom door, he paused. "This evening we'll watch the fireworks and make some of our own."

"Before we jump into bed, we'll need to talk about what I learn from my dad."

He grinned. "Over dinner."

After he disappeared into the bathroom, Astrid pulled on her sleep shirt and padded to the main room. She started coffee and assessed the refrigerator for breakfast items. When Duncan appeared, she handed him a steaming mug.

He inhaled. "Lifesaver."

"Milk and sugar?"

"Like mine straight and this is great."

"Would you like breakfast?"

"Would but I need to go home, shower and prepare for the day." He drained the mug and set it on the counter. "Meet me at the house around six thirty. If I'm not there, wait." He kissed her lightly and strode to the door.

Astrid sank onto one of the stools at the counter. She toasted a bagel and ate it. Once she finished, she straightened the bedroom, showered and dressed.

Were there more of the stolen items in the vault? She needed to check and also to remove the ones that had sent her into the past. She wanted to show them to her father and hoped the talk she'd long delayed would provide answers.

A short time later, she entered Antiquities. In case Clive arrived while she was in the vault, she took the inventory lists she'd begun. She paused in front of the rear shelf in the small room, closed her eyes and held out her hands. As though drawn, she touched a large box. When she pulled it free, she saw a smaller one had fallen behind and was wedged between the shelf and the wall. She extracted the box and carried it to the office.

When she dusted the top, she saw a piece of paper. Words

were scribbled and age-faded. Not her father's writing. "Medallions. Gold. Viking." The rest of the words were blurred.

She opened the catch. Gold circles, one large and one small were nested in cloth. She closed the box before the urge to touch one overwhelmed her. Not here. Clive would arrive soon to open the shop. With the box in her hand, she returned to the apartment and stretched out on her bed. She grasped the smaller of the medallions.

* * * *

The sun had barely risen above the horizon when Starr slipped from the house. She slid along the hedge enclosing the compound. Her tunic caught on a branch. She pulled free and crept through the opening. With care, she ran to the meadow. From several nearby homesteads, smoke rose and she prayed none of the other villagers would see the thegn's daughter make her escape from the day's chores.

She mounted her pony. A packet of food for her morning meal and a sack for her gleanings were tied to her belt. As the pony trotted toward the forest, she bent low.

Starr laughed. Though a skillful weaver, she preferred to be outdoors, free to explore the forest. Especially when the cloth she'd been ordered to weave was for her marriage clothes. Though no man had been named, she feared her father would name Kendel as her spouse. She didn't like or trust the man who owed half his blood to the invaders from the sea, the dreaded men who sailed the dragon ships.

If she'd been a boy, she could have spent her days hunting or tending the sheep, the way her older brother had. She chewed a kernel of grief. Ralf had been killed during a hunt and only she believed his death had been planned. She clenched her fists. She had no proof of her suspicions and without this, she couldn't make an accusation.

When she reached the forest, she tied the pony in a small clearing. The brook would provide water and the grass was lush. She checked her traps and found she'd snared several hares to add to the family's food supplies. She cleaned and skinned them. Then she ate her food and left her kill in a tree while she explored.

As she reached the edge of the forest where the land dropped toward the sea, she moved with caution. Several years before her birth, a raid by the dragon ships had left the fishing village deserted. She'd heard tales of what had occurred. A number of the people had sought refuge with her people, one being Kendel's mother. Starr's father had given the boy a home after his mother had cast herself into the sea.

Starr dropped to her knees behind a screen of briars and crawled to where the stream plunged over rocks to form a river to the sea. She muffled a gasp with her hand. The dragon ships had come again. Should she hurry home with a warning or watch to see what these men planned?

She stared at the four houses on the far side of the river. The men were building a palisade and covering the roofs. What did it mean? She saw several women, horses, cattle and dogs. Did they plan to settle?

From the lone hut near the falls, a woman emerged. A sound startled Starr. She looked down and her eyes widened. A tall man strode from beneath the cascading water. His shoulders and back were broad and rippled with muscles. His buttocks were firm and his legs long.

He turned and stared at Starr's hiding place. When he squeezed water from his long hair, she saw his male organ and held in a startled cry. The woman ran to him. He pushed her away.

Starr began a slow retreat. To be captured by one of these strangers could endanger the homestead. But she felt a deep yearning to be with the stranger and touch his sun-bronzed skin.

* * * *

Ragnar peered toward the cliff above the waterfall. He sensed someone watched, but he felt no threat. Perhaps a spy from the cluster of houses at a distance inland, the place where he intended to find a wife. In his meetings with his half-brother, Kendel, Ragnor had heard about the thegn's daughter. Kendel had plans to marry the older of the two, but he'd have to settle for the younger one, unless he took Dagmar into his house. Once again Ragnar heard his father's command.

"Found a settlement. Marry the daughter of a local leader as I would have done if I hadn't been married to your mother. Claim the land through her. Use your half-brother's desire to be acknowledged by me."

"Ragnar, why can't I move into your hut?"

Dagmar's throaty voice made him glower. He looked up. Her heavy breasts were bare. "Go away."

"Let me ease your mighty spear," she crooned.

He reached for his breeches. "Leave me be. Find Kendel. Bind him to you and when my father comes, he will free you."

She glided closer. Her large nipples thrust against his chest. "You have been without a woman for many weeks. That isn't natural."

"Leave me."

"Your father isn't here. He won't know that you make me your woman. I burn to have you fill me."

He pulled his tunic over his head. "Do your duty." He strode to the crossing stones. "Kendel has come. Go to him. If you wish to be free, you will obey."

She flounced away. Ragnar followed and watched her greet his half-brother. Kendel embraced her. With a glance toward Ragnar, Dagmar led the other man to her hut.

A group of men joined Ragnar. "That woman breeds trouble," one said. "Why was she sent with us?"

Another laughed. "You should know. You've been with her often enough."

Ragnar frowned. "Heed this. She must bind Kendel to our cause."

The first man snorted. "But you're all she talks about."

As they gathered for the midday meal, Kendel emerged from Dagmar's hut. He had the sleepy-eyed look of a sated man. He sat on a log beside Ragnar and speared a chunk of meat with his knife. "Your Dagmar is a lusty woman, but I'm sure you know."

Ragnar shrugged. "She's not to my taste. Tell me about the thegn's daughters."

Kendel grinned. "Starr is the oldest. She's wild and forever sneaking into the forest. Needs taming and I'll find pleasure in the process. Wina is quiet, sweet and biddable and will suit you quite well."

"Has he no sons?"

"He had two. The older is dead. An impetuous youth who went after a boar alone. The younger is sickly."

Ragnar noticed Kendel's sly smile. What part had he played in the death? "If you take the wild one as your wife, what will you do about Dagmar? Father sent her as a gift for you."

"And to pleasure the men on a long journey," Kendel said. "Don't worry. I'll keep her. When my wife needs a rest, Dagmar will be there. One woman isn't enough to satisfy my needs."

"Walk lightly. Dagmar's anger can be dangerous."

Kendel laughed. "You're the one she wants."

* * * *

Starr left her pony in the pasture. She slung the game bag over her shoulder and walked to the homestead. Her sister, Wina, caught her in the yard. "Where have you been? Mother's not happy with you."

Starr thrust her spoils into her sister's hands. "I was checking my traps and spying. There's a dragon ship in the cove where the fishers lived. Oh, Wina, I saw one of them step from the waterfall. He made me catch my breath. He's built like a stallion."

Wina's eyes widened. "He was unclothed."

"Bathing. His hair is long and his face is the most handsome I've ever seen."

Wina scowled. "Why do you take such chances? You could have been caught and harmed like Kendel's mother."

Starr made a face. "I was on the cliff and in no danger. Have you no curiosity?"

Wina shook her head. "About them? No. Maybe about Kendel. Don't you think he's handsome and wonderful?"

"Kendel!" Starr spat the name. "I don't like him. Not since Ralf was killed. I need to tell father about the ships."

"He knows. Kendel brought the news this morning. He's gone to spy on them. They trust him since he's half of their blood."

"They're fools if they do." Starr walked away.

"What do you have against him?" Wina caught Starr's arm. "He's brave and a good hunter. He killed the boar that attacked our brother."

Starr pressed her lips together. She couldn't tell Wina her suspicions. When Kendel killed the boar, Ralf's body had been so mangled any other wounds had been hidden by the slashes of the beast's tusks. "Just let it be." Starr entered the house.

Her father glared. "Where have you been?"

"In the forest. Spying on the dragon men."

"Pah. I know of them. Plan to build a settlement. Made an offer for their leader to wed one of my girls."

"Me?"

"Wina. You will wed Kendel in two weeks."

"No. No. I hate him."

Chatwin grabbed her shoulders and shook her. "You will do as I say. My people need a strong man when I'm gone. Since your brother's death, I have considered who will be my successor."

"Will you pass over my younger brother?"

"I must. Wulf is weak. He has the breathing sickness. He's not fit to be thegn."

Starr sank to her knees. "I had the breathing sickness when I was younger. It's gone now. Won't the same thing happen to him?"

"You're a woman and of value only through marriage. The men will remember Wulf's weakness and fear for the stead's safety. You will wed Kendel."

"I'd rather die." She rose and stumbled away. How could she wed a murderer? She would run away and this time she wouldn't come back.

Her mother grabbed her arm. "Where have you been? There's cloth to be woven."

"Father says I'm to wed Kendel. I won't."

Her mother embraced her. "Daughter, you have no more choice than I did when my father gave me to Chatwin. I don't want to see Wulf cast aside, but the choice isn't mine. Come and finish the cloth for your wedding clothes."

"They will be my funeral garb. I'll die before I wed the man who murdered Ralf."

"I know what you think, but no one saw what happened. All knew how daring your brother was. Without proof, there is naught we can do."

"Let Wina wed Kendel. She wants him."

Her mother shook her head. "We can't disobey. Wash your hands and be about the weaving."

When Starr sat at the loom, her anger curdled her thoughts. Instead of the soft colors, she wove black lines and scarlet slashes. When would her father make the announcement?

When Kendel was gone for three days, Starr began to hope.

* * * *

On the afternoon of the third day, Starr heard Kendel's voice and cringed. Wina entered the weaving shed. "He's back with gifts for Father. The dragon men want an alliance."

Starr shuddered. Turmoil roiled her stomach. Today, her father would announce his plans for her wedding with Kendel. She shoved her stool back. She had to flee.

Wina stared at the cloth. "What have you done?"

"It's for my wedding clothes."

"But those are the colors of death and mourning."

"That's how I feel about the man Father has chosen." Starr bolted from the hut and slipped across the yard. She skirted the house where the sound of men's voices rose and fell. Once she reached the meadow, she mounted her pony and sent him racing toward the forest. She didn't know where she would go, but anywhere would be better than being wed to Kendel.

At the edge of the trees, she dismounted and slapped the pony's rump. "Run, run. They will think I'm dead."

If the dragon men hadn't come, she could have sheltered in one of the huts near the shore. Cautiously, she made her way toward the waterfall, hoping for a glimmer of the man she'd seen bathing. She lay on her belly to watch the activity along the shore.

What were they doing? She wiggled closer to the edge. Earth crumbled beneath her weight and she began to slide toward the rocks below. She yelped and tried to grab bushes and tufts of grass to halt the plunge. She curled into a ball. Her head banged against a rock.

* * * *

Ragnar heard the scream and jumped from beneath the waterfall. He saw a figure rolling down the steep slope. He dashed and caught the boy before he landed on the rocks. Then he saw the braids. "By Odin, a girl."

He felt the rise and fall of her chest. Alive. Was she hurt? He checked her head, found a lump, but there was no bleeding.

A close study of her face made his breath catch. She was lovely. She was the one he'd been seeking. He held her against his chest and carried her to the hut he'd claimed. There, he placed her on the bed and lit a fire in the central pit. Though the season was summer, the nights were cool.

After pulling on breeches and boots, he knelt beside the bed and touched her chest. Her breathing was regular. He lifted her eyelids. The pupils seemed the same, not like the ones he'd seen on the man who'd been bashed on the head. Her thick braids must have cushioned her from injury.

Not knowing what more he could do, he left to collect his evening rations. Maybe when he returned, she would be awake. A short time later, he carried a jug of ale, bread, cheese and stew to the hut. He left them on the table and returned to check his guest.

She moaned. Her hand went to her head. She opened her eyes. "Who? Where?"

He shifted to the language his father had made him learn. "Ragnar. My house. Who are you?"

Her gray eyes clouded. "I'm ... I'm...." Tears spilled. "I don't know."

He sat on the edge of the bed. "You fell into my arms like a falling star."

Her brow wrinkled. "Starr. Yes."

Ragnar nodded. So this was the thegn's daughter. She was his, as she'd always been.

Her eyes closed. "I was ill, poisoned. Horses raced and I was thrown. He killed you. There was dust and fire."

He frowned. What did she mean? The day had been bright. The forest was too dense for racing horses. There was no dust and the only fire burned in the pit. "None of those things are true."

"They were."

Her body trembled. He brushed her lips with his. He unfastened the belt around her waist.

"What are you doing?"

"You fell from the cliff. I fear you have injured more than your head."

"Ah."

When her mouth opened, he seized the opportunity to taste her. Beneath his hand, he felt her nipples tighten. When the kiss ended, he felt ready to burst. He wanted to open his breeches and ravish her. "You are mine. Now and forever."

She smiled. "You make me feel like a burning torch."

He slid his hand beneath her ankle-length tunic and

slowly moved it along her legs. "No broken bones." He continued his exploration. She sighed and the sound vibrated through him. His fingers touched the nest of hair at the junction of her thighs. He pulled his hand away. He wanted her, but she'd been injured.

Ragnar rose and went to the table. His penis throbbed and he ached to spill his seed. Not yet, but soon he would take her again and again until her body swelled with his child.

"Do you think you can come here? Food's ready."

"I'll try." She swung her legs over the edge of the bed. She swayed.

He came to her. "You all right?"

"The room moves."

"Lie back."

"Thirsty." He brought her a beaker of ale. She drank greedily and choked. "Strong."

"Let me get you some water."

She grasped his arm. "You saved my life." She stroked his face.

He gathered her close, feasted on her mouth, tasted ale and breathed deep her intoxicating scent. He felt her nipples tighten against his chest. He wanted her. This time he wouldn't lose her.

He inched her tunic upward. Her skin heated. One hand caressed the cloth over her breasts. She moaned. His urgency to take her and seal her to him grew stronger.

A pounding on the door interrupted his concentration on the woman in his arms. The steady drumming continued. "What?"

"I have news."

Kendel, Ragnar thought. He released Starr. "Stay here." He couldn't let his half-brother see her. He knew of Kendel's plans to wed the thegn's oldest daughter. Ragnar had no intention of that happening. He lifted the bar and slipped outside.

* * * *

For a brief time, Starr cowered on the bed. She knew that voice. She'd heard the man's angry tones before. She didn't know his name but she feared him. She rose and smoothed her tunic. Chills shook her body. She rubbed her arms. Was the man a friend of the one who had rescued her? Would he give her to the one she believed was her enemy?

She reached the door and pressed her ear against the rough surface. The words were muffled. She searched the room, saw where light shone through a gap between the boards. She scurried to the place and peered outside.

Ragnar stood with another man. Murderer! Fear became terror. Her knees buckled. She slid to the floor. When the door opened, panic erupted. She pressed against the wall and shoved a fist against her mouth to muffle the scream clawing her throat.

She heard the scuffle of boots on the floor and tried to vanish into the wall. One man or two? She was too terrified to open her eyes. Then, she was lifted to her feet and enfolded in a tight embrace.

"Starr, what's wrong?" Ragnar asked.

With blinding force, all her memories flooded back. "Will you give me to him?" Her voice quavered. Tears trickled over her cheeks.

"To Kendel? Never."

"He killed my brother. There was no proof, but I know. My father wants me to wed Kendel."

"You'll wed no man but me."

She met his gaze and believed. His mouth covered hers. His tongue probed her lips, then slipped into her mouth to tangle with hers.

She felt feverish. Her breasts ached. Her heart thudded. What magic did he evoke? Her tears stopped and she rested her forehead against his chest. He made her feel safe. He made her wish. Once again, he inched her tunic up.

"Ragnar."

"Be easy. I will put my mark on you so no man will deny you're mine."

He stroked her back. His mouth devoured. She felt as though he seared his mark on every part of her skin. He drew her tunic over her head and pressed her against his body. He inched her back until her body touched the wall. When he stepped back, she reached for him.

"Soon." He placed a large fur on the floor at her feet. Then he sat on the bench to remove his boots. He stripped off his breeches. Her eyes widened. His male organ seemed much larger than the time she'd seen him step from beneath the waterfall. She stared. Heat surged along her skin.

He laughed. "Don't be afraid. What I do to you will be

good." He braced his arms on the wall and brushed his mouth back and forth over hers. No other part of him touched her. He flicked his tongue over her chin to lave her throat.

"What are you doing?"

"Making you ready for me."

He slid a leg between hers and moved his hands down the wall. When he drew one nipple into his mouth, her body jerked. She braced her hands on his shoulders. Surely, she would burst into flames. He grasped her hips and suckled the other breast. She moaned. The sensations flowing from his mouth were fire arrows piercing her lower abdomen. Her woman's parts throbbed. Her legs felt weak. She wanted, but she didn't know what or why.

He went to his knees. As he did, his mouth trailed over her abdomen. His tongue flicked her navel. He sat on his heels and spread her legs. His fingers delved between her nether lips. Her moans became a mewling cry. His tongue touched a place that sent lightning coursing. She grasped his head and called his name. She felt wet. Had she disgraced herself?

He sat on the fur and pulled her down so she straddled his thighs. He stroked and pulled her close for a kiss.

Slowly, he drew her closer. He grasped his organ and guided it toward her. When he pressed into her, her eyelids pulled open. She tried to pull away.

He stroked her hair. "It will hurt but once." He shifted position and laid her on the fur. He pushed inside. Her nails bit into his shoulders. He caught her cries with his mouth and remained still.

The pain ebbed, but the fullness remained. Starr moved. He released her mouth and thrust and withdrew again and again. She felt warm, then hot. Excitement built. She felt the way she did when her pony galloped across the plain. She caught his rhythm and moved with him. Sensations sped toward a peak. He roared her name. She cried his. He collapsed, pinning her beneath him.

"You're mine, now and forever. Time and time again we will do this. When you're with child, we'll go to your father." He rolled to his side and pulled her closer.

She stroked his chest and touched the pair of medallions. "As I have before, I will stay with you."

He kissed her. "Soon, one of these will be yours."
* * * *

For several seven days, Ragnar left the hut during the day to work, hunt and fish with his men. He found several tunics on the ship for Starr. After dark, he and Starr frolicked beneath the waterfall and made love. He told her of how trade had developed between her people and his. Though his men suspected he had a companion, they asked no questions. Even Dagmar kept silent. Hope blossomed in Ragnar's thoughts.

He entered the hut. Starr turned a fowl on a spit over the fire. She smiled and rose to kiss him. Then she carried the bird to the small table. "Come and eat."

He stood behind her and cupped her breasts. "I hunger for more than food."

"You must eat to maintain your strength."

Her nipples thrust against his palms. He ran his lips over her nape. "Will you feed my other hunger?"

"You know I will."

He removed his clothes and watched while she took off her tunic. When she turned toward the bed, he caught her hand. He went to the bench and pushed it closer to the wall. After filling a beaker with ale, he cut some bread. "Come here." He pulled her onto his thighs facing him. He bit a mouthful of bread and held the thick slab so she could eat.

She turned and pulled a leg from the fowl and offered it to him. He chewed on one side while she nibbled on the other. His gaze moved from her face to focus on her breasts. As the nipples peaked, he grinned. He dipped his fingers in the ale and rubbed them over her breasts. When he offered her his fingers, she sucked and he ran his tongue over her nipple, then drew it into his mouth.

His penis swelled and throbbed. He placed one hand on her buttocks and urged her to slide forward.

"Ragnar." The breathy sound of her voice further heated him.

He grasped her hips. "Guide me." When she closed her hand around his spear, he groaned. She inched toward him. "Take me," he growled.

She encased him and wrapped her legs around him. She ran her hands over his chest. "I love you."

He tilted her toward him. "I'll never let you go."

"And I will never leave you."

He planted his feet on the floor and began to rock. As he slipped his hand between them, she slid forward and back. He stroked and stimulated. Her body tensed.

"Ah. Ah. Ah." Her cries filled him. When her inner muscles spasmed, his seed spurted.

"I love you." He pressed her closer. No matter what happened, he would never let her go.

* * * *

Several days later when Ragnar left to be with his men, Starr curled on the bed. For the past seven day, she'd needed more sleep than usual. The leaves had begun to take on their bright autumn colors. How long had she been here? She hadn't counted the days. Perhaps Ragnar knew.

The creak of the door woke her. Ragnar strode toward the bed. He looked troubled.

Starr pushed into a sitting position. "What's wrong?"

"Kendel was here. He's arranged for me to meet with your father. I think my half brother suspects you're here."

"How?"

Ragnar shrugged. "Perhaps one of the men mentioned how close I've stuck to the hut and hinted I have a woman."

"I'll go to my father with you. I'll tell him we must wed."

He sat beside her. "There's more. Kendel will wed your sister and be named as your father's successor."

"Wina will be pleased. She wants him." Starr sighed. "How can my father set aside his own son? Wulf will be a good leader. Why can't my father see Ralf's blood on Kendel's hands?"

"Are you sure he's responsible?"

"I have no proof, but I know. Kendel flatters my father. He acts humble. Kendel envied Ralf, but my brother couldn't see his seeming friend's evil nature."

Ragnar took her hand in his. "He'll be punished. When I'm sure you're with child, we'll say our vows before my men. I'll give you the token and we'll face your father."

She looked up. "My moon time is late. Nearly two seven days. I'm sure I carry your son."

He lifted her and swung her around. "Then this night, I'll claim you." He set her on his feet. "I'll proclaim this as a night for feasting."

* * * *

Dressed in a new tunic Ragnar had brought from the ship, Starr held his hand as they crossed the stream. He led her to the huge fire on the beach. The sounds of laughter reached her.

At the fire, a cheer was raised for Ragnar. Some joking comments were made. He drew Starr to his side. "You know of my father's command. Starr is the oldest daughter of the thegn. She carries my son or daughter. Before you and by Odin, she is my wife." He lifted the smaller of the medallions, placed the chain around her neck, then pulled her into his arms.

His mouth found hers. His tongue caressed her lips and plunged into her mouth. Starr's arms encircled his neck. She pressed against him. Moments later, he sighed and released her.

Dagmar sauntered toward them. She scowled. "You dare take what belongs to another."

"Who is she?" Starr asked.

"Kendel's woman. My father's gift to him."

"How can he wed Wina if he has a woman?"

"He only beds Dagmar."

Dagmar stopped in front of them. "She can't have you." She tried to claw Starr's face. "Why do you give her what's mine?"

Ragnar grasped her hands. "Go to your hut."

"No. She can't have you. This time, you're mine."

"Not now or ever." He gestured to several men. "Take her. Bar the door of her hut. She'll remain there until Kendel claims her. On the morrow, I go to the ship for the bride price."

"What if Kendel refuses to listen?" one of the men asked.

"Send him to me."

As the men dragged Dagmar away, she fought and screamed.

Starr grasped Ragnar's arm. "What if my father refuses to accept our marriage? If he has named Kendel as his successor, he won't back down. My father is a stubborn man."

Ragnar kissed her forehead. "Would he have my men attack his people? Any day, more ships will arrive."

* * * *

The celebration lasted until well past moonrise. Ragnar and Starr returned to the hut, made love and slept. When they woke, he pulled her close. "Let it be this time. No betrayals. No loss."

"What do you mean?"

"We've loved and lost before."

She stroked his chest. "The dreams I had the day I hit my head." She shuddered. "All but once I died."

"Not this time." He kissed her until she felt dizzy.

A pounding at the door brought Ragnar to his feet. "What do you want?"

"Dagmar's gone. Escaped through some rotten boards. Should we send searchers?"

"She knows little about the land," Ragnar said. "When she's hungry, she'll return." He turned to Starr. "I must go to the ship."

"Take me with you."

He pulled on clothes. "I must row a small boat on the sea. I won't risk you and my child."

After he left, Starr washed in a basin and dressed. Soon, she and Ragnar would go to the homestead and face her father. She stood in the doorway of the hut and watched a small boat leave the dragon ship.

"Starr."

She turned. Kendel strode toward her. She backed away, but he grabbed her. "You will come with me. Your father expects me to wed Wina, but I have no taste for her. I'll tell him you were kept a prisoner and I rescued you. Once we drive these invaders away, you will be my wife."

"Do I look like a prisoner? I'm Ragnar's wife." She showed him the medallion. "Last night he gave me this before his men and his god." She tucked the gold piece beneath her tunic. "Help me!" she screamed. He put his hand over her mouth and hoisted her to his shoulder. She beat his back with her feet. Moments later, she was tossed over his horse.

Dagmar ran toward them. "Good. Kendel will teach you how to obey. Ragnar is mine." She reached for the chain about Starr's neck. Starr clamped her teeth on Dagmar's wrist. The other woman screamed.

"You can't have what's mine," Starr said. "Ragnar will come for me."

"And he will die," Kendel shouted. He mounted and prodded the horse into a gallop. The rough movement of the steed hurt Starr's abdomen. She feared not for herself but for the child.

Before long they reached the cluster of houses. Kendel dismounted. "Chatwin," he called. "I rescued Starr from the invaders who held her captive."

Starr slid to the ground. "He lies."

Chatwin stepped from behind the hedge. "What men?"

"The invaders."

"Call the men. We'll march against them."

Starr ran to her father and grasped his arm. "Kendel lies. The leader of the dragon men and I are wed in the sight of his men and before his god. He comes to bring the bride price. Kendel stole me from them. He is the one who holds me prisoner."

Kendel raised his hand. "If you're Ragnar's wife, why were you kept in that hut apart from the others?"

Starr flinched. "Because Ragnar lives there. You're his half-brother. You've betrayed him again." Starr looked at her father. "Kendel killed Ralf. He's poisoned you against Wulf. He's evil."

Kendel lowered his hand. "He's told her lies until she believes."

The older man nodded. "How did he know about Ralf?"

"Does it matter? Ralf was my friend. All who knew him knew how rash he was. You said I'd wed Starr. I'm to be thegn after you. I must wed her, not Wina."

"No," Starr screamed.

Wina stepped into the yard. "Father, you promised I'd wed him. Kendel, I've loved you all my life. I didn't tell anyone how you put grass in Wulf's bed so he'd get sick. Why do you want her?"

"To be thegn," Starr said.

Wina pushed Starr. "Why did you come back? You could have waited until Kendel and I were wed."

"He forced me to come."

"Liar," Kendel said. "You screamed for me to save you."

"Ragnar will come for me."

Kendel laughed. "Not after he hears Dagmar's tale. Go prepare for our wedding. I will be wed this day."

Starr slumped to the ground. Hurry, Ragnar, she prayed.

* * * *

Ragnar hoisted the small chest of gold and silver and stepped from the boat. Dagmar threw herself against him. "She's gone. Kendel came and she begged him to take her home."

"I don't believe you." Ragnar pushed her away.

"He said they would wed this day."

"And how do you know this?"

"I went to him. Told him how you'd kept her a prisoner. He'll kill you if you try to take her back."

"Do you think I fear him? You've failed and will be a slave until you die." He hailed his men. "You and you come with me. We go for my wife. Kendel has betrayed us and must die."

One of the men took the chest. Another brought mounts. Ragnar fingered his knife. There was no time to go for axe or spear. He mounted. "Come. If anything happens to me, see to Kendel and protect my wife. She carries my child." He urged the horse into a gallop. He had to reach Starr. She had no love for Kendel and would fight against marriage to him.

When he and his three followers reached the hedges surrounding the large house and several smaller ones, he saw Kendel, Starr and a group of people. "Kendel," he shouted. "Why do you disobey our father's orders?"

Kendel whirled. A knife appeared in his hand. "Obey a man I've seen but thrice. A man who despoiled my mother. She couldn't live with her shame and cast herself into the sea. I will have all and you none."

Starr ran to Ragnar. He caught her in his arms. "I knew you would come. Take me home."

An older man approached. "Let my daughter be. She's promised to Kendel."

"A man she risked death to avoid." Ragnar laughed. "Starr is my wife. She carries my child. Before this lunar ends, more ships and men will come. I wish peace. Do you want war?" In the periphery of his vision, he saw Dagmar. Several more of his men followed.

Chatwin turned to Kendel. "You will wed Wina. A child belongs to the father."

Kendel stepped toward Ragnar and Starr. "Then no man will have her."

Ragnar pushed Starr behind him and faced his half-brother. "Only a coward attacks a woman."

"Then face me if you dare." Ragnar drew his knife. He pushed Starr away. "Stay with my men. They'll protect you."

"Be safe."

Kendel lunged. His knife slashed Ragnar's chest. He laughed. "First blood." Ragnar twisted away. Kendel grabbed him. "I will gut you," Kendel yelled. His knife flashed.

Ragnar gasped. Pain radiated from the gash in his belly. He dropped to the ground.

Kendel laughed. "I've won. Starr, come here."

Through pain-hazed vision, Ragnar saw Dagmar. She plunged her knife into Kendel's back. "Fool. You were to kill her."

Starr's face swam into view. "My love, why must this happen every time?"

Ragnar felt her tears fall on his face. "The funeral boat. My father. Your child is mine. Don't mourn. Tears aren't the way of my people." He shuddered. When would this hatred and betrayal end?

* * * *

Starr sat on the shore and watched the men complete Ragnar's funeral boat. He'd lived long enough to say his vows to her father and the people. She pressed her fingers against the bridge of her nose to halt a rush of tears. She had to remain calm and protect Ragnar's child.

As the men carried Ragnar's body to the boat, she bit her lip. Tears welled but she couldn't seek that comfort until she was alone in the hut she'd shared with him. The men carried food, drink, clothing and weapons on board. They placed the offerings around the body. She clutched the gold medallion, a match to the one she wore. She must give it to his father, though she wished she could keep it for the gold was all she had of him. A cock, a dog and a horse were killed and added to the things Ragnar would take to Valhalla.

"You will join him."

Starr turned. "I carry his child."

"So you say. I don't believe you." Dagmar reached for Starr.

Starr rose. "You send Ragnar to his death. You told Kendel about me." When she saw the dagger in the other woman's hand, Starr backed away.

"A woman should be on the boat with Ragnar so his needs will be satisfied. You can serve as his slave in Valhalla." Dagmar sliced the air with the knife.

Starr continued to back away. She tripped and fell. Frantically, she groped in the sand for a weapon and found a piece of driftwood. She blocked the plunging dagger and scrambled to her feet. Dagmar struck again.

Starr felt a stinging on her arm. She swung the wood and connected with Dagmar's head. As her enemy collapsed, Starr felt relief. In part, she had avenged Ragnar.

Several men strode across the sand. "Odin has spoken. She will serve Ragnar." They lifted Dagmar.

"Is she dead?" Starr asked.

"Matters not. Come. First torch is yours. Tide's going out. May your son be as valiant as you."

They poured melted fat over the goods. One of the men handed Starr a torch. When the fire blazed, the boat was pushed into the water. When flames engulfed the entire boat, a shrill scream sounded.

* * * *

The echoes of a scream pulled Astrid from the past. Had the terror-filled cry been hers or the woman thrust onto the boat. She rubbed her temples with her fingers. Lorna Stinit. Astrid frowned. Why was she sure the betrayer had been Lorna?

With a shudder, Astrid headed to the shower. Once dressed, she packed the jewelry and letters in a shoe box and went to the car. She planned to eat lunch with her father and talk about the dreams. Also, she wanted to ask what he'd been looking for in the books.

When she reached the rehab center, she found her father had just finished a session in the pool. She waited in the hall while he dressed. When he opened the door, he grinned. The walker was gone. He held a cane.

"Well, look at you."

"Feel good. Another week, then home. Maybe even Friday."

"I'm glad. Want to stay here or go to the garden?"

"Garden. Order lunch first."

She smiled. His speech and gait were vastly improved. "What's on the menu?"

"Cobb salad. Blue cheese--"

"Stop there."

"Figures." He laughed and reached for the phone. As they left the room, he touched the box she carried. "What's in there?"

"I've a tale to tell." She led him to a shaded table. "Last night, Duncan told me about his search. Did you know there's a portrait in his foyer of a woman who looks like Grandma Logan must have when she was young?"

"Never been there." He settled on a chair. "Letters I want you to read. Cousin to your great-great grandmother. Lived with her until she died."

Astrid nodded. "Interesting."

"Might be woman in Duncan's journal."

Astrid nodded. "I think you're right."

"What's bothering you?"

"Remember when I was a child and touched old things, then saw pictures of ancient lands."

"I do. Weren't all old things, just certain ones."

"Really. I don't remember that."

He touched her hand. "When I found the letters, wondered if connected. She mentioned things Duncan described. One Egyptian necklace and a gold bracelet."

Astrid opened the box. "I think these are some of the things he's seeking."

Lloyd lifted the jewelry and placed it on the table. "Egypt, China, Babylon. You saw these places and others, too."

"What others?"

He closed his eyes. "Been ages. I think Japan, Pompeii."

She took a deep breath. "I dreamed I was in Egypt and other places. Lived other lives. The memories were hazy."

He placed his hand over hers. "Mermeshu."

Her eyes widened. "Yes. She fell in love with him. He was betrayed by a friend and then betrayed her. How did you know the name?"

"Saw it in a book. Commander of the Armies. Wanted to be Pharaoh. Never found more about him."

Astrid wanted to put her head on the table. As her father removed the jewelry from the box, she mentioned the other times. "I wish I could remember more. How do the letters figure into this mess?"

"Most from Madelaine. Written to the man she loved. Her father worked for Garretts. She loved Garrett's son. Were going to marry. Received threats. Father killed. She and her cousin fled."

"Did she steal the jewelry?"

"She took was the ring he gave her. She sold it so they could live. Madelaine died in childbirth."

Astrid leaned forward. "What happened to the baby?"

"Found nothing in the letters."

"That's a lot like Duncan's story."

"I know." Lloyd put the jewelry in the box. "Jewelry could be some stolen pieces. I think your dreams are true."

"I'm afraid they are," Astrid said. "What now?"

"Give them to Duncan." Lloyd reached for his cane. "Time for lunch."

* * * *

Duncan chuckled as the children in the three-legged race hobbled across the finish line. He cheered the winners and gave them their prizes. The other children received certificates for cones at the local ice cream parlor, making every child a winner.

With this race ended, his stint as a judge ended. He strode to the tent where the caterers served a variety of food. He snagged a soda, a burger piled with trimmings, potato salad and an ear of corn. He joined a group of employees at a table. The day would have been perfect if Astrid had come. He wanted her to know every facet of his life.

He nearly choked on the burger. Did this mean he was ready to make a commitment? No wrong moves this time, he thought. He frowned. He'd never felt the need to make a move toward anything permanent with any woman. Not until Astrid. Once again, strange thoughts arose. Like he'd done this before and wrong.

"So there you are."

Duncan looked around. He'd been so lost in thought he hadn't noticed when the others had left the table. Lorna slid onto the bench beside him so close her thigh touched his. "What do you want?"

Her tongue slid over her lips. Her eyes glittered. "What do you think?"

"I'm not going there with you, ever."

"I just want my bracelet. It's worth a lot."

"So sue me. I believe we determined ownership last night."

She dug her fingers into his arm. "I want what's mine. That's the last piece of jewelry my ancestor used to regain the fortune your family stole from mine."

He arched a brow. "The bracelet is described in my ancestor's journal. Looks like your family based their fortune on stolen property."

"It wouldn't be the first time that happened." A sly smile appeared. "You could make things right by marrying me."

He shook his head. "I don't want you now and I didn't in the past."

She glared. "You'll be sorry." She rose and stalked away.

Duncan shrugged. He would take his chances. He'd done nothing to harm her.

* * * *

Astrid reached the apartment just as Sarah was leaving. "Isn't the shop open?"

"Clive closed early to organize for the street fair tomorrow. How's Lloyd?"

"Much improved. Clear speech and he walks with a cane." Astrid halted on the steps. "Aren't there several canes in the shop?"

"I believe so."

"Let's go pick one and you can take it to Dad."

Sarah nodded. "Great idea. We were busy for a bit today. Will be busier tomorrow. Clive's sorting through boxes for items to put on the sidewalk tables. Said they're not good enough for the shop."

When they entered Antiquities, they found Clive in the vault. Astrid was glad she'd removed the jewelry she'd shown to her father. She noticed several boxes on the desk.

Clive emerged with another box. "Ladies, what brings you?"

"A cane for Dad." She pointed to the boxes. "Those?"

"For the street fair. Lloyd's always picking up odd lots with a few good pieces and the others not so good. People snatch them up at the fairs. Want the Antiquities boxes and bags. A bit of snob appeal."

"Guess you never know what people treasure," Astrid said.

"Canes," Sarah said. "I don't want to be late to dinner." She held one out. "What about this one?"

Clive laughed. "From the twenties. Actually, it's a flask. Don't think Lloyd needs one."

"Hardly," Astrid said.

"There's a great one with a brass knob," Clive said. "Very dashing. It's in the vault, right side, second shelf."

Sarah nodded. "Sounds perfect."

"Lock up when you leave." Clive waved and left the office with the box tucked under his arm.

A cry of frustration escaped when Astrid entered the vault. The shelves she'd neatly organized were a mess. Had Clive been searching for jewelry for the street fair or something else? She finally located the cane and left the vault.

Sarah smiled. "Wonderful and heavy enough to make a great weapon."

"Let's hope that's not necessary." Astrid followed the older woman to the door. "See you tomorrow."

"I'll be outside tending the table."

Astrid hurried to the apartment. Just inside the door, she halted. The sofa cushions were on the floor. The books she'd neatly stacked had been knocked over. She peered into her father's bedroom. Drawers had been pulled out and the contents strewn on the floor. Her room showed signs of the same frantic search.

She sank on the bed. "Who?" Good thing she'd taken the jewelry and letters with her. Was anything missing? Should she call the police?

She returned to the main room and checked the door. No signs of a forced entry. The only other way to open the door was with a key. Clive! He'd had her father's keys. He'd searched the vault. What had he been looking for? She needed to see if anything was missing. When she joined Duncan, she'd ask him to put the shoe box in his safe.

SWITZERLAND

Astrid stood in the middle of the apartment's main room. Scream or weep? Her emotions swung from fear to anger. Someone had invaded her space, had torn things apart. She rubbed her hands along her arms. At least the vandal hadn't trashed the kitchen. She took a deep breath and replaced the sofa cushions. Then, she straightened the books.

The doorbell rang. Astrid yelped and nearly knocked the books over again. Clive? Come to judge his effects on her nerves? She shook her head. He was sly, not bold. She looked at the clock. Too early for Duncan and besides, she was to meet him at his house. She went to the door and peered through the spy hole. "Paula, what are you doing here?"

"Checking on you. Stopped by the shop earlier to invite you to lunch. Sarah said you'd gone to see your dad. How is he?"

"Doing great. Should be home soon."

"That's wonderful." Paula perched on one of the stools at the counter separating the kitchen from the rest of the room. "Lorna came in while I was there. Dragged Clive into the office. Couldn't hear what they said, but she sure screamed. Shame the door blocked the words."

"A stethoscope would have helped," Astrid said.

Paula laughed. "Don't have one. Would you tell me what happened last night?"

Astrid frowned. "It's hard to explain." The talk with her father had brought as many questions as answers. "It's ... I'm not quite sure, but if you want to watch while I put things in order, I'll tell you what I remember."

The moment they entered Astrid's room, Paula gasped. "Good grief. Did you lose the crown jewels?"

"Not my mess. I came home to this. Seems I had a surprise visitor. Dad's room is worse."

"What was whoever looking for? All the valuables are down in the shop, aren't they?"

"As far as I know."

"That Egyptian necklace and crown is missing," Paula said.

"Not really. I put it some place safe. How did you know?"

"That's one thing I heard Lorna say. Accused Clive of hiding it. She said something odd. Carnelians aren't his usual style."

"When was that?"

"Around noon, just before she stormed out. He told her he'd checked the vault and it wasn't there." Paula sat on the edge of the bed. "Did you call the police about this?"

Astrid shook her head. "I'm not going to either. Whoever searched the place had a key. I thought there were only three."

Paula arched a brow. "And those belong to?"

"Me, Dad, and Sarah."

"She wouldn't do this."

"I know." Should she tell Paula about Clive? She knew how much her friend liked him.

Paula studied her intently. "I can think of two possibilities and one doesn't compute."

Astrid sighed. "Clive had Dad's keys. Gave them to me the day I arrived, but he could have made copies. I don't trust him." She reached for the pile of silky underwear. She had to wash them. She couldn't wear them knowing he'd pawed them.

"I don't like to think you're right, but you could be." Paula headed to the door. "Be right back. Need to make a call."

Astrid frowned. "Not the police."

"Someone else," Paula called.

Astrid carried her underwear to the washer. She paused to listen to Paula's end of the conversation.

"Jan, can you come over? I know it's a holiday weekend, but a friend of mine needs a new lock ASAP. Seems someone who shouldn't has a key to her apartment. Above Antiquities. Ten minutes. Thanks."

"Who and why?" Astrid asked.

"Jan's a locksmith. I'm sure you've passed her shop on Main. She'll install the lock and maybe the three of us can go to dinner."

"Wish I could, but I'm meeting Duncan at six thirty."

"Enjoy."

"Plan to. I could have a drink with you and your friend."

"Sounds good. Back to work. I'll start in your dad's room."

As Paula entered the other bedroom, Astrid sighed with relief. Paula had forgotten about last night and the unexplainable didn't need to be explained.

By the time Paula's friend had the new lock installed, the apartment was in order. Astrid changed into an ankle-length skirt and a clingy top. Duncan hadn't mentioned where they were going to dinner. This outfit would work anywhere.

"Meet you at the pub," Paula said.

"Where?"

"On Main across from the municipal lot."

Astrid tucked the shoe box beneath the passenger's seat. With luck, Duncan would agree to keep it in his safe.

Over drinks, she enjoyed learning about Paula's friend. They set up a lunch date for Friday. At a few minutes before six thirty, Astrid said goodbye and drove to Duncan's. As she parked the car, he drove up.

"Follow me." When he approached the wall, a gate opened. Astrid drove down a steep drive past what must have been a guest house. She parked behind a six car garage.

Duncan waited for her. "Let's go in. You can organize dinner while I shower."

"Sounds like a plan."

He led her up the back stairs to a spacious kitchen and gave her a quick tour of the drawers and cupboards. "You'll find about anything here. Leftovers from last night are in the fridge." He kissed her lightly. "See you in ten."

"Don't rush." She stood at the refrigerator and assessed the contents. A bowl of shrimp and one of crab inspired her. A salad with lemon vinaigrette would be nice. She took lettuce and tomatoes to the counter. After locating knives, bowls and plates, she assembled the salad. She sliced a half loaf of Italian bread and made garlic butter. Once she popped it in the oven, she put a selection of canapés in the microwave.

By the time the quick meal was on the table, Duncan appeared in the doorway. His tousled hair looked like he'd merely rubbed a towel over his head. The rumpled look was appealing. Astrid grinned. He took a bottle of chardonnay from the refrigerator. "This work?"

"Perfect."

They sat side by side and soon polished their plates. "Dessert later?"

She nodded. "How was your day?"

"Hectic but fun." He gave her the highlights of the employees' picnic. "Kids are fun. How's Lloyd?"

"Better than okay." She remembered the box beneath the passenger's seat. "I need to get something from the car."

"A present?"

"Sort of. Could you put it in your safe?"

"Sure, but what about the vault at the store?"

"Not a good idea." She told him what she'd found when she arrived at the apartment. "Had to be Clive."

"Doesn't Sarah have a key?"

"She does, but she has no reason to search. Clive does. Lorna wants the Egyptian pieces and I think she has some hold over him." She walked to the door.

"I hate to think he'd do something like this, but you're right about Lorna's influence." He followed her down the steps. "You're staying here tonight."

She laughed. "There's no danger now. The locks have been changed. A friend of Paula's came and did that."

"Can you trust Paula?"

"Why shouldn't I?"

"She has a thing for Clive."

Astrid took the box from the car. "She also knows he's not to be trusted, unlike some people who trust him."

He held up his hands. "He's a friend."

"And that excuses him?"

Duncan exhaled in a rush. "No. Takes a lot for me to re-evaluate my opinions. What's in the box?"

"Some letters that might give some clues to the mystery of your great grandfather's origins and what I believe are a number of the stolen items. I want you to put them in the safe."

"Can I look at them?"

"Sure, but I'm not touching them."

"Before we get involved with this, let's go to the apartment and get your clothes for tonight. I have plans that will take a long time to execute."

She laughed. "When do the fireworks begin?"

He chuckled. "Any time you want."

"Duncan, I meant the town's display."

"Around nine." He slid into the passenger's seat and took the shoe box. "I'll even let you drive."

Astrid started the car. "I'll be perfectly safe at the apartment."

"And I'd worry so much I'd be at your door like I was last night."

"All right." She drove to the apartment.

Since she would be gone overnight, packing took little time. She carried the overnight case into the living room. "I'm set."

"So am I." He grinned.

When they returned to the house, Duncan put the box on the desk and took her case to the bedroom. He returned and opened the box. He put the letters aside and removed the jewelry.

"Could you get me the journal?" Astrid asked.

He opened the safe and handed her the leather-bound book. Slips of paper marked the detailed descriptions. Astrid read them and Duncan lifted the pieces. "I think these are the ones. So what's left?"

Astrid flipped the pages. "Jeweled silver cross found in Switzerland. A netsuki, whatever that is, from Japan and a silver and gold disc from Peru. Do you think Lorna has the other things?"

"I'm not about to ask her."

"Any idea what happened to Chester and Bonnie?"

"Chester left town around the time Madelaine disappeared. Bonnie's family lost their money and moved." He put the jewelry in the box. "Why won't you touch them? Afraid of another fainting spell?"

"Actually, yes." She sucked in a breath. "When I was a child...." She began the tale. "So you see when I touched the jewelry, I had dreams--like I was living other lives. When I wake, I don't remember much."

He frowned. "Do you wish you did?"

"I don't know. Might give me some idea about what's happening now."

He put his arms around her. "I like what's happening.

Ready for fireworks."

She laughed. "What kind?"

"An aerial display, courtesy of Rockleigh." He brushed his lips over her mouth. "Later for the other kind." He led her to the balcony outside his bedroom.

* * * *

With a final explosion and a magnificent blaze of red and white spirals and circles, the fireworks ended. Astrid turned to Duncan. "That was wonderful and this is the perfect viewing spot."

He pulled her into his arms. "This will be as exciting." He nipped her lower lip, then slid into a devouring kiss.

She inhaled his scent and slowly slid her tongue into his mouth. She pressed against him. "Duncan," she whispered.

"We need to take this inside before I forget."

She nodded and moved away. After rising, she held out her hands to him. "I want you."

"You drive me crazy."

She gulped a breath. He made her want the things she wasn't sure he could give--a home, a family, a commitment that he would be beside her every night.

He guided her into his bedroom. The maleness of the room engulfed her. Huge bed, dark mahogany furniture. Browns and rich blues in the carpet and draperies. He circled her waist and pulled her hips against his. She felt his erection and raised her head for a kiss.

He groaned. "Been like this ever since you got out of your car."

She tasted his lips. "I think I can handle what's to come."

"Keep on and I'll forget that I owe you one and take what I want." He slid his hands beneath her top and then along her spine. "Front fastener?"

"Why don't you check?" She pulled the clingy material over her head.

Duncan sat on the edge of the bed. "Undress for me, then I'll return the favor."

Astrid watched his face as she unfastened her bra and let the straps slide down her arms. His eyes darkened and his gaze was focused on her hands. She cupped her breasts. Then, she opened several buttons on the skirt. The soft cloth slid to the floor. As she moved her hands to the top of her thong, he shook his head. "Leave it. I'll do that later.

Come here."

She glided toward him and stood between his legs. He ran his hands along her ribs, then took one throbbing nipple into his mouth. She rested her hands on his shoulders and purred. "Duncan, I want you. All of you."

"And you'll have me." He lifted her and put her on the bed. "My turn. Never done this before."

"Want music?" she asked.

"I can manage without." He removed his shoes and socks and rose from the bed. He stepped back and pulled his shirt over his head.

Astrid moistened her lips and itched to stroke his chest, to feel his muscles expand and contract beneath her fingers. When his hands unbuckled his belt, she sucked in a breath, then laughed. "Your briefs match mine."

"Blue's one of my favorite colors."

She gave him a once-over, then studied his briefs. You'd better prepare now. This time, I want all of you inside."

He sauntered toward the bed and took a condom from the bedside stand. Astrid leaned forward and ran a finger along his silk briefs. "Take them off."

"Why don't you?"

She slid her fingers under the elastic and peeled the briefs down. She caressed his scrotum and stroked his penis.

He stepped back and kicked off the briefs. Then he grasped his shaft and slowly rolled the condom over the length. "Ready for payback?"

"And eagerly waiting."

He grinned. "Just lay back and enjoy."

Astrid settled against the pillows. When he knelt of the bed, she reached for his erection. "All of you."

He sat back on his heels. "You can look, but not touch."

"You're cruel."

"We'll see." He drew one of her feet onto his knees and massaged the sole. She groaned. He moved to her other foot, then stroked her calves, inching toward her thighs. When his fingers delved into her cleft, she moaned.

"Duncan, now."

He shook his head. "Patience. Isn't that what you told me?"

She made a face. "Guess I did."

He brushed his lips over the flesh above her thong. As he

slowly inched the cloth away, his mouth followed.

She sighed. She whimpered. She bent her knees and braced her feet against the mattress. He drew the thong over her legs and tossed it on the floor. His fingers played magic on her clitoris.

"Duncan, come into me."

His mouth replaced his fingers. Her body thrummed with need. He nipped, licked and sucked. Heat rose like the tail of a rocket and sent her soaring. While her body pulsed with aftershocks, he thrust inside. He captured her mouth and thrust his tongue in synchrony with his rocking movements. When he raised his head, his thrusts grew harder. Astrid felt her body take fire. She cried his name as he shouted hers.

He collapsed atop her. She stroked his back and his arms. He slid to one side, cupped her face and kissed her. "Never been like this before."

"For me either," she whispered.

"Astrid, I--"

She curled against him. If he said more, she didn't hear. Sleep claimed her.

* * * *

The noise, the voices, the strains of classic, rock and country blended into a cacophony of sound. Astrid looked at Duncan. "I love street fairs."

He laughed. "Never had the pleasure. My grandfather called them the invasion of peasants. He was a bit of a snob. Dragged me off to the mountains or the shore. Avoiding street fairs became a habit."

"You missed a lot of fun. Every summer when I stayed with Dad, I was in the thick of things. After my mom died and I came to live with Dad, my friends and I looked forward to street fair Sundays. This one's on Monday, though."

He clasped her hand. "I should have come. We might have met."

"Or passed each other as strangers in the crowds. Come on, to the park and food."

Duncan shook his head. "Don't you want to look over more of the tables?"

"We will."

"I'd like to buy you something to mark the day."

She tugged on his hand. "Food first."

A short time later, they sat on the grass to eat hot dogs smothered with everything, greasy fries and soda. Duncan chuckled. "If my grandfather could see me now."

"He'd avoid you. You've ketchup on your chin." She leaned over and flicked it with her tongue.

"Want to go back to the house?" He waggled his eyebrows.

"In due time. About your grandfather. Would he really be upset?"

"He was a gentleman to the core and we have our position to maintain." Duncan reached for the soda. "He had standards and rules, but I loved him."

"That's what counts." She studied her hands. "My mom and dad split soon after I was born, yet I always knew they loved me. She taught English and had a dozen lovers. Dad had none I knew of. I always hoped he and Sarah would make a match."

"They're friends. Could be they don't want more." He wiped his mouth. "What now?"

"We'll look at the jewelry and visit Sarah. First I want cotton candy." She walked to where a man spun sugar into clouds of sweetness.

Duncan laughed. "I'll pass."

Astrid took the paper cone from the man and took a bite. She held it out to Duncan. "Try."

He bent his head and kissed her lightly. His tongue swept along her lips. "Sweet. Could be addictive. I'll just share."

Astrid danced away. "No way."

Moments later, he had his own. They held hands and threaded through the crowd, pausing to browse at tables where people sold jewelry, crafts and toys. They paused to peer through kaleidoscopes.

Finally, they reached the Antiquities table. Sarah looked up. "Come to find a bargain?"

"Maybe," Astrid said. "Also to give you this." She handed Sarah a key.

"What's this for?"

"Had to change the lock on the apartment yesterday. Had an uninvited visitor."

Sarah glanced into the shop. "Clive?"

"Looks that way. Tell you more later." Something tugged

at Astrid. She studied the contents of the table. Her hand hovered over a tarnished silver cross. Gems had been pried from the setting.

"Duncan, would you buy that cross for me?"

"That? It's junk." He stared at the piece. "Do you think?"

She nodded. "Buy it and we'll go to your place." She felt a need to explore another time and maybe find answers to what was happening now. Maybe she could discover for certain Duncan was the lover found and lost. Maybe she wouldn't, but she had to know before she tumbled completely in love with him.

Duncan paid a dollar for the cross. "Cheap present."

"Maybe not." She held his hand as they strode up the street. As they crossed the foyer at his house, she glanced at the portrait. She and Duncan could read the letters later. Then, she would tell him about her grandmother's uncanny resemblance to the woman in the painting.

They entered his bedroom. Duncan rested his hands on her shoulders. "Are you sure you want to do this?"

"Yes."

"Promise you'll come back."

"Why wouldn't I?" She kicked off her shoes and lay on the rumpled sheets. Duncan lay beside her. As she grasped the tarnished cross, he kissed her forehead.

* * * *

Esther slid her cloak from her shoulders. Though the party was high in the mountains, the sun beat down. She stared toward the alpine slopes. Excitement filled her. She was coming to the place she'd always thought of as home. She glanced at her father who rode at her side. His face was grim. Was he angry that he'd had to come to the home where his beloved wife had died? Not her mother, but his second wife, the one he had married for love. His marriage to Esther's mother had been for wealth and power.

She turned to look at the carts. One held baggage and the other supplies. Her young half-sister and the aging relative who acted as nurse and companion rode in the second cart. A troop of men surrounded the party for there had been trouble in the mountains. Men had formed bands to fight against the taxes collected by the king and his counts.

The carts had added to the time spent on the road. Esther had had time to remember summers spent in the mountains where the air was cooler than in the lower lands and in Count Rudolf's castle. Here, she'd had friends who didn't court her for her father's wealth and status.

Trude and Berwin had been her playmates. Berwin was the son of one of the town's elders and Trude, the daughter of one of the castle's maids. Had the pair married? That had been Trude's plan to escape the lowliness of her mother's place in the community.

At the end of the pass, Esther stared at the shining waters of the lake below. Mountains cupped the lake. By evening, they would reach the town on the shore and the castle on a slope above the town. She wanted to race past the dark green firs and the trees just turning autumn bright.

She gulped a breath. Gerald would be here. A distant kin of the count, he'd been sent to gather the taxes. Months ago, he'd cornered her and taken a kiss. Fortunately, she'd escaped before he'd done any harm. She didn't like him and had no intention of being forced into a marriage.

The sun was low on the horizon when they rode through the town. Esther glanced at the shops and hoped Mathilde would allow her to visit places she had as a child. They reached the castle, though the structure was more like a moated manor house than the massive structure where she'd lived for most of her life.

Berwin and his father waited in the hall. A fire burned in the massive fireplace. Esther removed her cloak and stood beside the fire. She glanced at Berwin.

He was so tall, so broad-shouldered, so handsome. His brown hair held streaks of gold and his eyes were the color of the lake in sunlight. He was nothing like the boy she hadn't seen for years. He looked up and their gazes meshed. She felt heat shimmer through her body.

He stepped toward her. "Esther, you've changed."

"She's a lovely young lady," his father said. "We've missed you and your father."

When the servants brought food to the table, Mathilde came to Esther. "Adelle is nearly asleep. I'll take her to our room."

Esther turned to her father. "Should I go up with them?"

He shook his head. "You're my hostess. Any business will be discussed later." He gestured to the guard who stood at the door. "Where's Gerald?"

"Gone, my lord. He's overseeing the harvest and collecting the taxes."

"Harvest Festival is next week," Berwin said.

Esther sighed. She would love to go, but this was not the time to ask for permission. Her father looked so drawn, so old. She felt sure he wished they hadn't been forced to come.

* * * *

Berwin glanced at Esther. He felt edgy. Eight years since she'd last been here. The change had taken him by surprise. She was lovely, but not for him. Though his father was a town leader, she was as distant as a star. While he could adore her, he could never speak of the desire that stormed his body. Her father had taken a young woman from the town as his second wife. Esther wouldn't be permitted to wed below her high station.

"How's Trude?" Esther asked.

Berwin grimaced. "She works in the barracks."

"Then you didn't marry her." Esther smiled. "She said she would when she grew up."

"Rather not talk about her," Berwin said. "She wanted things I couldn't give her. I'm a forester and trapper. Don't earn much." He couldn't tell Esther Trude was Gerald's woman, that her friend slept with the man who bragged Esther would be his spouse.

Berwin swallowed. When she placed her hand on his arm, he felt strange. The light brush of her fingers made his member throb.

"Berwin," his father said. "George has suggested you escort Esther to the Harvest Festival."

Esther smiled. "I would like that. Mathilde says town is too far to walk and she hates to ride. Do you remember when we were younger and got sick on apple cake?"

Berwin nodded. "We had fun."

"So you'll take me?"

He looked away. What should he do? He had agreed to meet with several men from other cantons to talk about how to stage their next act of defiance. Rumors about the shadow leader's presence had stirred Berwin's curiosity. He saw the eagerness in Esther's eyes and made a decision.

"I would be pleased to be your escort." He would find a way to speak with the men. If he missed the shadow leader, there would be other times to learn his identity. Berwin planned to tell his fellow conspirators that Sir George would listen to their petitions. All knew the count's representative was an honorable man.

A commotion outside the doors brought the guards to attention. Berwin reached for his knife. Had the rebels gained entrance?

The doors opened. Gerald and his arms men entered. He stopped and bowed. "My lord, I didn't realize you were coming. Had I known, I would have been here to greet you."

Esther grabbed Berwin's arm. Her fingers trembled. He felt a need to protect her, a need so strong he nearly leaped to his feet to challenge Gerald. He looked at her. "I won't let him hurt you."

She nodded. Berwin's heart stuttered. He desired her. He had always loved her. The expression in her eyes told him she felt the same. If they had been alone, he would have gathered her into his arms and tasted her lips.

She left her chair and kissed her father's cheek. "Papa, I'll retire now. I'm sure you have matters to discuss."

"Good night, child."

When she vanished up the stairs leading to the upper floor, Berwin stared at Gerald. The other man's gaze followed Esther. His expression spoke of greed and lust. I won't let him hurt her, Berwin vowed. Gerald had already ruined Trude by playing on her desire to be more than a servant.

* * * *

Esther spent the next few days overseeing the household and avoiding Gerald. Much needed to be done. The servants had grown lax under Gerald's hand. Her father had been busy. He'd met with the town leaders and spoken to Gerald. The encounter had produced shouting and a sullen anger in Gerald's eyes. On the few occasions when Esther was in his company, his manner had been charming, but his eyes had remained cold and calculating.

Though Esther knew Trude worked in the barracks, she seemed like a shadow, often glimpsed but never met. What's wrong, Esther wondered.

Determined to speak to her friend, she hid in a doorway. She saw Trude leave the wooden building where the soldiers slept. When the other girl walked past, Esther grabbed Trude's arm. "Why are you avoiding me?"

Trude whirled. Her scowl made her appear ugly. "You're always stealing what should be mine. Remember how I wanted to marry Berwin?"

Esther nodded. "I expected to find the two of you wed and with a child or two."

Trude made a face. "After you left, all he talked about was you. Every summer, he waited for your return. I got tired of hearing your name. I still am."

"But we were friends."

"Hah! I found a man who gives me money and buys me things. Then, I learned he plans to ask your father for your hand."

"Who?"

"Gerald."

Esther shuddered. "I won't wed him. I don't like him. He's sly and greedy."

Trude laughed. "If your father says you will wed him, you'll have no choice. This I will tell you. Gerald has no taste for maidenly protests. He's a lusty lover who enjoys having a woman fight and scream."

Esther shivered. "You can have him with my blessing."

Trude laughed. "I will have him and when he leaves me, Berwin will be mine. Why did you come back?"

"Count Rudolf sent Father. The revenues Gerald sends are not what they should be."

"Rebels," Trude said. "They steal the tribute." Her smile became sly. "Ask Berwin what he knows of them. It's said in the village he knows who they are and that he's one of them."

Esther released Trude. She wouldn't believe Berwin would do something to bring shame to his father and she knew her father was fair to those who served him honestly.

She went inside and hurried to her room. On her bed was a dress, a plain one, not of the expensive fabrics she usually wore. When she went to the festival, she would look like the other girls. She held up the dress and the undergarment. The wide sleeves would allow the tighter ones of the underdress to show. There was also a cloak with no fur trimming.

That night, she decided to eat dinner with her sister.

Adelle clapped her hands when Esther came into the room. The young girl ran to her. "I'm so glad you came."

"How did you spend your day?" Esther asked.

"Mathilde taught me my letters. Why must we learn to write the words we hear only in church? Why don't we write the ones we use every day?"

Esther laughed. "I'll admit it makes no sense, but Papa says it's so we can deal with people who live in other lands."

Adelle sighed. "Even when we don't know them."

Esther nodded. "We must learn for Papa has no sons." She sighed. Not only had Adelle's mother died, but so had the son her father had desired.

Adelle patted her hand. "Don't be sad."

"I won't. Tomorrow I'm going to the Harvest Festival in town. What would you like me to bring you?"

"Apple cake. A big piece."

"I will."

Mathilde arrived. "Adelle, wash your hands. Dinner is on the way." She turned to Esther. "I'm glad you dine with us. Adelle misses your company."

"And I miss hers. Now the house is in order, I'll have more time."

Esther joined the pair at a small table. She felt on edge. The things Trude had said troubled her. Tomorrow, the day would be spent with Berwin. Esther put a slice of meat on her plate and cut it with her knife. Trouble brewed and she was sure whatever happened now, the seeds had been sown in the past. She forced a smile. There was no reason to upset Adelle and Mathilde with these thoughts of doom.

Tomorrow, she thought.

* * * *

When Berwin arrived to escort her to town, Esther's troubled thoughts vanished. He helped her mount. The feel of his hands brought shivers of delight. When he smiled, her emotions avalanched and made her feel weak. They rode to town and left their mounts tied at the edge of town near a stand of trees. Hand in hand like two children, they walked to the commons.

She didn't feel like a child. What about Berwin? Was he to remain no more than a friend?

Music filled the air. Esther saw dancers and envied their

grace. The milling crowds laughed and talked. Esther spotted the black-robed priest and her father. A chill washed over her. Was he speaking about a betrothal?

As she and Berwin mingled and looked at the things the merchants had to sell, Esther saw among the crowd men with sullen faces. Why? This was a time for celebration.

Berwin handed her a mug of cider and a piece of apple cake. The cider was cold and sweet, the cake warm and rich with spices. "I must take a piece of cake to Adelle," Esther said.

"We'll buy some before I take you home." He glanced around and frowned. Esther's gaze followed his. Was that man signaling?

Gerald sauntered over. "Berwin. Esther. Your father said you would be here. I've missed seeing you at dinner these past few days."

"Adelle needs my company since there are no children as there were when I was young." She turned to leave, but Berwin had vanished. Why had he left her with this man?

Gerald pulled her toward the circle of dancers. "Your escort has abandoned you. Come into the circle with me."

She shook her head. "I'd rather not."

He pulled her closer. "Then we can leave. I can show you many more things than that peasant."

"I'll wait for Berwin."

"You're mine." He tightened his hold on her and brought his mouth toward hers.

She twisted away from his questing lips. "Let me be." Someone jerked on her hair. She cried out.

"I warned you," Trude said. "You won't have what's mine."

Gerald grabbed Trude. "You dare harm your betters."

Esther backed away. Trude struggled with Gerald. Esther fled. When she looked back, she saw the pair locked together and stumbling toward the shadows.

"What have we here?"

A man's slurred voice startled Esther. When he grabbed her, she jerked free. "Let me alone."

"A kiss or two won't hurt." A second man appeared beside the first. "I want her."

Esther froze. She was trapped. Tears threatened. "Go away."

"Be off."

For a moment, she didn't recognize the voice. Tears trickled down her cheeks. She looked around and saw Berwin. The men shambled away.

Berwin drew her into the shadows of the trees not far from where they'd left the horses. "What happened?"

She wiped her tears on her sleeve. "Gerald tried to kiss me. I fought. Trude came and pulled my hair. Then she and Gerald fought. I ran and those men found me."

He tightened the embrace. "I shouldn't have left you."

She rose on her toes and slid her arms around his neck. Her lips brushed his. She'd only intended to thank him, but he held her flush against his body. His mouth slanted over hers. His tongue danced over her lips.

This was meant to be, she thought. As it's been time and time again, to love him is right.

She opened her mouth. His tongue darted inside to touch hers. Delicious sensations arose. Her fingers threaded through his hair to stroke his nape. Her body caught the rhythm of the motion of his tongue and she danced against him. She felt light and happy. Her emotions cascaded like water plunging over rocks during a spring thaw.

* * * *

Berwin knew he should pull back, but having her in his arms brought back his childhood dreams of being with her forever. He wanted her as an adult. He wanted to kiss her until her desire matched his.

He couldn't. Esther was too far above for him to touch. She was the daughter of the man who oversaw these lands, a wealthy lord. Esther was his heiress and a child of those he'd decided were invaders. Reluctantly, he pulled away.

She reached for him. Moonlight filtered through the leafy canopy. He saw desire, yearning and need in her gray eyes. He was sorry he'd stirred a fire that had to die.

"I'll take you home," he said.

"What if I don't want to go? I would stay with you."

"You can't." He clasped her hand.

She sighed and he caught the echo of a sob. "Apple cake for Adelle. I promised."

He led her to their horses and lifted her onto the saddle. "Wait here. I'll fetch the cake."

"Berwin, why are you doing this? Why are you pushing

me away?"

"I must."

As he hurried to the square, he felt as if two armies warred in his head and his heart. He wanted Esther as a man wants a woman. She could never be his for more than one reason, but the one that put miles between them was that he stood with the men who wanted to end the power of the foreign rulers.

When he returned to Esther, he handed her the cloth wrapped cake. Without speaking, they rode to the castle. He didn't know what to say or how to tell her the kiss had been a mistake.

Once they crossed the moat, he dismounted and lifted her down. She looked into his eyes. "I love you. I always have. This isn't the first time we have met and fallen in love."

He nodded. "And each time, we make the same mistakes and lose each other again."

"Maybe this time we can do the right thing." She feathered her fingers over his face. "If only we knew what to do and what to avoid."

He swallowed. The right thing would be to walk away and he wasn't sure he could. He pulled her into the shadows and kissed her. "Good night," he said. Goodbye, he thought.

He turned on his heel and mounted. Tonight there was a meeting and he was late. The shadow leader would be there. Berwin wanted to meet the man who provided money and planned the attacks on those who collected the taxes.

He left the horse at his father's house and set a rapid pace along the trail to the abandoned shepherd's hut where the men were to meet.

When he entered the clearing, several men left the hut. Trude's brother hailed him. "You're late. He's gone." The young man's smile was sly. "Shame you always seem to miss him. One would think the two of you were avoiding each other."

"I had something my father made me do. What was decided?" Berwin frowned. What did Trude's brother mean? Was the shadow leader avoiding him? He thought of all the times he'd missed the man. Did the leader really come from another canton?

"He'll let us know. Shouldn't be more than a few days of

waiting. He said this would be an important strike and we'll be well-paid."

"Paid? I don't do this for money," Berwin said.

* * * *

Esther spent days dreaming of Berwin and the kiss that had left her aching. Though several times his father had come to speak to hers, Berwin hadn't come along. His father said he was preparing his hut for the winter when he cut wood for the village and hunted fur-bearing animals.

One evening, her father came to the door of her room. He looked old and sad. "Papa, are you ill?" she asked.

He shook his head. "I must talk to you. I've had an offer of marriage for you."

She got to her feet. "Does the offer displease you?"

He nodded. "I won't keep you from a marriage you want. He assured me he has your favor. I just never considered Gerald as a man I'd gladly see you wed."

"Gerald!" Esther's hand flew to her mouth. "No, Papa, I never said I wanted to marry him. I don't like him. He's sly and greedy."

He caught her hand. "I'll deny his suit. I married your mother by arrangement. She didn't love me. Her father and mine were pleased. I don't want you to be unhappy."

"Papa, thank you." She wanted to tell him of her feelings for Berwin, but she didn't know what he felt for her.

Her father reached held out a packet. "A gift. To keep you safe."

She unwrapped the cloth and found a silver cross on a chain. Gems adorned the cross. A diamond, a ruby, an emerald, a sapphire and a topaz. "Papa, it's lovely." She hung the cross around her neck.

"Gerald and I leave in the morning. Once I've collected the rents and taxes, we'll leave for home. My men will stay here to keep you and your sister safe."

"Be careful. I have heard tales of attacks by rebels."

* * * *

For days, Berwin waited for someone to summon him to a meeting. Sir George and Gerald had ridden off to make rounds of the farms and villages to collect the count's due. Berwin believed they had no right to take men's harvest or hard-earned coins. Though this was custom, the herdsmen and farmers received little for their offerings.

He stopped in the tavern in hopes of seeing others of the band of men who were determined to drive the overlords away. He frowned. None of the men were there. Had they been called and how had he missed the summons?

Trude carried a mug and sat beside him. "Finally come out of your cave."

He frowned. "Is your brother around?"

She shook her head. "He's with the men. The day has come."

"What?" Berwin got to his feet. "Why didn't they send for me?"

Her smile mocked. "Maybe they don't trust someone who has his eye on the overlord's daughter. Or maybe their leader didn't want you along."

He pushed his chair back and grasped her arm. "What do you know?"

She sucked on her lower lip. "That the day has come and a new star will rise in the sky. You won't have her. Gerald will."

Berwin released her arm and strode to the door. He donned his cloak and grabbed his bow and quiver. He had to find the others. He believed they intended to attack Esther's father.

As he raced toward the meeting place, he realized why he'd never met the shadow leader. Even in disguise, he would recognize Gerald. The man had no plans to drive away the tax collectors. His plans were meant to elevate himself.

* * * *

Esther stood at the narrow window of her room and opened the shutters. Her father should return today and in a few days they would depart. Should she tell him of her love for Berwin? Though her father wanted her happiness, Berwin wasn't a noble. Would her father drag her home and find another man for her to wed? Some noble whose wealth matched hers.

She spotted the troop of men in the distance. As they drew closer, she knew something was wrong. There were no wagons filled with harvest tribute. She saw what looked like bodies slung over the horses. Holding back a cry of fear, she ran to the stairs. She hadn't seen her father in the lead where he always rode.

Mathilde came from the room she shared with Adelle. "Esther, what's wrong?"

"The men are returning and I don't see Papa."

The older woman gasped. "I'll see to Adelle and then come down."

By the time Esther reached the hall, the doors opened and Gerald strode in. "I bring ill news. We were set upon by rebels and your father is dead."

Esther balled her fist against her mouth. What could she do? "Have the body brought to his room and send for the priest and a coffin. Mathilde and I will prepare him. We'll leave in the morning to take him home."

Gerald grasped her shoulders. "As he was dying, he begged me to see to you. When the priest comes, he will perform our betrothal."

Esther tore free. "He would never have done that. He said you asked for my hand. I told him no and he was pleased." She ran to the stairs where Mathilde stood.

"You will marry me," he said. "I will speak to the priest. You need my protection."

Panic roiled her grief-filled emotions. She moved into Mathilde's arms. "What can I do?"

"We'll see to the body. You must move in with Adelle and me until we leave for home."

Esther nodded. That was one solution. If she could get word to Berwin or his father, maybe they could help. Why had the rebels killed her father? He would have listened to them.

She followed Mathilde to her father's room. They placed a clean sheet on his bed. When the men carried him in, Esther burst into tears. She cried until her chest and stomach ached.

"Look at this," Mathilde said.

Esther wiped her eyes and went to the bed. "What do you see?"

"He was back-stabbed. The arrow in his leg wouldn't have killed him."

Esther held an anguished scream inside. "Gerald did this. What can we do?"

"Don't say a word to him or the priest," Mathilde said. "When we return home, I will tell Count Rudolf. Even if you're forced into a betrothal as long as he doesn't bed you, the count can say no to the marriage."

Esther nodded. Not speaking would be hard. How could she swear before God that she would wed Gerald? She ran her fingers over the cross her father had given her.

She and Mathilde dressed her father. Esther kissed his cheek and went to her sister. She held Adelle and wept with the child.

When Adelle fell asleep, Esther put her in the bed. She turned to Mathilde. "I'll fetch my things and then sit vigil with Papa."

"I can get your clothes."

"You're tired. I won't be long."

Esther hurried to her room. When she stepped inside, arms imprisoned her and a hand covered her mouth. She tried to free herself.

"I'll make sure a marriage is necessary." Gerald turned her to face him. He ground his mouth against hers.

Esther tried to loosen his hold. She opened her mouth to scream. He thrust his tongue inside. She bit. He yelled. She raised her knee and shoved against him with all the force she could muster. He doubled over. She grabbed the heavy pitcher from the wash stand and smashed it against his head. He sprawled on the floor.

She grabbed a cloak and ran to her sister's room. "Mathilde, Gerald attacked me. I hit him with a pitcher. Take Adelle to Berwin's father. He'll protect you." She sped down the stairs and through the doors. As she raced across the moat, she heard Gerald shout.

"Stop her."

Instead of taking the road to town, she raced into the forest. She had to escape. She would rather die than wed Gerald.

Branches tore at the cloak. They scratched her face. Even when she no longer heard Gerald, she continued to plunge heedlessly. She tripped on some rocks and scrambled to her feet. On a rock strewn slope, she stumbled and rolled into the icy waters of an alpine stream. She reached the far shore and crawled onto the bank. There, she collapsed.

"Esther!"

The call spurred her to move. She crawled several yards and fell again. Fear and exhaustion tumbled over her grief. She couldn't move. Chill from her immersion in the stream seeped through her body.

* * * *

When Gerald turned back to the castle, Berwin continued to follow Esther. He'd known her father's death would devastate her, but why had she run? He'd been on his way to offer her comfort when she'd bolted into the forest. He'd noticed the blood on Gerald's head and wondered if the man had been wounded in the fight.

Berwin had nearly reached Esther when she tumbled into the stream. He leaped to the other bank. "Esther, it's Berwin."

Her body shook. Her eyes were wide with panic and he wasn't sure she knew who he was. The icy water and the chill wind made him realize he needed to get her to shelter. She could die.

He lifted and carried her to the shepherd's hut. Town was too far and so was his hut. Until he knew why she'd run, he couldn't take her to the castle. The shepherd's hut would provide shelter and he could build a fire. Surely, none of the men would come this way for several days. Berwin was so convinced the death of Esther's father had been Gerald's goal, especially after he'd overheard the men speaking of Gerald's actions during the attack.

When Berwin pushed the door of the hut open, he put Esther on one of the chairs. Though the hut was cold, the absence of the wind helped. He had to start a fire and find a way to warm her icy skin.

He stripped Esther's soggy clothes and draped them on the table. When he carried her to the cot, he stroked her silky skin. He sucked in a breath as desire raged. Quickly, he covered her with several thin blankets. He pushed away from the cot. Once a fire burned in the fireplace, he searched the shelves for food and found nothing. He wished he could have carried her to his place higher in the hills. His hut was well-provisioned for the coming winter, but there had been no time to carry here there.

He returned to the cot. Her body shook so hard the cot moved. He brushed his fingers along her shoulder. So cold. Too cold. With shaking hands, he stripped off his clothes and hung them to dry. He would give her his heat.

He slid beneath the covers and wrapped his arms around her. She whimpered. As he stroked her, his hand touched her breast. A surge of fire swept through him. His organ swelled and throbbed. When her buttocks pressed against him, he sucked on a breath. She turned and plastered her body against his. Her puckered nipples pressed his chest. Just one kiss, he thought. One taste.

When his lips touched hers, he felt like he was drowning. She opened her mouth to his probing tongue. She inched closer. His penis probed the junction of her thighs. She eased her leg over his hip and sighed. Berwin tried to draw back, but she clutched his shoulders. Her eyes fluttered open.

"I knew you would save me." Her breath flowed over his face. "He killed Papa. Not the rebels. He says the priest will betroth us. He tried to...." She shuddered.

Berwin rolled to his back. She clung to him and lay atop his body. "Esther, be still. You fell in the stream. I had to find a way to warm you."

"You have. Kiss me again." Her mouth touched his.

He was lost in the flames that threatened to consume him. He had to stop, to move away before he did what he'd dreamed of each night since her return. He tried to slide from beneath her. "Esther, we can't."

"Why not?"

"If I don't move, we'll go beyond what's proper."

She wiggled her hips. Her moisture laved his shaft. "It's like fire spreading through the forest. This feels good and right."

He groaned and rolled so she was beneath him. "You're warm now."

She clung to him. "Just once, please. Let me know what it's like to be with the one I love. When I return home, I'll be given in marriage to someone chosen for me."

He tried to move away. "I mustn't."

She pulled his head to her breast. "They ache so for your touch."

His lips brushed her nipple and he lost the desire to make further protests. He rolled his tongue over the tip, then sucked. She stroked his back and cried out. He slid a hand between her legs and felt her dew. As he suckled her breast, he stroked along her cleft. Her body writhed. Her hips pumped. When he thrust inside, she cried, not in pain, but with welcome.

He stroked, he thrust, he plunged. And he knew they were meant to be together. Her cries built to a crescendo. Her body tensed and her inner muscles tightened around his shaft. He spewed his seed until there was no more.

He found her mouth and drank deep of her sweetness. He rolled to his side and gathered her close.

When he woke, bands of light filtered through cracks in the shutters. Esther stirred and opened her eyes. He brushed her lips with his. "I'll take you to town."

"I can't go there. He'll be waiting. He'll drag me to the priest. Let me stay here with you."

"Not here. Others know of this place. If they see you, they'll tell Gerald."

She sat up. Her eyes filled with tears. "If you take me to town, I'll flee again. I won't let him touch me."

He took her hand in his. "I know a place where you'll be safe until I can take you to the count. We must dress and be on our way before anyone comes."

She kissed his cheek. "Adelle and Mathilde will worry about me. Don't tell them I'm alive. I told them to go to your father. He'll keep them safe."

"And I'll protect you."

* * * *

They stayed in Berwin's hut until the leaves had fallen and a dusting of snow covered the ground. Love filled their nights and laughter their days.

"I need to go to town," Berwin said. "Will you be all right alone?"

Esther nodded. "I'll miss you." She stood in the doorway and watched him leave. After she closed the door, she hugged herself. When he returned, she had to tell him that she carried his child. In the morning, she'd been able to hide her nausea until he left to check his traps or cut wood to take to the village to sell.

Should she tell him about the odd dreams she'd had the past few nights? She'd heard voices. They had argued and cursed each other. The woman was with child and the man had denied the babe. What if Berwin did that?

As dusk, he returned. He hung his cloak on a hook inside the door. "I have much to tell you."

Esther put a bowl of stew on the table and filled two mugs with tea. "Are Adelle and Mathilde all right?"

"They accompanied your father's body home. They grieve for you. Soldiers came for Gerald two days ago. He fled into the forest."

"Will he find us?"

"I pray not." He caught her hands. "Let me take you home before the passes are closed."

She shook her head. "I love you. I want to stay with you. I've dreamed and in these dreams we cursed each other because of betrayals. We have a chance to end what happened ages ago."

He settled her onto his lap. "I feel we've been together before, but you should be with your family. You're beyond my reach like one of the stars we see in the night sky."

She turned to him. "I must stay. I am with child."

He kissed the corner of her mouth. "Then we must go to town and see the priest to say our vows."

"Yes."

"Then we'll go in the morning."

At daybreak, snow swirled through the air. Berwin looked at the sky. "I fear the snow will be heavy by nightfall." He put some food in his pack for them to eat when they stopped to rest.

Esther donned her cloak and fought to control her stomach. She followed Berwin from the hut. Snow fell heavier and she couldn't see far ahead. They reached the ridge above the town. How different the houses and the lake looked from when she'd arrived.

"We must take care," Berwin said. "The path is steep and the snow will make the way slippery." He caught her hand.

"Esther!"

She froze. The voice belonged to Gerald.

Berwin tugged on her hand. "Come. If we reach town, we'll be safe. He's a hunted man."

Fear welled and spewed over. Esther pulled her hand from Berwin's. Every time they met, happiness ended in betrayal and tragedy. She ran. She heard someone behind her. A figure loomed through the wind-driven snow. She changed direction. Someone grabbed and she fell. Her body hurtled down the slope.

"Esther!"

This time, she heard Berwin. "Here." Arms enfolded her. She continued to slide. She heard a rumble that grew louder. She and her captor rolled.

"Avalanche! Esther, no!"

* * * *

Astrid opened her eyes. Duncan cradled her against his chest. Just like the man in the dream. "They're dead. They found love and were destroyed by greed. When will it stop?"

"Who?"

She took a deep breath. "The ones who have sought each other time and again."

He frowned. "I don't understand."

"During their first meeting, they cursed each other. They had enemies, a man and a woman who wanted to possess and destroy." She shuddered. "One of them was me. An avalanche killed her. She was pregnant and shouldn't have been." Astrid sat up and wrapped her arms around her knees.

"Do you remember more?" Duncan asked.

She met his gaze. "Clive ... Lorna ... Dad...."

"What?"

"I think they were there in different guises." She yawned. "I need to sleep. Every time I go into these dreams, I'm more exhausted when I wake."

"No more trips then," he said.

She shook her head. "I don't think I should stop. I believe it's important to see this to the end. Madelaine fled when she could have ended the curses."

He pulled her against his chest. "What if you get lost in one of these dreams?"

What if she did? She didn't think she would be, but she was too tired to continue the discussion.

When Astrid woke, she stretched and scurried to the bathroom. After splashing cold water on her face, she went to Duncan's study. He'd spread the jewelry including the gold bracelet on his desk. "What are you doing?" she asked.

He looked up. "Putting them in order of age. The Egyptian pieces are the oldest."

"And that's where it began," Astrid said. "Dad told me he found a reference to a leader of the armies named Mermeshu. He was the lover in the first dream. I also remember the double curse."

"Which was?"

"He coveted power and wealth. She believed duty and honor were stronger. Her curse was he had to learn love was more powerful than power and wealth. He told her love was more important."

"Heady stuff. Does he equate duty and honor to power and wealth?"

"I'm not sure. I can't remember enough."

He gazed into her eyes. "I wish you'd leave this alone."

She put her hands on his shoulders. Did he care that much for her or was he trying to control her life? She wouldn't ask. "I think I've gone too far to stop. I need to reach the end."

"Why?"

The ring of the phone interrupted the conversation. He reached for the receiver. Astrid walked to the computer and logged on. There were two more items and she intended to find them.

* * * *

"Garrett here."

"Rick reporting on your request for information. Figured you'd want a briefing, especially when you ruined my weekend."

"Sorry about that." Duncan sat on the arm of the couch. "So what did you learn?"

"I'm faxing you a full report. Your Lorna Stinit isn't a nice woman and she's not who she says she is. She's a con artist and usually works with a partner. Though the Stinits were once residents of Rockleigh, she's not related to them. They left after they lost their fortune. Had one daughter named Bonnie. She set out to marry your ancestor but when her plans fell through, the family left town. She went with them. They settled out West. She married a rich miner and had one child, a son. There are no more Stinits who once lived in Rockleigh."

Duncan frowned. "Then who is she and where did she come from?"

"Hopefully have that for you tomorrow."

"What about Clive?"

"Nada yet. Wasn't he your college roommate? Can't find a thing on him before that."

"Odd."

"Sure is. I'll start tracing him from college and see what I can find."

"Good enough." Duncan frowned. What was going on? Had Clive been planning whatever since college or before?

"Come here a minute," Astrid said.

Duncan joined her at the computer. He stared at the images on the screen. "What are they?"

"Netsuke. Carved from ivory. In Japan, they didn't use jewelry. Some kind of laws or custom. The netsuke was called a purse toggle. They hung things from their obis, some sort of boxes they kept things in. The boxes had strings and were held together by these that were tucked beneath the sashes. These are small, seldom larger than two inches."

He frowned. "I remember seeing something like that when I was a child. Even played with one."

"Where?"

"I can't remember. Maybe it will come to me." He rose. "Are you sure you want to continue this search?"

"Yes."

The fax began to spew paper. Duncan turned to collect the pages. "We'll go somewhere for dinner and read what's here."

"And that is?"

"Information on Lorna. She's a bit of a mystery woman."

Astrid logged off. "How so?"

"Evidently, the Stinit family died out when their only child, a daughter married." He gathered the papers and put them in a folder. "Ready."

"Let me get my bag. Tell me where you want to eat and I'll meet you. I need to go to the apartment and change."

He arched a brow. "Your staying there alone is another thing we'll discuss."

JAPAN

Astrid put her overnight case in the car. So Duncan didn't want her staying at the apartment alone. How nice, but she wasn't going to be bullied into remaining here. Not with the way she felt and the way he didn't. If it weren't for her reactions to the artifacts and the connection between them, she could walk away. Every moment spent with him sunk her deeper. She feared he would become essential to her existence. He wasn't one for long term. Unfortunately, she was.

Duncan caught her hand and pulled her into an embrace. "Emilio's in fifteen minutes."

She couldn't think when he held her. "Half hour. I need to shower and change."

"And pack for an extended visit."

Her hands fisted. "You're being ridiculous. With the new locks, the apartment is safe." Myriad emotions flashed in his eyes and none was the one she wanted to see.

"You're safer with me."

She tapped her foot against the asphalt. Safer? Hardly. She was completely in danger of losing her heart and having to fuse the pieces when he walked away. "Forget dinner. I'll eat at the apartment."

He threw up his hands. "Fine. If there's trouble, I have I-told-you-so rights."

"Granted." She slid behind the wheel.

He waved the folder. "Come to dinner. I'm sure you want to know what Rick discovered."

She nodded. "Dinner. Then information and no badgering. Just because we had sex doesn't mean you can run my life." The stubborn set of his jaw irritated her.

"We made love," he said.

"Same thing." She closed the door and drove to the apartment where she showered and changed. Before leaving, she checked the answering machine for messages. Then she walked to Emilio's.

Duncan waited at the table where they'd eaten the first time. Salads and rolls were waiting. He shoved the papers he'd been reading in the folder. "Your things in the car?"

"I walked and no things." She opened the menu and moments later, ordered. "The folder." Duncan handed it to her and she quickly skimmed the pages. "Lorna's quite a piece of work. Wonder how and when she and Clive met."

"Rick will find out." He waited for the waiter to serve their entrees. "So what do you think she wants?"

Astrid tapped the folder. "Not enough information here to form a theory."

"I know." He grinned. "So let's talk about other things."

"Like what?"

"Where you're sleeping tonight."

She put her fork down. "Already decided. I'll be at the apartment and you'll be at your house."

"Astrid."

She looked up. "We've discussed this before, but let me repeat. It's not your place to tell me where I'll sleep." She slid along the bench away from him. "I don't need a man running my life."

"What if Clive comes to your door?"

"I'll tell him to get lost."

"But--"

"Enough." She rose. "Look, tomorrow I'll be in the shop finishing the inventory. If he wants, he can ambush me there. That doesn't mean I won't go."

"Will you be alone?"

"Maybe. I can handle Clive."

He frowned. "Just be careful."

"Always. I'll be working in the vault. Maybe I'll find the netsuke and the Incan necklace."

He caught her hand. "If you do, call me. I don't want you tripping in the past when you're alone."

Astrid sucked in a breath. What was with him and these orders? Don't stay at the apartment. Don't touch the artifacts. One more order and she would smack him. He was her lover, not her keeper. "I'd better go before I say something I'll regret."

"I'll walk you home."

She pulled free and strode to the door. She wouldn't scream, not in public. She pushed the door open and headed down the street. Her sandals slapped the pavement. Duncan caught up and matched her pace.

At the foot of the steps leading to the deck, he put his arms around her. "Why are you so angry?"

She clenched her teeth. "Your dictatorial manner. You're acting like a Victorian husband."

"Hold on. I'm concerned about you. When you slip into one of those fugue states, you're vulnerable. What if someone attacked you? How could you protect yourself?"

She shrugged. "I'm careful about where I am."

"What about the first time?"

"Took me by surprise." She glared. "I won't take a trip without letting you or someone I trust know. Is that enough?"

"No. We're a couple until the fire dies. Go pack a bag."

"Absolutely not." She stormed up the steps.

Sarah's door opened. "Astrid, are you all right?"

"I'm fine. He's not." Astrid smiled. "Didn't I promise to tell you about the new key? Now's a good time." She opened the apartment door. "Duncan was just leaving."

"I'm not finished."

"I am. Thank you for dinner and the interesting entertainment. If you find the netsuke, give me a call. Otherwise, don't bother." She steered Sarah inside and closed the door.

"What was that about?" Sarah asked.

"Men are dumb. Once they sink their teeth into a position, they won't let go." Astrid opened the refrigerator and took out the iced tea container.

"He cares."

"Not enough and not in the right way."

Sarah carried a glass of tea to the front window. "And if you're wrong? Men find speaking about their emotions hard. I've loved your dad for years. He didn't speak so I kept silent. We settled for friendship when we could have had more."

Astrid joined the older woman. "I told Duncan how I felt and he said nothing."

"Give him time."

"Why don't you tell Dad how you feel?"

"I just might."

"Good." Astrid sipped the tea. "How were sales today?"

"We sold a lot of what Clive calls junk. I think many of the cloisonné pieces are lovely and some of the old costume jewelry isn't bad. Clive only cares about jewelry that has precious or semi-precious gems."

"I've noticed they've removed most of the inexpensive pieces from the showroom."

"Clive has pushed your dad into seeking a different clientele. At least Antiquities looks less like a flea market booth."

Astrid nodded. "I'm not particularly business-minded, but I think there should be a few inexpensive pieces on display."

"Agreed." Sarah put her glass down. "Tell me about the new key. Wasn't that why you dragged me in?"

Astrid related the tale of the searched apartment. "Had to be Clive."

"I think you're right. Will you be in the shop tomorrow? He asked me if I knew."

"I want to finish the inventory so I can get on with my life. Why don't you join me?"

"Sounds like a good idea. What time?"

"Say ten or so. I've my run, then breakfast and some chores here."

"I'll be there." Sarah put her glass on the counter. "See you in the morning."

* * * *

Duncan strode up the street. He scowled. Had he really expected her to agree to come to the house? He hadn't believed, only hoped.

Thank you for dinner and the interesting entertainment.

Was that all the weekend had meant to her? Maybe he'd come off a bit strong, but his concern was valid and logical. He knew she didn't trust Clive and wouldn't let him into the apartment. What about tomorrow when she was alone in the shop? As she had said, Clive could ambush her there or during her morning run.

So what do you plan to do? Lock her up and only let her out when you can be with her?

He groaned. She would never agree unless he made the commitment he didn't plan to make for years. He could lose her. He wasn't sure how that made him feel. He cared more for her than any woman he'd been with. Did that mean she was the one?

He pushed those thoughts aside, entered the house and stopped in the kitchen for some beer and a bottle of iced tea to stock the mini-refrigerator in his study. Once he reached his lair, he opened the safe and took out the letters Astrid had brought with the jewelry.

After he read them, he knew why Madelaine and her cousin had fled. They'd been brave to leave with little money and no real skills, especially when Madelaine soon learned she was with child. She had survived long enough to give birth. Her cousin had made sure the baby was sent to his father.

He read the first letter again. So Chester, his great-great grandfather's cousin, had killed Madelaine's father. He had also left town. Had he followed the women or had he run to escape being caught?

Duncan finished a beer, took a shower and turned on the television. He gazed at the bed and wished Astrid was here.

We had sex. Call me when you find the netsuke.

Was that all there was? He rubbed his temples and stared at the television. He watched the end of a Yankee game and caught the news. All the while, thoughts of Astrid stirred. He had to make a decision about her. Did she really love him, or was she only caught up in the dreams?

He sat up. The netsuke. He recalled the small figure of a Japanese warrior. The beach house. The ivory carving had been among the toys he'd played with on rainy days. Was it there? His grandfather had packed the toys away when Duncan had become a teen. They would be in the storage rooms above the garage. He would call Astrid and she could help him search.

The next morning, he handled a few business matters and wrote several scenes for his new book. He reached for the phone to call Astrid. The fax hummed.

As the papers emerged, he scanned them. He shook his head. What was Clive up to? When they'd graduated, Clive had gone to work with a jeweler and had learned to appraise gems. He'd traveled to Europe and then returned. Several times, he'd come under investigation when pieces he'd appraised had been discovered to have paste instead of jewels. He'd never been arrested because there'd been no proof he'd been responsible for the substitutions.

Duncan frowned. Had Clive been playing that game at Antiquities? What would happen if someone who had bought a necklace or pin discovered the jewels were fakes? Lloyd would be held responsible. Duncan groaned. He had to tell Astrid about the latest development and they had to find a way to deal with Clive.

When the last page emerged, Duncan sat on the couch to read the entire report. What a narrow escape, he thought. Lorna and Clive were married. Duncan shuddered when he thought of the scandal that could have erupted if he'd succumbed to her blatant overtures. A second tidbit shocked him. So Clive was really a Garrett, a direct descendant of Chester.

He dialed Clive's apartment and left a message. When he tried the cell phone, he was shunted to voice mail. Would Clive respond to any of the calls?

* * * *

At a few minutes before nine, Astrid entered Antiquities. She sealed and marked the boxes remaining from the street fair and carried them to the office. After opening the vault, she groaned. What had Clive been searching for? She would have to restore order and check the inventory list she'd begun.

She printed the running list of articles purchased and sold since Christmas. She put it with the inventory list.

At a few minutes after ten, Clive arrived. Astrid frowned. Where was Sarah? Being alone with Clive wasn't Astrid's choice. He stood in the vault doorway. "Sorry about the mess."

She brushed past him. "You destroyed hours of work."

He shrugged. "There were things I needed."

"Such as."

"Doesn't matter. I'd stay to help but it's my day off and I have a dozen things to do."

"Sarah said she'd give me a hand. She should be here soon."

"Can you cut me a check? Lloyd should have added my name to the account."

"When you see him, you can ask. Why do you need a check?"

"Some purchases I made at the fair and for some gems to repair a few pieces. Five grand should do it."

Astrid choked back a gasp. "Give me the sales slips."

He scowled. "Can't you take my word? The slips are at home. Your father never questioned me."

"I'm not my father."

"How well I know." His gaze roamed her body.

She tensed. Was he about to make another unwelcome pass? "I'll see Dad tomorrow and ask him how to handle money matters."

"Fine." He strode to the door.

Astrid returned to the vault and finished straightening the shelves. There were eight pieces missing. Had they been put on display or sold? She heard the bell above the door and closed the vault.

Sarah waved. "Sorry, I got tied up on the phone."

"I've finished the vault." Astrid left the office. "Let's work out here. You call off the numbers and I'll check them off."

When they finished, Astrid frowned. The total of missing items had reached a dozen. "Are you going to see Dad today?"

"I'm leaving as soon as we finish. I'll cheer him on with his exercises and have dinner with him."

Astrid retreated to the office. "Could you take these lists with you? There are eight pieces missing from the vault and four from the showroom. Some of them could have been sold. Dad and Clive are bad about paperwork."

Sarah nodded. "You're absolutely correct about that. Sunday, I had to nag Clive several times to log the items he sold."

"Ask Dad about these items."

"Why?"

"A hunch. I've been thinking about having the locks down here changed. I'll explain why to him tomorrow. Haven't told him about the apartment being searched."

"Want me to make the suggestion?" Sarah asked.

Astrid shook her head. "I will." The phone rang. Astrid took the call. "Antiquities."

"Astrid."

She gripped the receiver. Was Duncan going to push her again? "What do you want?"

"I know where the netsuke is, but it's going to take a bit of searching."

"Where?"

"In the storage room above the garage. Would you like to help?"

"When?"

"Say three. I've some business to finish. I'll leave the gate open and meet you."

"I'll be there."

At precisely three, she drove down the long driveway and parked beside Duncan's car. He motioned her over and opened a door on the side of the garage. As she followed him upstairs, he flicked on the lights. Astrid looked at the stacks of boxes and the jumble of furniture and groaned. "We'll be hours. You could have a perpetual garage sale."

He laughed. "Another of my grandfather's traits. Never know when something will come in handy, and if you've thrown it away you'll have to buy another."

"How do you expect to find a small ivory figure in all this?"

"With luck, the boxes will be labeled." He pulled one from a stack and set it aside. After examining four, he lifted a fifth. "Beach house. Duncan's toys. This should be the one."

He carried the box to a table and slit the top. He and Astrid removed the contents. She gasped when she touched a cigar box. "Here, I think."

"Let me." Duncan took the box. "Don't want you collapsing here. No room to stretch out." He opened the box and sorted through the contents. "Here it is."

"Let me see."

"Come to the house."

She followed him down the stairs and across the drive to the house. When she reached the bedroom, she kicked off her shoes and lay on the bed. She hadn't planned to be in this room again. After she tripped in the past, would she be able to resist the temptation of finding comfort in his arms?

"Are you sure you want to do this?" he asked.

"Very." She held out her hand and he placed the small carving on her palm. She closed her fingers.

* * * *

The early days of summer heated the air, but Hoshi felt cold and alone. Her father was dead. He had been betrayed by the man who stood on the other side of the bier. Saburo, who had forsworn the ways of the samurai and sought power in the emperor's court. No one would accuse him but she knew.

Why hadn't her father broken the betrothal made just before her younger brother's birth? In those days, Saburo had been a warrior-in-training and a perfect match for the daughter of a samurai. That was no longer true.

She lowered her gaze and fought to keep from smiling. The step she was about to take would end that hated union. If her father's death had come a lunar later, she would have been wed. She glanced at Saburo. His smug expression and the lust in his dark eyes made her ill.

Hoshi fingered the netsuke warrior, once her father's and now hers in trust for her younger brother. Keyoshi stood tall and proud at her side. In four years, he would be of age and stand as the head of the family. She would choose the best warriors and scholars as his teachers. He would be a great leader.

She blinked tears from her eyes. This was no time to display weakness. Her grief would remain buried beneath the determination and anger she felt. Until her brother stood as the head of the house, she would put aside her woman's life and stand as samurai. A rare choice, but one permitted when the heir was too young.

With measured steps, she approached the bier. She lifted her father's sword and held it aloft. "Those who are born must die. Those who meet must part. Samurai, here stands your heir, Keyoshi, not yet of age. Thus I stand in his place until he is ready to hold this sword."

Gasps followed her words. Saburo glared and stepped toward her. He reached for the sword he'd thought to gain through treachery. Two of her father's guards blocked his path.

"My bow will bend with strength," Hoshi said. "My arrows will fly in straight paths into the hearts of our enemies. I will hold this sword until Keyoshi takes it from my hands. Today I wear women's clothes for the last time until my service ends. Now, my father, you can depart in peace. Your grave is prepared."

She signaled the men. Holding the sword point up, she walked to the grave. Keyoshi matched her pace. Once the body was lowered, they returned to the house.

Chika, nurse to Hoshi and Keyoshi wept. "This is the saddest day."

Hoshi nodded. "Dry your tears, foster mother. Send Ishi with food and tea."

Keyoshi touched her hand. "Will you really stand for Father? Saburo will not like that. He is very angry."

"What he wants does not matter. I will do my duty. Before your birth, I was the heir. Once we knew you thrived, I stepped aside as I will again."

"I will be as great a warrior as Father."

She nodded. "You will be greater for you will learn all the ways of leadership and the ways to find treachery so no one can betray you as they did Father. Let us eat and remember him."

"I have so much to learn."

"You will."

A commotion startled her. Saburo burst into the room. Two guards followed. "What foolishness are you about, girl?"

"Foolishness?" Hoshi rose. She wouldn't remain in an inferior position before him. "I do what my father trained me to do."

He snorted. "He was a fool. You are a woman and no warrior. You are my betrothed."

"No longer. Would you care to test my skills with the sword? As I recall, I defeated you twice. Will you make it thrice?"

"We were children and I knew not to harm a girl." His eyes narrowed. "This house is weak. I would have brought safety. The emperor would have cast his shade over the house and no one would dare touch anyone who serves him."

Hoshi sucked in a breath. "This is a house of mourning. I am the one to decide what course we will take. You have no status here. Return to the emperor. Leave us to our remembrances."

Saburo caught her hands. "You would have been my love. You would have shared my position in the court. Should matters change, I will not wed you, but take you as my concubine for I would have you in my bed, not in men's armor."

"Never. Leave and don't return. The guards will not admit

you." She waited until he was gone before sinking onto the mat. Tomorrow she would cut her hair and put her women's clothes away.

* * * *

Hoshi spent the next day organizing the household. She put Chika in charge of the servants with Ishi as her assistant. She spoke with the guards and named the oldest as the leader. She found padded armor and had it adjusted to her size. Once her brother was settled for the night, she went to the garden.

What would Keyoshi do if she died before he came of age? She must select strong men with ties to the house as his teachers and name them as guardians if she fell. Who had the knowledge, skills and honor? She considered a number of distant cousins and selected two. In the morning, she would send for them.

The scent of summer flowers sweetened the air. She knelt before the massive black stone set on a sea of sand. Silently, she pledged herself to the heart of the house. She thought of what she must do tonight. The hilt of her knife dug into her palms.

In this time of trouble, fathers turned against sons and brothers against brothers. The cloistered emperor sought to walk in the world. What did he know of warrior ways? Yet, his ambitions had set her on the path she had to take.

A rustling noise startled her. She gripped the knife and listened carefully. Had Saburo sent an assassin? Her aging nurse appeared. "What is it?" Hoshi asked.

"A man seeks the head of this family."

Who would dare intrude on a house in mourning? Surely word of her father's death had spread through the city. "Did he ask for me by name?"

"No. For your father. Should I send him away?"

Hoshi wanted to say yes. The hour was late for a caller and she feared some plot of Saburo's. Yet, as her brother's guardian, she had to face all challenges. "Send him in and have the guards remain nearby. Pray he doesn't come with a challenge. I'm not ready to face one."

"They must let you grieve in peace," Chika said.

Moments later, the elderly woman led a stranger into the garden. His richly embroidered silk robe spoke of wealth and ease. She frowned. Why had a courtier other than

Saburo been sent? Did this man stand with or against her former betrothed?

He strode toward her. Hoshi stared. He was tall, broad-shouldered and lean. His face surely brought sighs to every woman he encountered.

Their gazes meshed. She felt a jolt of recognition. Though she'd never seen him before, she knew him and her body responded to his presence with yearning. She tore her gaze away. How could she know he was the man she'd always wanted to find? While she maintained the honor of the house, there could be no man in her life. "Why have you come?"

"To speak to the head of the house. Where is he?"

"Here."

He frowned. "But you're a woman."

Hoshi drew a deep breath. "My father was buried yesterday. Until my young brother stands here, I head the family."

"Then I greet you and am sorry for intruding on your sorrow. I have been away from the city and didn't hear the news." He bowed low. "Yemon, servant of the emperor."

Hoshi gestured to Chika. "Have tea brought." She needed time to compose her thoughts. Why was she drawn to this man? She didn't understand her response to his presence. Did he bring danger to her and to the house?

* * * *

Yemon felt as though lightning had seared his flesh and jolted his heart. This Hoshi was the star to light his life. He'd sought her forever. Why had he bowed to his father's wishes and accepted the betrothal to Akako, a woman who didn't want him? She desired another, but her father had courted Yemon. Since that day his life had been miserable. Still, the coming union would unite wealth to power and benefit both families.

He sat on a low bench. A frown furrowed his brow. Why did Hoshi carry a knife? Did she fear an attack by an enemy of her house? Had she planned to take her own life? He couldn't allow her to do that. If she accepted what he'd come to offer, she would be safe.

Their glances met. In her gaze, he read an awareness akin to what he felt. First he would present the emperor's words, then he would offer her his heart.

The servant arrived with the tea makings. Hoshi performed the ceremony with all the grace of the most practiced geisha. She was all Akako wasn't.

He took the cup and sipped. His gaze traveled from her face over her body. He noticed slight changes that signaled her interest. Her cheeks colored. Her breasts seemed to swell beneath her robe. She sighed and shifted in a restless dance. If he touched her, would she burst into flames only he could quench?

When he finished the tea, she rose. "Why have you come? Tell me quickly for there is much I must do."

"The emperor wishes to offer your family his protection. In these days of rebellion, he must stand strong. Long has your house been among those who serve the throne. Will you give oath of fealty to him?"

She turned away. "We have served. We have kept our honor. Promises were made but those promises were not kept."

He nodded. "Of this the emperor is aware. Others made those promises and failed. This time they will be kept. I would like to be the one who brings your house to him."

Hoshi frowned. Was he competing with Saburo and were several factions vying for favor? Had her father's death made the family appear weak? "This is not a decision I can make lightly. I will consider the request."

"I can ask no more of you for the emperor." Yemon rose and went to her. "There is another question I would ask." He placed his hands on her shoulders. He craved her as his body needed air, drink and food. She stiffened. As he stroked her neck, the muscles relaxed. He pressed his lips to her ear. "I desire you. You are the star to light my night." He caught her lobe between his teeth.

She shivered. "I can belong to no man. I have my duty."

"As I have mine. Do you believe duty is stronger than love? We have walked this road many times and have turned our backs on love. Duty, power and wealth always win."

She faced him. "What you ask is impossible. You must go."

"I can't leave you." He pulled her into an embrace. He brushed his mouth lightly across hers. He pressed her against his rigid erection. "I'll go, but I'll return every night until your body burns and you join me in the flames."

She grasped his shoulders. "I cannot. I stand as my brother's guardian. I have a duty to my family."

He kissed the corners of her mouth. "Can you say you have no desire for me? Can you say you didn't know me the moment our eyes met?"

She looked into his eyes. "You know I can't. Please leave. I must lay stones so I can cross the boiling lake of temptation."

He stepped away. "I'll go, but remember this. Our fates are twined as tightly as the strings of a bow." He strode from the garden.

* * * *

Hoshi sank to her knees and pressed her forehead against the cold stone of the bench. Why had he entered her life now when she must put aside all thoughts of love? She lifted the knife and began to cut her hair to the proper length for a warrior. A tear, then a flood flowed over her cheeks.

Tears were wrong. A samurai had no time for weeping. She sliced the last piece and gathered the long strands into a ball. She buried the hair beneath the cherry tree and wiped her eyes.

When she reached her sleeping room, she lifted her father's sword and held it blade high. She gazed at her moon-lit reflection in the polished metal mirror. "Ho, warrior."

* * * *

Yemon left Hoshi's house. His emotions churned. He had no desire to spend time with his betrothed, yet her father had summoned Yemon to a meeting. The man expected to hear a report of success. The rivalry among the senior courtiers was strong. The one who succeeded in persuading one of the warrior houses to swear to the emperor would gain wealth and power. Akako's father craved power. Yemon's wanted wealth.

As he entered the front gate, he heard laughter from the garden. Yemon recognized Akako's voice. When a man spoke, Yemon frowned. Didn't his future father-in-law have a lighter voice? Yemon left the path to the entrance to the house and walked to the garden.

Lanterns on the trees dappled the area with pools of light.

When Yemon neared the pond where carp were kept, a figure in dark robes hurried away.

Akako wheeled. A thin smile erased her scowl. "Yemon, I didn't expect you."

"I had a message from your father to attend him here tonight."

"How odd. He isn't here. He was called away." She sidled toward him.

He caught the odor of her arousal and stepped back. He wouldn't finish what another man had begun. Who had been here? If he could catch her with another man, no one would blame him when the betrothal ended.

"Where's your maid?" he asked.

"With her friends." She licked her lips. "I've no need of her when you're here."

He stepped back. "It's not proper for us to be alone. Tell your father I was here."

She appraised him like a housewife at the fishmonger's stall. "Don't you get tired of being proper?" She ran her fingers over his chest. "Let me give you a taste of what will soon be yours."

Yemon turned and strode away. His back tensed. He tried to assure himself the prickles he felt didn't foretell a dagger in the back.

"How dare you walk away from me," she cried. "You reject me when I need you. You will be sorry."

He already was. He paused outside the gate. Where should he go now? He had no desire to return home and face his father's questions. With brisk steps, he headed to the section of the city where tea houses abounded. He was certain to find a few friends.

As he entered the lane to his favorite house, he heard the raised voices of two men. One voice belonged to Saburo. Yemon ducked into the shadows. Since Saburo's arrival at court, he had acted as though Yemon was his rival and enemy. Yemon had felt the same antipathy.

"Why should I pay you?" Saburo asked.

"The man you wanted dead was buried yesterday," the other man said.

"You were to wait until I said the time had come."

The other man laughed. "You're the one who is a fool. The time to strike is when the opportunity arises. Pay me. I need to leave this place before they find me."

Saburo laughed. "Then here. Payment for a botched job."

When Yemon heard a yelp cut off too quickly, he hurried away and paused at the door of the tea house. Who had Saburo paid an assassin to kill? Yemon tucked this tidbit away. Learning the answer might add an arrow to his quiver.

A burst of laughter from inside drew Yemon into the first room. He saw his friends gathered around a table. He slipped off his sandals. The geisha hostess led him across the room. She handed him a hot wet towel for his hands. The subtle aroma relaxed his tension.

"Yemon, welcome," one of his friends said. "Wait until you hear the latest news."

Yemon waited for the geisha to bring hot sake and fill the tiny cup. As he sipped, his thoughts returned to the scene he'd overheard. Had Saburo killed the man he'd hired? "So what is this great story?"

"Saburo has lost his betrothed," one said.

"You mean the betrothal was broken," another said.

Braying laughter erupted. "Lost and broken. His betrothed's father was killed and she has vowed to stand as the head of her family until her brother comes of age."

Hoshi, Yemon thought. Had to be her.

"In ten days, they would have been wed and he would have been head of the family. You know what that means."

Yemon smiled. Now he knew one of Saburo's secrets. He leaned forward. "Perhaps his plan failed."

"What do you mean?" one of the others asked.

"I heard some ronin challenged the head of a family and killed him. Could be he acted too soon."

"And Saburo did himself in."

"Perhaps." Yemon filled his sake cup again and raised it for a toast. "To plans gone astray."

The conversation turned to other matters. When Yemon's favorite geisha paused at his side, he shook his head. The thought of being with any woman but Hoshi made him feel cold.

When he reached his father's house, he hurried to his sleeping room. He took a piece of parchment to the low table where his brushes and ink waited. To honor his feelings for Hoshi, he wrote a tanka.

A woman appeared.
Clothed as a man, standing proud.
Woman--all beauty.
Star of the night in glory.
Disguised, a sword in her hand.

Hoshi, he thought. She was a woman made to please a man. She was too beautiful to be a warrior. He fell asleep and carried her image into his dreams. As he tumbled into dreams, her face changed, but he knew the woman was Hoshi.

* * * *

For Yemon, the next day seemed endless. All he could think of was Hoshi and how he would find her in the garden of her house. At dusk, he dressed in dark clothes and slipped from the house. He hurried along the streets. He found the rear gate to her garden and entered. There, he hid behind a tree for Hoshi spoke to someone.

"Tomorrow, you will recite the duties of a samurai. When your teachers arrive, you must show them you are a child who can learn."

"When can I use a sword?"

"When your teachers come, they will tell you. You must practice the steps of the dance until they are ingrained. Your teachers will also help me hone my skills."

"What if you must face a challenge before then?"

"I'll do my best."

"Why did Father lose? I thought he was the best samurai in the land."

"The other man he fought cheated. He used a poisoned blade."

"Who was he?"

"A ronin. Someone paid him, but he escaped so we never learned who. Now off to your room. Write your duties three times."

Yemon waited for a time before he left his hiding place. Hoshi sat on a bench with a sword in her lap. He must have made a sound for she leaped to her feet. She held the sword in a two-handed grip. "Who is there?"

"Yemon."

She lowered the sword. "Why do you come like a thief in the night?"

"To see you. To speak of my heart's desire."

She sheathed the blade. "Your heart and not your mission?"

"Since last night, your face has been with me. I saw you in my dreams. Even when your features changed, I knew you. I learned how over the ages, we have loved and lost. Fate has granted us another chance."

She sank to the ground. "Perhaps what you say is true, but I can't give you what you want. For four years, I must remain a warrior. When my duty ends, I will resume my life."

Four years, he thought. By then, he would be wed. If not to Akako, to another of his father's choosing. He had to persuade Hoshi to be his. He sat beside her. "I burn for you. Can you say you have no desire for me?"

"No."

"How can you wait four years to fulfill our destiny?"

"I must."

Clouds slid away from the moon and he saw her clearly for the first time since he'd entered the garden. "Your hair." Why had she cut it before she heard his offer?

"I am samurai. My decision has been made. It is my duty to stand as family head until my brother comes of age. Now I am neither man nor woman."

He pulled her to her feet and into his arms. "How can you deny the need that beats like a pulsing heart?"

"I have no other choice." She met his gaze. "To accept the emperor's offer is to put my house into the hands of the man I believe betrayed my father. To step aside would bring me into a marriage I don't want to a man I despise. Go. Please."

Yemon stroked her back. "I will return. Think on this. Is duty greater than love?" He strode away. He had to find a way to end his betrothal and also to protect Hoshi from Saburo.

His wanderings took him to the house of his betrothed. He paused at the garden gate. Voices on the other side came closer. Yemon stepped into the shadows. The moon, well-hidden by clouds, cast no light. The gate opened.

"Go. My father has returned and he dare not find you here," Akako said.

"I'll come tomorrow and show you new ways to pleasure me."

"And perhaps I'll have some ideas of my own."

"A shame your skills will be wasted on your betrothed."

Akako laughed. "When I wed him, you can still come to me."

The man laughed. "Every day."

His voice sounded familiar. As he darted away, Yemon followed. The man ducked into an alley and vanished. Yemon smiled. He would catch the pair together. He'd be free. No one would expect him to wed a faithless woman.

* * * *

For the next seven days, Hoshi worked with her brother. She was exhausted, but the days had been peaceful. Saburo hadn't returned. Neither had Yemon.

After the evening meal, Keyoshi had gone to his sleeping chamber. Hoshi bathed and donned a robe and sandals. She entered the garden and sat beneath a cherry tree. Soon she would have help. The teachers were on their way. Though she should be abed, she was too weary to sleep. She drifted in thought.

Something touched her hand. Her eyes flew open. A shock wave rolled along her skin. "What are you doing here?"

Yemon smiled. "I said I would return."

Before she could order him to leave, he leaned forward and brushed her mouth with his. The lightest touch, but she felt as though typhoon driven waves rushed over her. His tongue moved feather-light on her lips, then slipped to caress the lower one. Her mouth opened. His tongue touched hers and moved in a pattern causing her breasts to ache and her nipples to tighten.

She slid her tongue over his and tasted sake. Had he needed to find courage in rice spirits before he came? His hands slid over her shoulders and kneaded the taut muscles. His fingers stroked her nape. Delicious warmth cocooned her and leached her resistance away.

Without breaking contact with her mouth, he rose and drew her with him. His arms circled her, imprisoning her arms against her sides.

He raised his head to snatch a breath. "Hoshi, Hoshi," he whispered. "Let me show you. Let me love you." His tongue flicked the skin of her neck sending shivers along her spine.

When his lips nuzzled her collarbone, she sighed with pleasure. She wanted what he offered, but she couldn't accept. "Yemon, this is wrong."

He pulled her closer. "How can what we feel be wrong?"

"I am samurai."

He nipped her lips. "And do warriors never feel passion? Do they spend their lives alone?"

His question puzzled her. Warriors had passion for battle. "They take wives so they can have sons."

"What about love?"

"I don't know."

"Show me where you sleep so we can find the answer."

His mouth covered hers. The movement of his hands on her body stirred a fire deep in her belly.

She tangled her hands in his hair. He grasped her hips and rocked against her. Wetness gathered between her legs. Her breasts, her woman's parts throbbed. She raised her head. "Come." She led him to the sleeping room.

Would she regret this moment? She prayed he would give her memories to carry her through the next four years. Hoping he would be free when the time came was foolish, but she would have this night.

She unfastened her obi and let the robe slide to the floor. When she turned, she saw he was also nude. Moonlight bathed his muscular body. A light breeze carried the scent of the garden into the room.

He caught her in an embrace. His mouth found hers. They stood locked together while his tongue probed her mouth and his hands moved over her back. She rose on her toes. When he spread his legs, she felt his penis slide along her cleft. She pressed her legs together and when she moved exquisite sensations stormed her.

He released her and led her to the mat. With a graceful movement, she lay on her back and held out her hands. He knelt between her legs, found her mouth, and then suckled her breasts. The waves washing her were like the fiery streams pouring from a mountain. He sank back on his heels and guided himself to her threshold. Slowly, he entered. When she tensed, he eased back then advanced. With a finger, he rubbed a spot that raised heat and vanquished her fears. He thrust again and paused. With his hands braced on either side of her, he began to move.

He clasped her hands and rose to his knees. She wrapped her legs around his hips. "Yemon, oh, Yemon," she cried.

"Hoshi." He growled her name and sent her soaring.

They moved together. Waves of pleasure swept through her. His name became a chant. She rode the waves of sensation over the crest and felt his seed gush deep inside. He collapsed and heaved great gulps of breath. She smoothed his hair. Never would she forget this night.

He rained kisses on her face and throat. "I will have you as my wife as soon as this can be arranged."

His words acted like water from a wind-driven winter storm. "I can't be any man's wife until my duty to this house is completed."

He rolled on his side. "How can you dismiss what has happened here? I've been with other women, but never have I felt as I do now, satisfied and triumphant."

She edged away. "I have my duty."

"Tell me you don't yearn for me."

"I can't. If I could, I would gladly be your wife. For four years, I must remain alone."

He rose and dressed. "I'll come tomorrow night."

A cry burst from her lips. "Once again, we have made the wrong choice. We have doomed ourselves. Go now and think about what I've said."

* * * *

When Yemon left Hoshi, anger roiled in his thoughts. He remembered the eagerness of her responses. How could she send him away? How could she say they had made the wrong choice? He would go to her and stir her until she confessed her love for him. She hadn't been able to deny the attraction. How could she deny love?

When he finally calmed down, he sought his bed. His dreams were filled with images of strange places and death.

In the morning, he went to the emperor's court and spent the day listening to bits of gossip. He hoped he might learn the identity of Akako's lover. Once he knew, he could make plans to catch the pair. On the way home, he purchased a silk robe and sent it with the tanka to Hoshi.

That evening, he stopped at his betrothed's house and found her maid. Perhaps she knew when the lovers would meet again. The young woman had a bruise on her face. Yemon handed her a coin. "What happened to you?"

"My mistress was angry. Last night I came to the garden to tell her the master wanted to see her."

"And she hit you?"

The maid nodded. "She was on her knees before a man licking his organ."

Yemon smiled. He gave the young woman another coin. "When will she meet him again?"

"Tonight. I heard her tell him to come. Why would she want another man when you are her betrothed?"

Yemon shrugged. Instead of going to Hoshi, he entered his favorite tea house. His friends were gathered at the table. He would listen to their gossip and perhaps find clues to the identity of Akako's lover. Though the young men were full of stories, he heard nothing he could use. Once the moon rose, he left and walked to Hoshi's house.

Silently, he entered the garden. He stopped to pick one of the long stemmed lilies then made his way to her room.

Hoshi sprawled face down on the mat. Yemon studied her nude body. A narrow waist gave way to wider hips. The sight of her firm buttocks inflamed him. He stripped and knelt between her legs.

As he ran the lily along her spine, he saw a hint of a smile on her face. She started to roll to her side, but he pressed his hands against her buttocks. "Stay as you are."

"Yemon?"

"Who else would creep into your bed to steal your breath and make your body burn?" He leaned forward and nipped the skin of her shoulders. He ran his tongue along her nape and massaged her taut muscles.

She sighed. "That feels good. I'm sore from practice. Ishi's hands aren't strong enough to knead deeply."

"Oil?" he asked.

"On the table."

He rose and found the bottle. When he returned to her side, he poured oil into his hands to warm. Then he began to stroke and massage the knots from her shoulders and the tension from her spine.

Her skin was smooth and silken. Her moans of contentment brought blood surging into his penis. He slid his oiled hands from her spine to massage her buttocks. Her cries changed to those of arousal. He smiled and his strokes became caresses.

"Yemon," she whispered.

"Soon I will come into you and we will soar," he said.

"We shouldn't."

"But we will." He kissed her shoulders and ran his tongue along her spine. He slid his hands beneath her body and stroked her belly. She raised her hips. His fingers found her slit and he caressed the tiny nub he knew would make her wild.

Her cries raised his ardor. The movement of her body enticed. He spread her legs and thrust inside. Deep growls rose from his depths. He would claim her in this life as he had in those visions of the past. He thrust harder and faster. Her inner muscles convulsed. His seed spurted then gushed until he was breathless.

As though strings had been cut, she collapsed. He rolled from her and pulled her into his arms. His mouth found hers and took greedy tastes. "As you have always been, you are mine. I have dreamed of strange places when time and again we have met and loved."

She sighed. "To love is right, but to forget honor is wrong."

He nipped her lower lip. "To put duty first is wrong. I love you now and I always will."

"If what you say is true, you will stay away from me until I'm free."

"How can you say that? I'm willing to give up my quest for wealth and power. Can't you turn away from this duty you've assumed, a duty that shouldn't be yours? Surely there are other males in the family who can stand as your brother's guardian."

She turned away. "If I hadn't claimed the position, I would be Saburo's wife. He's the one who arranged my father's death."

Yemon recalled the scene he'd overheard in the alley. But the ronin was dead. "Have you proof?"

"No. Believe me or not. Saburo is evil and treacherous. Go find another woman for your house."

"I love you."

"Now isn't the time for love. Leave me. From this night, there will be guards at the gates."

Yemon rose and dressed. As he departed, he considered her words. He would find a way past her guards. His plans came to naught for he was sent from the city on another mission for the emperor.

* * * *

Two lunars passed without a visit from Yemon or Saburo. Keyoshi's teachers had arrived and Hoshi's days were spent honing her skills with bow and sword.

As she bound her breasts, she winced. Why were they so tender? She couldn't remember being struck on the chest during a practice bout.

Ishi reached for the padded coat. The maid frowned.

"Is there a problem?" Hoshi asked.

"Are you in truth no longer a woman?"

'Why would you ask that?'

The girl stared at the floor. "You haven't had your woman's time since before your father's death."

Hoshi sank on a stool. What Ishi said was true. Hoshi knew what her tender breasts meant. She recalled the day years ago when her mother first knew she was with child. Hoshi had bumped her mother's chest and her mother had cried.

Hoshi grabbed Ishi's arm. "Tell no one."

"Not even Chika?"

"I will speak to her." She prayed the older woman would have a solution for the problem. Surely there were ways to undo what had happened. She donned the armor and went to practice with the men.

* * * *

A sound woke Hoshi. She grasped her knife.

"Hoshi."

"Yemon, what are you doing here?"

"I would have come before, but I was sent on a mission. I have returned and we will make plans so we can be together."

She tensed. She couldn't let him love her. He would discover the changes in her body and force a marriage. He served the emperor and as her husband, he would become her brother's guardian. "How can you think to make plans? My servants have heard tales of your betrothal. Your wedding will be soon."

"The betrothal will be broken."

"Then leave. Do not return until you are no longer bound to this woman."

He pulled her into his arms and sought her mouth. Her body responded to the urgings of his mouth and hands. "How can you send me away when you ache for me?"

"If I scream, the guards will come and end your life." She held an anguished cry inside. "We cannot make love again and I won't have your blood on my hands."

He released her. "I'll leave. In the morning, I'll send a gift that expresses my feelings for you."

His anger vibrated the air. What did he plan?

* * * *

Yemon clenched his fists. How could he persuade her to accept his offer of marriage? First, he had to end his betrothal. Akako had had two lunars to enjoy the company of her lover. Would she have grown careless? He walked to the house where she lived with her father and paused at the garden gate. With care, he slipped inside. Even if she wasn't with her lover, he would confront her with his knowledge.

The soft murmur of voices was followed by the cries of a woman in the throes of passion. Yemon ran along the path. Did he have his proof?

He reached the entwined couple in time to see the man climax. Yemon grabbed the man's hair and pressed a knife to Saburo's throat. Akako screamed. "Assassin."

"Faithless woman," Yemon spat. "You have betrayed me and shamed your father."

Servants and guards ran into the garden. Yemon kept his hold on his enemy.

Akako's father arrived. "What is happening here?" He roared a curse and grabbed his naked daughter. "Shameful. Have you no honor?" He shook her and flung her away. He approached Yemon and the struggling Saburo. "Betrayer." He plunged a knife into Saburo's chest.

Yemon released his hold on the body. He glared at Akako. "The betrothal is ended."

She spat. "If you think to find another, you won't. You'll be sorry you harmed Saburo. He knew who you visited before you left the city. He told me and she will pay." She ran to the house.

Yemon turned to Akako's father. "You will declare the betrothal is ended or I will have her examined and her shame published for all to know." He left the garden and went to tell his father what had occurred.

* * * *

Hoshi looked at the fugu fish and read the note that had arrived this morning. This must be the gift Yemon had promised. Had he written the note? She had seen his writing but once and had thrown the tanka away. Who else would have sent the fish? She read the message again.

This gift shows my sadness. Can you accept the challenge?

Would he try to kill her? Was this a test of her courage? She cut a piece of the flesh and ate. How long would it be before she knew?

Ishi appeared at the door. "A man begs to see you."

"Send him in."

Yemon entered. He stared at the fugu. "What is this?"

"Your gift and I have eaten."

"I did not send it."

"Who then?"

He groaned. "Last night, I found my betrothed in the garden with Saburo. They were unclothed and in a compromising position. Her father killed Saburo. I believe she sent the fugu."

"Why?"

"She blames me for his death. She vowed revenge. Saburo must have seen me entering your garden. "

Hoshi opened her mouth to speak. Garbled sounds emerged. She gasped for breath.

Yemon sliced a piece of the fugu and ate.

"Why?" Hoshi managed to gasp.

"I love you more than wealth and power. Since I can't be with you in life, I will be there in death." He gathered her in his arms and held her when the convulsions began. "Would that you had chosen love over duty. This you must remember when next we meet."

* * * *

Duncan stared at Astrid's convulsing body. He plucked the netsuke from her hand and caught images of a man and woman. He began to shake. He opened his hand. The small ivory carving fell on the floor.

Astrid's body stilled. Duncan held her in his arms. If this had happened when she was alone, she could have died. He would forbid her any more sessions.

Forbid? How could he do that? He was her lover of the moment, but not forever. Why not?

Astrid's moans cut off those thoughts. Her eyes fluttered open, but they were unfocused. "Why did you eat the fugu? Why did you choose death?"

"Astrid, its Duncan."

Awareness crept into her eyes. "Death. Always death."

Duncan kissed her forehead. He offered comfort, not the desire that would consume them. "Tell me all you remember."

She took a deep breath. "You must remember to choose love over duty." She met Duncan's gaze. "They almost succeeded in breaking the curses. He did. She didn't. There were two who opposed them. The evil ones won again. She was with child when she died. They should have kept their love apart from the physical." Tears filled her eyes. "It's a jumble."

He stroked her back. "How did she die?"

"She ate from a fish she thought her lover had sent."

"A fish?"

"Puffer fish. Fatal in at least fifty percent of those who eat the poisoned flesh. Kills in ten minutes to four hours. Even cooking doesn't destroy the toxin."

He shuddered. "Remind me never to eat any."

She stretched. "I need to see my dad."

"Why?"

"To get his permission to change the locks on Antiquities. I think Clive has been stealing."

He nodded. "You're in no condition to drive. Take a nap. When you wake, I'll show you the information I received about Clive."

He held her until her body relaxed. After covering her with a sheet, he went to the office to complete some business matters. Then he tried Clive's numbers and left a message for his friend to call.

Astrid slept until evening. She stepped into the study. "Is it as late as my watch says?"

He nodded. "You hungry?"

"Famished."

He pulled two bottles of iced tea from the small refrigerator. "Let me order pizza. Then we'll talk."

"Sounds great."

Duncan made the call. "Be here in twenty minutes. I need to go down and unlock the gate." He strode to the door. "Don't think you'll get to see your dad tonight."

"I'll go tomorrow." She followed him downstairs.

By the time the pizza arrived, Astrid had made a salad and eaten several mouthfuls. Duncan put the box on the table. Astrid slid a slice from the box and took a large bite. In a short time, she reached for a second slice.

Duncan chuckled. "You weren't joking about being hungry. Feeling any better?"

"Much. So what did your hound sniff out on Clive?"

"Could you make that a bloodhound? Rick would like that for a title." He told her what the detective had learned.

She frowned. "That means Dad will have to check every jeweled piece sold since he hired Clive."

"Afraid so. There's more. Seems Clive and Lorna are married."

Astrid's eyes flashed with anger. "So they play a double game. Substituting paste for gems and luring you into an affair. What if you had become sexually involved with her?"

"I'd have ended up at the center of a nasty divorce or blackmailed into a large settlement."

Astrid looked up. "Or dead with Clive to step in as your nearest relative."

Duncan felt a chill slither along his spine. "Never thought of that."

Astrid arched a brow. "Looks like you're the one in danger."

"Maybe not. Our meeting thwarted their plans. They might want revenge. Stay here with me."

She studied her hands. "I can't."

"Why not?"

She rose and walked to the door. "Because I'm falling in love with you. I can't be just another fling." She started down the stairs.

Duncan rose to follow and sank back on the chair. What now? He cared for her, but did his feelings go deeper? Until he knew the answer, he had to let her go.

* * * *

Astrid entered the apartment and leaned against the door. Why had she told him about her feelings? She could have kept quiet and just vanished from his life. Was that possible? For the next two years, she would be living in Rockleigh or nearby. There would be chance encounters. How long would it take to get past the hurt? Love had to be mutual or it was not worth the heartache.

She entered the main room and saw the answering machine flashing. She listened to the messages. One puzzled her. A woman identifying herself as Astrid's advisor for the Master's program announced a mandatory meeting for Thursday from nine until noon.

Astrid called Paula. "I've a problem with our lunch date. Have to be in the city until noon."

"No problem," Paula said. "I'll call Jan and we'll reschedule for Friday."

"Thanks. See you then." Astrid dropped the receiver in the cradle.

PERU

Astrid opened the apartment door and stepped onto the deck. If she left now, she'd be at the rehab center in time to watch several of her dad's therapy sessions. Might give her a clue of what to do when he was discharged. She wondered when that would be. She took a deep breath. Over lunch, she had to tell him about her suspicions of Clive.

Sarah appeared at the foot of the steps. "I'm glad I caught you. Clive hasn't come to open the shop."

"Let me get the extra keys. Keep them in case he doesn't show." Astrid returned to the apartment. Moments later, she dropped the keys in Sarah's hand.

"Thanks. Don't know what's with him lately."

Astrid shrugged. Though she'd shared her belief about Clive and the apartment search, she couldn't tell Sarah everything that had been learned. The older woman might let something slip and Clive would be gone before her father learned the truth. "How was Dad last evening?"

Sarah rolled her eyes. "Antsy. Stubborn."

"How so?"

Sarah chuckled. "He wants to come home last week."

"That doesn't surprise me."

"When I told him about the apartment, he refused to believe Clive was responsible. He said he should have changed the locks years ago. Was a bit upset you didn't call the police."

"I'll talk to him." Astrid recalled the report Duncan had shown her. "Better, I can give him something he might believe. Just have to make a call I'd rather avoid."

"Duncan?" Sarah asked.

"Yes. I've decided not to see him again."

"Sorry to hear that. What did he do?"

"Nothing." A knot formed in Astrid's gut. "I told him how I feel and he didn't say a word, just snapped orders." She swallowed. "I fell in love and it's hard to know he hasn't."

"Are you sure?" Sarah asked. "I've seen the way he looks at you."

"That's lust. He has said how good we are together. Sex isn't love." Astrid opened the door of Antiquities. "Let me make that call." She entered the office and reached for the phone. Unless her father saw proof in black and white, he'd never believe Clive was a thief.

"Garrett Enterprises."

"Astrid Logan here. I'd like to speak to Mr. Garrett."

"I'll buzz him."

Moments later, Duncan came on the line. "Change your mind?"

"No. I'm on my way to see Dad and I'd like to show him that report on Clive. When Aunt Sarah told him about the apartment, he said Clive couldn't be responsible."

"Are you in a rush? I'm tied up here for about a half hour."

"I'll wait. Thanks."

Astrid booted the computer. Might as well see how bad things could be. She printed the list of sales made since Clive had begun to work at Antiquities. With a red pencil, she circled the ones she knew were jeweled. The phone rang. "Antiquities."

"Ms. Logan, please."

"Speaking."

"Susan from Rehab Inc. Your father said if you weren't home, we might reach you here."

"Is he all right?"

"He's fine. He'll be discharged tomorrow. You'll need to be here between ten and eleven."

Astrid groaned. What now? There was the mandatory meeting in the city. Now this. She'd better learn how important the meeting was. She couldn't be in two places at the same time. She dialed the university. After being transferred to the Nursing Department, she asked for the advisor.

"Ms. Trainor isn't in today."

"I need to speak to her about the meeting she scheduled for tomorrow morning."

"That's odd. Nothing here. Guess she forgot to tell us."

"I need to reschedule. A family emergency. Could you

either give me her number or take mine with a message to call me?"

"I can leave the message on her voice mail."

Astrid recited her number. "Thanks."

* * * *

Duncan dictated a final letter and grabbed his car keys. "Be back in a bit," he called to his secretary.

Before going to Antiquities, he stopped at the house to copy the file on Clive. He wasn't sure what to do with the information, but if Lloyd ran into problems, the material would go to the police.

His thoughts turned to Astrid. Could he persuade her to see their affair through to its natural ending? He groaned. How? If she believed she loved him, she would want to protect herself. She would want a commitment he wasn't ready to make. Since he'd met her, he'd felt like he was part of a runaway train. He had to apply the brakes, especially when he felt some force was pushing them together.

What did he want? She was everything he'd ever desired in a woman. Why hadn't they met a few years from now?

When he reached Antiquities, he greeted Sarah and the clerk. "Astrid at the apartment or here?"

"The office," Sarah said. "She looks like the world's problems have been dropped on her head."

"Let's hope I can help." He moved away before Sarah could ask the questions he saw in her eyes.

"Come in," Astrid called.

Duncan stepped into the room and felt his body shimmer with need. Her scent wafted toward him. He wanted her as much as he had the first time he'd seen her. Then he noticed the worry lines on her forehead and wondered if she would accept his offer of help. "Here's the file."

"Thanks."

He leaned on the desk. "What's wrong?"

"A problem in logistics. Dad's being discharged tomorrow. I have to pick him up between ten and eleven, plus at the same time attend a mandatory meeting at the university."

"I can solve that problem. I'll go for Lloyd and make sure there are no further charges on the bill."

She placed her hands on the desk. "Thanks. I'd ask Sarah,

but she has to be here to open the shop."

"Glad to help."

She looked up. "You will let me know how much you've spent."

"Why?"

"If Dad can't repay you, once I finish the Master's and have a job, I will."

He shook his head. "Not an option. Lloyd and I will sort things out."

"If he can."

"What do you mean?"

"Almost fifty jeweled pieces have been sold since Clive started here. Dad will have to replace all those gems."

Duncan covered her hands with his. "No problem. I'll help. I owe you."

"Excuse me."

"It's only money." He traced circles on the back of her hand. "Have dinner with me tonight and we'll discuss the matter."

"I can't."

"Don't you mean won't? Don't toss away what we have. We're good together."

She met his gaze. "I love you. I have time and again. Each meeting ends in death. I'd rather walk away now."

Duncan shook his head. "We're not going to die unless we buy these dreams. I'm not sure I do."

"Doesn't matter. I'm walking away."

"I see." He turned to leave. Even if he didn't love her, he had to help. If he hadn't lived in Rockleigh, Clive wouldn't be here. "See you around." He waved and strode to the door.

* * * *

Astrid glanced at the gathering of dark clouds. Would the storm break before she returned home? The sinuous mountain road would be treacherous when the roads were wet. The metal guardrail didn't seem strong enough to keep a car from plunging into the deep wooded gorge. Though living upstate had given her skills for driving in hazardous conditions, she didn't want to use them today.

She glanced in the rearview mirror. Was the dark car the one that had followed her from the highway? The car was too distant for her to see the driver or read the license plate.

When she pulled onto the road leading to the rehab center, the sedan followed. Her heart raced. She pulled into a space in the visitor's lot. The other vehicle continued to the staff lot. Astrid laughed. Chalk one up to a vivid imagination. She took the folder from the passenger's seat and walked to the entrance.

Her father met her in the foyer. They walked to the dining room. "You are late."

"Clive didn't open the shop. Then there were a few phone calls."

He led her to a table for two. "A reuben all right with you?"

"You know it is. This place is going to spoil you for ordinary food."

"Maybe. What time should I expect you tomorrow? I'll have the bags at the door."

"There's a slight change of plans. I've a mandatory meeting in the city with my advisor. Duncan offered to play chauffeur unless I hear from her this evening." She cut a piece of the open-faced sandwich.

"That'll work. He and I need to talk. I'm considering an offer of a partnership to Clive." He held up his hands. "I know you think he searched the apartment, but I can't figure why."

"The Egyptian necklace for starters. Lorna wants it and she'd push him until he gave in."

Lloyd laughed. "Clive isn't one to be under some woman's thumb."

Astrid lifted the folder. "Before you make the offer, you need to read this."

He read each page slowly. "I don't believe this. There has to be another answer."

Astrid shook her head. "It's true. The report came from a detective Duncan trusts. I've a feeling you don't want to believe you're being cheated."

Lloyd sighed. "You're right."

"Another thing bothers me. Clive hasn't been around since the day after the street fair when he asked me to cut him a check for five thousand dollars."

"Did you?"

"Hardly. Told him to produce the sales slips." She rose. "I have given him checks before this. They total several thousand."

Lloyd frowned. "With sales slips?"

She nodded. "I'd like to change the locks at Antiquities."

"With what's in this report, that's a good idea." He frowned. "What if he arrives in the morning and can't get in? He could run before we learn exactly what he's done."

Astrid took the folder from the table. "I'll ask Aunt Sarah to open early."

"Good enough. I'll be home tomorrow. He'll have some questions to answer."

"Let's hope he doesn't vanish." She kissed her dad's cheek. "Monday, I'll start an apartment search."

He grinned. "Might not have to. Doing what I should have years ago. Asking Sarah to marry me. If she accepts, you can have her apartment."

"Good luck."

When she reached her car, she glanced at the sky. The clouds had thickened. By the time she reached the road, a steady drizzle had begun. My luck, she thought and turned on the wipers.

Before long, wind drove the rain against the windshield. Though she wanted to speed, she slowed. As she rounded a sharp curve, a dark vehicle sped out of a side road and clipped her rear fender. Astrid's car spun and slid toward the guardrail.

She eased off the gas, gently turned the wheel, then tapped the brakes. The dark sedan had vanished. Astrid's car skimmed past the guardrail and slued toward the rocky slope edging the road. When she finally gained control and stopped, the passenger's side was in the drainage ditch.

She dragged in gulping breaths. Her heart thudded. Tears flowed down her cheeks. As visions of what could have been stormed her thoughts, she clutched the wheel. When the tremors stopped, she climbed from the car to assess the damage. Rain and wind assaulted her.

Two tires were in shreds. The rear fender bore a dent. She returned to the car and grabbed a towel from the back seat to dry her face and hair. Then, she reached for the cell phone.

A short time later, the police arrived. The policeman gave her the number of a local gas station with a tow truck. "We'll fill out a report, but I doubt we'll find the car." He looked at the fender. "The other car might be wearing some of your paint."

By the time they finished the report, the tow truck had arrived. Astrid rode with the driver and waited for the tires to be replaced and the car checked for other problems. Finally, she returned to Rockleigh.

Antiquities was closed. Sarah's car was gone. Astrid walked to the apartment and called the locksmith. "Jan is out of town for the day. Leave your name and number. I'll get back to you as soon as I can." Astrid hung up. She would call in the morning.

She rubbed her arms. Her body ached. With a groan, she pushed away from the counter and headed to the bathroom. As the tub filled with steaming water, she poured in herbal bath salts. She sank into the heat and felt her muscles uncoil. When the water cooled, she pulled on a sleep shirt, heated soup and turned on the television.

* * * *

The next morning when Astrid returned from her run, she headed to the shower. She had time before she had to leave for the city. As she stood under the spray, she heard the phone, but by the time she reached the main room, the answering machine had clicked off.

She dressed and toasted an English muffin, then listened to the message. "Ms. Logan, Greta Trainor here. There seems to be a misunderstanding. I haven't scheduled a meeting for today. See you in September."

Astrid stared at the machine. What was going on? Who would want her out of the picture? Clive and Lorna, maybe. But why? Did they know her father was coming home today? Unless Aunt Sarah had said something, they didn't.

She dialed Duncan's number. Perhaps she could catch him before he left. He wasn't at home. His secretary said he'd be out of town for the morning.

Next call, she thought and dialed the locksmith. "Hi, Jan, it's Astrid Logan."

"Caught me on my way out the door. We're on for lunch tomorrow, right?"

"We are. That's not why I called. We need the locks on Antiquities changed."

"Let's see. I'm tied up until eleven or so. Why don't I meet you at the shop?"

"Sounds good. See you around eleven." Before leaving for the shop, she gave the apartment a quick cleaning.

At the foot of the steps, she stopped abruptly and stared at the dark sedan parked next to hers. She approached the vehicle. When she saw a bit of paint on the right fender, she frowned. Was this the car that had tried to force her off the road? Whose was it? She needed to let the police know, but what if the owner drove away before they arrived?

She made a decision. Whoever owned this sedan wasn't leaving until she had some answers. She crouched and let the air from one of the rear tires. She moved to the second and then to the front. Something jabbed her back.

"What are you doing?"

"What does it look like?" Astrid asked. "Did you try to run me off the road yesterday?"

"And what if I did?" Lorna asked. "Get up and walk ahead of me."

"Why?"

"Because I have a gun,"

Astrid got to her feet. She slipped her cell phone from her pocket and started to dial. The phone was knocked from her hand and slid across the asphalt.

"Don't be a fool." Lorna prodded her back. "Move."

Astrid walked ahead of Lorna. Did the other woman really have a gun? For a moment, Astrid debated, but the risk of Lorna telling the truth was too great. She rounded the corner and entered Antiquities.

"Look what I found," Lorna said.

Clive held a pair of silver goblets. "I thought you had a meeting in the city this morning."

Astrid heard the door close behind her. "Someone was playing a trick."

Clive put the goblets in a box and reached for the second pair. "Who would do a thing like that?"

"You. Lorna."

"Shame you learned the truth." He finished clearing the shelf.

"Just what are you doing?"

He laughed. "Taking what I'm owed." He closed the box. "Your presence presents a difficult problem. What am I going to do with you?"

Lorna giggled. "Get rid of her."

Clive shook his head. "I'm not crossing that line. No killing. The time for that is past."

"Who would suspect us? They'll think she interrupted a burglary."

Astrid sucked in a breath. "You're wrong. The door was opened without force and the alarm was turned off. Will look like an inside job. Not to mention the information Duncan's detective found. They'll know."

Lorna grabbed Astrid's hair. "What information?"

"Clive's habit of substituting paste for real gems. Your marriage. Other things." She glanced at them. "Sarah should be here any time to open."

"Wrong," Clive said. "I called her yesterday to say the shop would be closed today to make up for the Monday street fair."

Astrid swallowed. "Jan's meeting me here to change the locks. Should arrive any minute." Though the locksmith wasn't due for an hour, they wouldn't know.

Lorna glared. "So bright boy, what now?"

"Never fear." Clive's smile sent a chill along Astrid's skin. "I know the perfect place for her. Depending on how soon someone figures where she is. We should be long gone by the time they do."

"And broke," Lorna said. "Will take us time to liquidate our assets."

"I've a better idea," Clive said. "I know who'll be willing to hand over cash to free her."

Lorna snickered. "So she messes up one plan, but falls into another. I like it."

Clive dragged Astrid to the office. The vault door was open. Astrid grabbed the back of a chair and tried to pull free. "Clive, don't do this."

"No options left. We'll be far from here by tonight." He jerked and she lost her hold on the chair. The chair crashed on the floor. He shoved her into the vault and thrust something into her hand. "A little gift. Pity the emerald's flawed. Would have been worth a bundle."

Astrid's knees buckled and she sank to the floor. The vault door closed. Though she fought, she felt herself being swept into another time.

* * * *

The last rays of the sun colored the distant snow-covered

peaks. Coyllur stood in the courtyard of the Sun Temple and stared at the road beyond the entrance. Her father was late. Since she'd been taken to the temple after her mother's death, he had come every lunar for a visit and to bring fresh fish for the temple. Her shoulders slumped. He wasn't coming. The sea harvest wouldn't arrive this lunar. What had happened? Unless there had been trouble, he would have been here by now. Tears threatened, but she held them back.

She saw movement on the road and felt a hope quickly extinguished when she identified the runner. A chasqui held his quipu. The knotted string dangled from the messenger's hand. What news did he bring?

Moments after the chasqui disappeared into the temple, a Sun Priestess appeared. "Child, I have news of your father."

Coyllur approached Chaquira. "Has he been hurt?"

The priestess took her hand. "It is not known how or where my youngest brother is. A floating fortress came near the shore and spawned small boats. Strangers came from the boats. They took your father and some others when they left."

Coyllur blinked tears away. "Then I will believe he lives and I will see him again."

"You will." Chaquira held out her hand. "Come with me. There are things I must tell you. For many nights, I have dreamed of strange places and people. Last night, the visions drew to an end and I know what they mean."

Coyllur followed her aunt to her cell. A prophecy meant change. Was she to be sent to the Sun Temple in Cuzco? Was she to be a Chosen Woman to serve the Inca in life and death?

Chaquira sat on a stool. Coyllur sat at the priestess' feet.

"A time of change approaches for the land and for you. Strangers came and will return. Among them is one tied to you by the strings of an ancient curse given in a land beyond your imagination."

Coyllur frowned. Were these strangers the ones who had taken her father?

Chaquira leaned forward. "This I say to you. When you see his face, you will love him. This love must remain pure until you are bound together. There are three who will help and two who wish to prevent this union. Time and again, they have manipulated and succeeded. This time, they must not."

Coyllur frowned. She was too young to join with any man. Besides, she belonged to the temple. If she was to have a mate, the Inca would choose him. "I hear, but I do not understand."

"In time, you will."

Coyllur sighed. "When?"

"In many turnings of the moon." Chaquira patted her head. "Seek your mat."

"A good night to you." Coyllur scurried away. As she hurried to the room she shared with the other girls, a priest beckoned. She tensed. Though Suka was handsome, something about him made her fearful.

He caught her arm. "Why aren't you with the other girls? Were you seeking me?"

She stared at the floor. To meet his gaze would expose her fear. "I was with the Sun Priestess Chaquira."

He lifted her chin with his fingers. "You are lovely, but too young for the pleasures I could show you." He laughed. "You won't be young forever."

Coyllur backed away. "I must go."

"Tell Sumac I await her. She is late for her lessons and I would see her at once."

Coyllur ran the rest of the way to the sleeping chamber. Sumac sat on her mat. The older girl was near the end of her training. Soon she would be a priestess. What kind of lessons did Suka teach? Coyllur shuddered. None she wanted to learn.

Her friend, Coca, waved. Coyllur stopped before Sumac.

The older girl glared. "What do you want?"

"The Sun Priest, Suka, awaits you."

Sumac undulated from the mat. Her icy smile chilled Coyllur. "Your turn will come, but I doubt you'll enjoy the lessons. He'll punish you for your haughty ways. Just because your hair and skin are lighter than most doesn't make you a treasure."

Coyllur frowned. Was Sumac one of her enemies?

Coca waited until Sumac left. "Let's go bathe. I waited for you."

Coyllur picked up a clean dress. "Why does she go to

Suka?"

Coca laughed. "To learn how to please a man. I watched through a spy hole once. He mounted her like the llamas do."

"But the Chosen are virgins."

"Not all. Some of the priestesses serve the priests."

"He said he will teach me. I don't like him. What can I do?"

"Don't let him catch you alone." Coca stepped into the heated pool. "Did your father send the chasqui?"

Coyllur joined her friend. "The chasqui came to Chaquira. Coca, my father has been taken away by strangers."

* * * *

Five years passed, but Coyllur clung to the belief she would see her father again. Her skills grew and she became a weaver of the finest cloth.

"Coyllur, wake up."

She rolled over and rubbed her eyes. "Coca." Her friend was dressed, yet the sky remained dark.

Coca bent closer. "Chaquira woke me and told me to bring you without waking the others."

Coyllur rose and pulled her dress woven from vicuna over her head. She overlapped the sides and fastened the belt. With her sandals and shawl in her hands, she hurried after her friend. They trotted down one of the inner passages and emerged outside the temple.

Chaquira stood beside a litter. "Inside. When we are on the road, I'll tell you why we leave."

Once Coyllur and Coca were settled, the priestess took the place across from them. The bearers lifted the poles. A man carrying a torch led the way from the town. Chaquira released the side curtains and enclosed them in darkness.

"Where are we going?" Coyllur asked.

"To where the Inca waits for a call to Cuzco. I must warn him about the strangers. He must destroy them before they bring his doom."

"Are these the ones who took my father?"

"Perhaps. All I know is they bring danger."

Coyllur sighed. "I must believe my father lives. If you dreamed true, he is one of the ones who help."

"Are you sure?" the priestess asked.

"Coca woke me from a dream. Faces changed until they

were ones I know. You, Coca, my father,"

Chaquira leaned forward. "What of the Inca?"

"He wasn't there, but not all the faces changed."

Coca frowned. "Will the Inca listen to you? If the gods have called, we can do nothing."

"No matter. I must warn him," Chaquira said. "Rest now. The day will be long."

Coyllur dozed until the sun was high. She lifted the curtain. Dust stirred on the hard-packed earth of the road. Walls lined the sides providing protection from landslides. Coca woke and they ate from the basket of provisions.

As the sun set, the bearers lowered the litter to the ground. Coca lifted the side curtain and climbed out. Coyllur helped the priestess to her feet and led her to the tampu. The way station guardian showed them to an inner room where food was brought for the evening meal.

The journey continued for days. Finally, they reached the palace where the Inca waited. They found places in the women's quarters.

Coyllur stopped just inside the door. "Why is Sumac here? Wasn't she sent to Cuzco?"

Coca shrugged. "She is beautiful. The Inca must have chosen her."

"But she and Suka are ... you know. Do you think he's here?" Coyllur feared the answer. If the Sun Priest was here, she and her friend could be in danger.

* * * *

Coyllur and Coca found places among the women who wove the cloth for the Inca's clothes. He wore a new set every day and the old ones were burned. Several days passed before Chaquira bade Coyllur to attend her when she spoke to the Inca. Coyllur followed the older woman into the Inca's presence. The sight of Suka among the Sun Priests brought a rush of fear.

"I would speak," Chaquira said. "I bring news of the strangers come to this land. I have fasted and meditated. There are prophecies."

Suka sprang to his feet. "The Inca knows of the gods who have returned as they promised. Be gone, old woman. Take your prophecies of doom elsewhere."

Atahualpa held up his hands. "Priest, you dare insult a Sun Priestess. I have heard of this one's prophecies and would listen to her words."

Chaquira knelt at his feet. "It has been said when the gods who brought great gifts of learning to the people departed, they promised to return. Strangers have come. Men with pale skin and hair on their faces. Some say they are the gods come again." She stared at the Inca. "This I know. When the gods walk among men, sometimes they come to test, sometimes to teach, sometimes to bring change and often to destroy. Weigh carefully the actions of these men before you trust their words."

The Inca nodded. "I will think on what you have said."

Suka waited until Chaquira moved away. His gaze lingered on Coyllur. He licked his lips as though anticipating a treat. Coyllur tore her gaze away and found herself staring into Sumac's hostile eyes.

The Chosen Woman's eyes held anger. Coyllur felt as though arrows pierced her serenity. Why does she hate me? Sumac had no reason, except--Sumac must be one of the two enemies from the past born into a new body. Coyllur was so lost in thought she missed Suka's first words.

"...the strangers have come to aid your struggle. Did they not reach these shores on the very day Huascar died? They have come to honor you. You must welcome them. Take them into your service so they can carry you in triumph to Cuzco. Can't you envision the glorious precession through the Golden Enclosure?"

The Inca smiled. "You present a grand picture. I will weigh your words, but the decision is mine."

When the Inca retired, Coyllur followed Chaquira to the women's quarters. What would happen now? If the Inca believed Chaquira what would happen to the strangers?

* * * *

Fall drifted into winter and nothing changed. Even when word arrived about the rape of the priestess of the Sun Temple in Caxas, the Inca remained silent. Spring arrived and still the strangers didn't arrive. Atahualpa remained in his refuge near Cajamarca. Chasqui brought news of the strangers; Coyllur listened and hoped for word of her father.

"These men ride beasts like large llamas. The beasts have silver hooves. The men bear things that send killing thunderbolts. They wear moon metal shells. With them are ones who speak both tongues."

Atahualpa nodded. "Perhaps they are not the gods, but I will wait. They are few and we are many."

Suka smiled. "My Lord Inca, you are wise. Yes, wait until they come to you."

Chaquira drew Coyllur into a corner. "I will make plans to send you and Coca to a safe place. There is a small village in the mountains where you can hide."

Coyllur shook her head. "I can't go."

"There is danger here."

"The dreams. One face became a man with fair skin and dark hair. Sumac and Suka are in these dreams. They are the evil ones. I must be here or I fear they will destroy the man."

Chaquira sighed. "So we stay."

* * * *

Coyllur and Coca joined Chaquira in the Inca's presence. They sat with the Sun Priestesses. Courtiers and Sun Priests milled about the room. Sumac sat at the Inca's side. Suka stood behind her. A chasqui trotted into the room. He knelt and held out the knotted string.

"Speak," the Inca said.

"The strangers have reached the town and have taken several houses on the square. With them are some of our people who speak the stranger's tongue. They came on their riding beasts and carry their lightning weapons."

One of the war leaders rose. "Let me lead the army against them and bring an end to this."

Suka rose. "My Lord Inca, Son of the Sun, remember the promise of the gods. They vowed to return. Let these strangers lead you to Cuzco and your rightful place."

Chaquira faced the Sun Priest. "Or lead him to his death. These men could be tricksters. They seem to be mere men with men's appetites. Haven't you heard how they despoiled the Sun Priestesses and stripped gold and silver from the temples?"

Suka raised his fist and strode toward Chaquira. Coyllur grasped Coca's hand.

"My Lord Inca, the strangers have sent a party to speak to you," a guard said.

"Bid them enter. I will hear what they have to say."

"You must come to the plaza. They must remain on their

beasts for they fear the animals will attack someone."

"Then we will go." Atahualpa motioned to his bearers. They lifted his chair and carried him outside. Suka whirled and joined the priests and courtiers.

Coyllur's eyes widened when she saw one of the beasts race across the ground and halt beside the others. The creatures were large. The men gleamed in the sunlight. A man on foot approached the steps. Coyllur grasped Coca's arm.

"What's wrong?" Coca asked.

"That man is my father. I must go to him."

Chaquira clasped Coyllur's shoulder. "Not here. A way will be found so you may speak in secret."

The man who had raced to join the group spoke to her father. Then she saw the man's face and her breath caught. "That one is the man from my dreams."

"Ah," Chaquira said. "Tonight, I will go to the town."

Coyllur's father bowed to the Inca. "These men from Spain have a gift for you." He placed a small box before Atahualpa.

"I have gifts for them." The Inca clapped his hands. Two servitors carried a pair of stone fountains. Another brought lengths of fine woven vicuna.

"The men of Spain would have you come and share a meal in their company."

"I cannot come this day. I will come tomorrow. Tell the leaders I give them the houses on the square." Atahualpa raised a hand. Servitors arrived with gold cups, one for each mounted man. Another poured liquid from a silver pitcher. "Tell them the cups are theirs."

Coyllur watched the faces of the strangers. All but one, the man from her dreams, grasped the cups and grinned. She stared at the man she knew. Her gaze meshed with his.

* * * *

Guerro stared at the young woman. When he'd joined Pizarro's men, he had thought he wanted adventure, wealth and power. Those reasons vanished. He had come for her, the one who had flitted through his dreams always out of touch.

Who was she? He prayed she wasn't the ruler's wife. If so, she was in danger. Pizarro and his men craved the gold that seemed as common as stones in this land. The gold and silver they had already acquired had only whetted their greed. And the priests saw only souls ripe for conversion.

He noticed Qhari also stared at the young woman. Guerro called the interpreter to his side. "Do you know her or is it the women with her?"

Qhari nodded. "One of the young women is my daughter. The older is my sister."

Guerro sucked in a breath. "They must be warned of their danger."

Qhari frowned. "I'm not sure I can reach them. If they're among the Chosen Women, they will be guarded."

Guerro noticed one of the men who wore a large gold medallion also stared at the three women. "That one." He pointed. "Who is he?"

"I don't know his name. He is a Sun Priest. The woman he touches is the Inca's companion."

"How could your daughter be one of these Chosen?"

Qhari toed the ground. "When her mother died, my sister took her to the temple. There she was cared for and taught. Every lunar, I visited her. Then your people came and took me away. Let me stay here and try to see her."

"You must return to town," Guerro said. "Pizarro will want to know what was said." He wheeled his horse and rode toward the town. Qhari followed.

* * * *

The next morning when Coyllur woke, Chaquira was gone. Coyllur and Coca dressed, ate and went to the weaving room. Where had the priestess gone? Coyllur sat at a loom and began to work. She ignored the conversations around her. The chatter of the women halted abruptly. She looked up and froze.

Suka sauntered through the room. He pointed to several of the younger women. He nodded to Coyllur and Coca. "You and you. Go to the baths. You will travel with the Inca to his meeting with the gods. Perhaps he will give you to them. Don't look to Chaquira. She can't help you."

Coyllur shivered. Had he harmed her aunt? Had the priestess deserted them? Coyllur rose and followed Coca to the baths.

* * * *

Guerro frowned. Who was the woman sitting in Qhari's room? Guerro and the translator had become friends during the voyage and Guerro had been assigned as the man's guard. The interpreter placed his fingers on his lips. "My sister. Chaquira is a Sun Priestess."

"We're alone." Guerro looked closer and recognized the woman he'd seen during the visit to the Inca. "Is your daughter here?"

Qhari shook his head. "Chaquira came alone. She has a tale and a favor to ask."

Guerro sat on a stool with his back against the wall. "I listen."

Qhari translated the woman's words. "That's the story." He looked up. "What do you think?"

Guerro smiled. "The moment I saw your daughter, I knew I'd come to this land to make her mine and keep her safe."

"Then you will flee with us when we leave?" Qhari asked. "You may not see your home again."

"Matters little. When I joined Pizarro, my father disowned me. I'm but a younger son and have no thought of inheriting anything. There is little in Spain for me." He rose. "I need to learn what Pizarro plans for the evening. When I return, we'll discuss the rescue."

* * * *

Coyllur and Coca took their places in one of the litters. Coyllur frowned. None of the Inca's guards were armed. Why had he eschewed protection? Did he believe these strangers were the gods who had promised to return?

Sumac sat at the Inca's side. Coyllur studied the others. Where was Suka? Once he'd made his selection, he had vanished. The bearers lifted the poles and the long line set forth for Cajamarca.

When they reached the town, the sun was setting. The distant mountain peaks were stained with the color of fresh blood. Coyllur swallowed her fears. Was this an omen? No one waited in the plaza to greet them. What had gone wrong?

Two men appeared. One wore a robe the color of the night. He carried a black object in his hands. Coyllur's father was the second man.

The dark-robed man spoke then Coyllur's father said words. "This man of God says you must swear fealty to his god and king." The priest held the black object toward the Inca. "Place your hands on this and give oath to Christ, the greatest king of all."

Atahualpa jerked back. "I rule these lands. I will meet your king as a brother, not a servant."

The black priest's eyes narrowed. His face flamed. He raised his hands and dropped them. A boom resounded. As men fell to the ground, Coyllur screamed.

"Santiago." The cry came from the strangers.

Men burst into the square. Their shouts blended with the screams. The litter bearers tried to flee, but there were too many bodies in the way. Coyllur watched the one holding the Inca topple. Her litter tilted and she slid toward the ground. She screamed for Coca.

Someone grabbed her. Who? As she was carried into the shadows, she saw the Inca and Sumac being dragged to one of the houses.

The man who held her lowered her so she could stand. She looked into the face of the man from her dreams.

"Safe," he said. "Qhari friend."

She turned to look at the chaos in the square. "Coca, my friend. Where is she?"

He shook his head and pointed to her. "You Coyllur. I Guerro." He raised her hand to his lips.

Coyllur felt threads of heat circle her heart. This was right and good. He pulled her into his arms and brushed her lips with his. His tongue slid along her mouth. She breathed in the scent of him and knew this closeness had happened before. His hands moved along her arms. She wanted him to caress her flesh the way he had in those dreams.

"Qhari. Come. Need words."

"I teach."

"Come." He led her to the house where the men had taken the Inca. While some of them tried to grab her, he pressed her against his side. He spoke and they moved away. Coyllur saw her father and the Inca. She broke from Guerro and ran to the man she hadn't seen for years. "Father."

"Coyllur." He kissed her forehead. "Chaquira and Coca wait for you."

She turned to look at the Inca and gasped. What had these men done to him? His clothes were torn. Streaks of dirt stained his skin. His eyes were wary and haunted.

She looked at her father. "What have they done?"

"Made him a prisoner."

Coyllur sighed. The Inca was doomed. A condor could not live in a cage.

Sumac rose. She grabbed Coyllur's arm. "So your father betrayed him. For this, you will die and so will he. Suka remains free to seek vengeance."

The Inca shook his head. "Take no action. Fate marked us for this event." His smile reflected sadness. "I will offer them gold and silver if they let me go."

Guerro pulled Coyllur toward the door. A group of men appeared. He pulled her into the shadows.

The black-robed man headed the group. The ice in his dark eyes made Coyllur grasp Guerro's hand. Would the Inca die today and would she be one of the women to accompany him?

The Inca rose. He nodded to Qhari. "Tell them of my offer. I will give them enough gold and silver to fill this room."

Qhari related the message. One of the men laughed. "I would see this done. Tell him he will live this day."

The black robe nodded and left the room. Guerro drew Coyllur outside.

* * * *

Guerro didn't like the way the other men had looked at Coyllur. She was his and not one to be passed around. He hurried her to the small house he shared with Qhari. Chaquira and Coca were preparing a meal. He left Coyllur with them and went to find a priest. He was delighted when he saw the secretary. This man would be a good choice for what was needed.

"Can I help you, my son?"

Guerro nodded. "I wish to wed one of the native women."

The priest frowned. "Why?"

"To protect her. She is Qhari's daughter. He has served us well. I fear when the Inca dies, the natives will kill her."

"Why would they do that?"

"Their custom is to send virgins with the Inca when they die. Also, she has an enemy at the Inca's side. This woman threatened Coyllur's life."

The priest tented his hands and nodded. "She must convert willingly. If she agrees, come to the square near that building tonight." He pointed to the Sun Temple.

"She will agree."

"What will you do if my superior is angry? What about your family in Spain?"

"Your superior should be pleased since I will not commit a sin by laying with a woman not my wife." Guerro hung his head. "I am a younger son and my father cast me off. Please, Father, this must be done."

"Then I will."

Guerro returned to the house. Qhari was with the women. Guerro reached for a bowl of stew. "What is happening with the Inca?"

"In the morning, he will send chasquis to begin the collection of gold and silver. Months will pass before the treasure is assembled."

"Then he will die," Guerro said.

Qhari nodded. "Before that day comes, we must be gone. What of my child?"

"I'll marry her tonight. You must explain to her what will be done. Like you, she must swear to God and the Christ."

Quari turned to the women and spoke. The priestess nodded and spoke. Though Guerro understood some of the words, he waited for the interpreter to speak.

"We will leave tonight after the ceremony. There is a place where we can stay until it is safe. Coca and my sister will go soon and gather things we need for the journey. I will stay to guide you." He beckoned to Coyllur. "Come. I will tell her what she must do."

* * * *

Coyllur followed her father and Guerro. "What did you say to him?"

"Tonight the Spanish priest will marry you and Guerro. Once this is done, you will lead us through the temple."

She nodded. "I know the way. All the temples are the same. Tell me more of what I must do tonight."

"The priest will ask you questions. You must agree to do all he says."

She nodded. "But I don't know their tongue."

"I will tell you what he says."

She heard a sound and turned. Guerro stood in the doorway. "Will you do this?" he asked.

"I will be your wife."

After dark, they left the house and made their way across the square. A figure slid from the shadows. "Coyllur."

She gasped. Suka stepped into view. He held a knife.

"Coyllur, in the days to come, now or in the future, all you love will die and you will know when all I have done comes to pass. When you see the emerald in a cage of gold and silver, you will know. Stranger, I will find a way to take your wealth."

* * * *

Guerro thrust Coyllur into her father's arms. "Who is he?"

"Sun Priest. Enemy." Coyllur's whisper reached his ears. When the Sun Priest spoke again, Guerro cursed his poor understanding of the native language.

"What is he saying?" Guerro asked.

"He says, 'Coyllur, I have marked you for death," Qhari said. "You will die with this stranger. He cannot win over what he set in motion in the far past. Greed for wealth and power rule him now as then."

"Not so," Guerro said. "I have no wealth other than love."

"Suka, Sun Priest." Coyllur's words came slowly. "You are the one who thirsts for power. You betrayed the Inca and your lover, Sumac. She will follow Atahualpa into death."

"Do you think I care?" Suka ran toward Guerro.

Guerro kicked the Sun Priest's arm. The knife clattered on the ground. Guerro's fist connected with the native's jaw and knocked him backwards. His head hit the ground.

"Bind and gag him," the Spanish priest said. "I'll take him to where the other prisoners are kept."

Coyllur said something. Her father translated. "Put him with the Inca so he can spend his last days serving the man he betrayed."

The Spanish priest smiled. "A good move. Now for the ceremony. Kneel and take each other's hands. I will hear your pledges." With Coyllur's father speaking the priest's words in Quecha, the pledges were made. The priest drew them to their feet. "Go with my blessing. I will inform Pizarro you should have a few days with no duties."

Guerro gave the priest the gold cup he'd received from the Inca. "With my thanks, Father."

When the priest and his prisoner vanished, Guerro pulled Coyllur into his arms. He started to lead her to the house where he could feast on her body.

Qhari touched Guerro's arm. "We must leave now.

Chaquira has found a change of clothes for you."

Guerro groaned. His time with Coyllur must wait.

* * * *

Guerro growled with frustration. Long days of travel with stops at the way stations had kept him from consummating the marriage. His companions didn't seem to understand the necessity. Until he and Coyllur were united in body, the marriage wasn't valid. If they had wed in Spain, observers would be waiting to view the stained sheets. He had other reasons to wish the union was complete. His desire for Coyllur grew stronger every day. He feared when they were finally alone, he would fall on her and satisfy his needs with no thought to hers.

They left the main road and traveled along a narrow trail into a high valley. When they arrived, most of the people were in the fields. An old woman greeted Chaquira and showed her two small houses that were vacant and ready to be occupied.

Chaquira sent Qhari and Coca into one. "I will join you after I have blessed this pair." She stood in the doorway of their house and drew an emerald wrapped in a cage of gold and silver wire. She placed the gem in Coyllur's hand. "May the Sun and Moon bless your union and the emerald bring you the fruits of the earth."

"Thank you." Guerro smiled. The days of travel had given him an understanding of the native language. He took Coyllur's hand and led her into the second house. At last they would be alone. His body reacted to the thought. His engorged organ rubbed against the breechcloth. Eagerness for Coyllur warred with the need for care.

Just inside the doorway, he drew her into his arms and kissed her the way he'd yearned for so long. He explored her lips with his tongue and ran his hands over her back until they reached her buttocks. He pressed her against his erection and urged her mouth open.

He thrust his tongue into her mouth. His hold on her tightened. The sweetness of her response urged him to rush. He couldn't. He had to make this time a wonder. He explored her mouth and savored the timid touches of her tongue on his.

When he freed her mouth, he sucked in deep breaths and stepped back. He drew his tunic over his head. She touched his chest lightly and smiled when his nipples tightened. Lightning shot to his groin. His penis throbbed.

He opened her belt and tossed it aside. He slid his hands beneath the open sides. Her skin was smooth, silken.

"Guerro," she sighed.

He smiled. "Soon you will be my wife by deed." He slid the dress over her head and admired her body. Full breasts, narrow waist, flaring hips and the long legs he ached to have wrapped around him. "You are beautiful."

A flush spread over her body. "No man has seen me thus."

His smile broadened into a grin. "I like what I see." He removed the breechcloth. His penis sprang free. The thick rod pulsed. He stepped toward her and ran his fingers over her breasts. The nipples tightened. He rolled them between his fingers and heard her gasp.

"Guerro, what should I do?"

"Come into my arms and touch your lips to mine."

She moved closer. He put his hands on her shoulders and drew her against his chest. Her erect nipples thrust against his skin. She opened her mouth to his probing tongue.

His hands glided over her back, stroking and massaging. He wanted to lay her on the mat and thrust until his seed filled her womb. He couldn't. To rush would cause her pain instead of the pleasure he wanted to bring.

She raised her mouth from his. "I feel strange. Hot."

"As do I." He lifted her into his arms and carried her to the mat. He lay beside her. He grazed his fingers over her face then leaned forward to nip her mouth. When he turned on his side, he propped himself up with one elbow. He cupped one breast. His tongue trailed from her mouth, across her chin and along her throat.

Her sighs made him smile. When he lapped her nipples, she moaned and reached for him. "Guerro, please."

He raised his head. "Soon, my star." He pressed his hands on the mat and rose over her. Her legs parted and he knelt between them. With hands and mouth, he explored her breasts and her abdomen. The sounds she made raised his desire to a peak.

His fingers stroked the nest of hair between her legs. As he stroked, he felt moisture form. Soon she would be ready. He found a spot that made her moan in a restless dance. He thrust a finger into her passage, then two and three in hopes of making her ready to receive him.

"Guerro, Guerro." As she cried his name, she tightened around his fingers.

He drew them out and thrust into her. She gave a gasp. He caught her mouth in a fierce kiss and began to thrust and withdraw. She wrapped her legs around his hips and grasped his shoulders. As one, they moved. He raised his head. The pressure built and erupted. "Coyllur," he cried. "Mine now. Mine forever."

* * * *

Astrid groaned. Where was she? She pressed her hands against the floor. The vault! She fought panic that bordered on incoherence. Once her heart rate slowed and her breathing became less than panicked gulps, she wrapped her arms around her knees. Memories of the dream trip to Peru circled in her thoughts.

We broke the curses from Egypt. Why did the trouble continue? Then she recalled the Sun Priest and his ravings. Years ago, Madelaine's father had been killed, but not the others who were the loved ones. What else had he said? The wealth.

Clive had wanted to bleed Duncan through blackmail. That scheme had failed.

What now? She needed to escape, but there was no way to open the door from this side. How long could she survive in here? There was air, but no water or food.

She pressed a button on the side of her watch. Eleven fifteen. Had Jan arrived? Would she wait or leave? Duncan and her father could be here any time. Would they come to the shop? She wondered if there was a way to let someone know she was here.

After feeling her way to the door, she pressed her ear against the metal. Oh for a stethoscope so she could hear if anyone was in the shop. She kicked the door and heard a dull thud. With renewed hope, she groped on the shelves for something to use to bang on the door.

* * * *

Duncan reached the rehab center at nine thirty. Before going to the billing offices, he loaded Lloyd's suitcases in the trunk. The financial end was easily handled. Shortly after ten, he and Lloyd headed back to Rockleigh.

"I will be glad to be home," Lloyd said.

"Imagine you will."

Lloyd heaved a sigh. "Have to ask you something."

"Go ahead."

"I know she's an adult and it's not my business, but what's happening with you and my daughter?"

Duncan gripped the wheel. "Right now, nothing." He sucked in a breath. "She said she loves me, but she doesn't want to see me."

Lloyd nodded. "How does that make you feel?"

"Confused. If I'd met her down the road...."

Lloyd leaned back. "Know how you feel. That happened with Sarah. Met her too soon after my divorce, so I thought. We settled for friendship, but she never said how she felt about me."

"Astrid doesn't mince words."

Lloyd chuckled. "Guess she doesn't. Last night I asked Sarah to marry me. Says she will. I think of all the time we wasted and groan. Can't tell you what to do though."

"I don't know either. " Duncan looked at the older man. "Part of the problem is those dreams she's having. She thinks we're fated to love and die. Spooks me."

"Can't say I blame you. Think on this. If you believe you would love her in a few years, why not now?"

Duncan frowned. He had no answer for the question.

When they reached Rockleigh, they parked behind the shop. Duncan frowned. "Why is Astrid's car still here?"

"Maybe she went to the city by bus, or she could have gone with Sarah. She said she had some shopping to do there."

"Could be." Duncan carried Lloyd's suitcases to the apartment. "Need anything?" he asked.

"Can't think of a thing. Thanks." Lloyd clasped Duncan's hand. "We'll talk about a bit of payback once I learn how much Clive siphoned off. Still can't believe he's a thief."

Duncan nodded. "Makes two of us. No hurry on the payback. It's only money and I have plenty."

"Hope you didn't say that to Astrid."

"Afraid I did."

"Then good luck in your chase."

"Right." Duncan headed down the steps.

As he strode to his car, he noticed a cell phone on the

ground. He stooped to pick it up. As he straightened, Jan dashed around the corner. "Have you seen Astrid?"

"No."

She frowned. "She was supposed to meet me here around eleven. I was a bit late."

"Maybe she's delayed in the city."

"She didn't say anything about going there. The odd thing is the door of Antiquities is unlocked and ... the place doesn't look right."

"I'll check." Duncan hurried around the corner and slipped into Antiquities. When he looked around, he noticed the open cases and though he wasn't sure, there seemed to be pieces missing. He reached for his cell phone to call the police when it rang. "Garrett," he said.

"So where are you, my friend?"

"Clive."

"Yes."

"What are you up to?"

Clive laughed. "I'm a man in need of cash and you're the one with a ready supply. Have some things that belong to a friend of yours and one that belongs to you. How does a million sound?"

"Pardon me."

"Astrid. She's in a safe place. When I have the money, I'll tell you where."

Duncan felt cold. What had Clive done? He heard Lorna's laughter. "Tell him she's in the dark. A safe, dark place."

"Where?" Duncan asked.

"The money."

"Do you think I can get that much in a short time?"

"Maybe not, but you can get a quarter mil with no problem. When I have that in hand, I'll tell you where Astrid is. With the rest sent to an account in the Caymans, I'll tell you where the jewelry and things are. Lloyd's going to have a lot to explain, and if you're thinking to do what I figure, you'll want to help him, too."

"Two hundred and fifty thousand. Where and when?" Duncan asked. He'd bargain with Clive, but once Astrid was safe, he'd think about the rest. Clive didn't know how much dirt he had on him.

"The beach house. As soon as you can manage. She won't survive in the safe place forever."

"Will do. Give me three or four hours." Sure, he thought. Not if he could locate Astrid first. He sent Jan for Lloyd and tried to think of which accounts he could tap.

Where could they have taken her? He heard a tapping noise from the office. He walked toward the open door and saw the overturned chair. The steady beating grew louder. The vault! Numbers he hadn't wanted to hear flashed in his thoughts. He tapped the numbers and opened the door.

Astrid nearly conked him with a metal bar. He swept her into his arms.

* * * *

Just as Astrid aimed another blow, the door opened. To keep from slamming the bar into Duncan's head, she opened her hand. The metal clanged on the floor. Duncan captured her mouth in a kiss that seared a path to her lower abdomen. For a time, she surrendered to the need threatening to destroy her vow to forget this man.

She pulled away. "Move. We have to stop Lorna and Clive. They've looted the shop."

"They won't get away. Your dad's calling the police to report the burglary."

She heaved a sigh. "Too late. They've had two hours to get away."

He shook his head. "They've left Rockleigh, but I know where they are."

"Then let's go."

"And jump into danger. Not a good idea."

She pushed past him and left the office. Her father stood at the counter. "Dad."

He turned. "Where were you?"

"Clive locked me in the vault. If Duncan would tell me where Clive and Lorna are, I'd go after them."

Lloyd put a hand on her arm. "No need. The police are on the way."

Duncan joined them. He reached for a pen and jotted on a scrap of paper. "I have somewhere to go. Tell the police they'll be there for at least three hours. They're waiting for a ransom."

Astrid stared at the paper and memorized the address. Must be the beach house. She started to the door.

"Astrid," Lloyd called. "Where are you going?"

"To make sure they don't escape." She dashed outside

and sprinted around the building for her car. Duncan grasped her shoulders. "You can't go after them."

She whirled. "Why not? I can't let them make off with Dad's things."

"Let the police solve the matter."

She tried to shrug him off. "I'm going."

He pulled her against his chest. "Then we'll take my car."

She slid into the passenger's seat and fastened the seatbelt. Duncan started the car. When he reached the street, he turned away from the bridge. "Where are we going?" she asked.

"To my house. We need to talk."

"I've said all I'm going to."

He turned his head and flashed a grin. "I haven't."

She slumped against the seat. "We have to see this to the end."

"We will. After they're arrested. No sense putting ourselves at risk."

Astrid clenched her fists. "We're not in danger. The curse ended in Peru."

"You had another dream."

She nodded. "In the vault. Clive shoved an emerald he said was flawed into my hand. He knew about the curses. In Peru, he was a Sun Priest. When the Spanish priest married Coyllur and Guerro, the curse was broken, but the Sun Priest vowed to kill those she loved and to take his wealth."

"Looks like he partially succeeded. Madelaine's father was killed."

"But the others lived. This time, no one has died." She looked at him. "He could still take your money."

Duncan pressed the opener for the gate. "He tried and failed twice."

"Twice?"

"Through Lorna and then the ransom for you and the goods from Antiquities." He parked the car and got out. At the passenger's side, he opened her door and unfastened her seatbelt. "When he told me he had you hidden in a safe place, I knew I loved you."

Astrid stared at him. "You what?"

"Love you, need you in my life forever." He tugged her hand. "Let's go inside and decide where we're headed."

Once they were in the hall, he closed the door and pulled her into an embrace.

Their lips touched. The kiss raised liquid lightning that seared a path to her core. He stroked her back, nibbled her mouth. She felt his erection grow full and hard.

Need bubbled inside. She dug her fingers into his shoulders. Her back pressed against the cool plaster of the wall. He slid his hands beneath her silk shell and skimmed the cloth toward her head. He released her mouth and pulled the cloth over her head. He ran a finger along the edge of her bra. Her nipples thrust against the satin.

"Duncan." She grasped the open neck of his shirt and fumbled for the buttons. Unbuttoning would take too long. She wanted to feel his flesh beneath her hands. She gripped the cloth and ripped. The buttons flew.

Duncan laughed. "A bit impatient."

"I want you." She ran her hands over his chest, savoring the ripple of his muscles. She touched her tongue to his skin and tasted salt. His aroma stoked her desire.

"You'll have me deep and hard." He unfastened his trousers and pushed them down. After he stepped out of them, he popped the snaps of her bra. He dipped his head and teased her nipples with his teeth while he dragged her skirt to her waist. When he hooked his thumbs in the sides of her thong and drew it toward her feet, she unfastened the waist of her skirt and let it fall.

Duncan rose and feasted on her mouth. The plaster felt cool against her back, but his hands were hot and fevered on her skin. He slid his tongue into her mouth. She rubbed her erect nipples over his chest.

"Now, now," she cried.

"Soon."

When he gripped her waist, she raised one leg to his hip. He clasped her buttocks and lifted her. While he grasped her thighs, she leaned back and reached to guide him inside. A contented sigh flowed from her lips. He opened his mouth over hers. Tongues thrust and parried. She braced her hands on his shoulders and began to move. He matched her rhythm.

Astrid pressed her shoulders against the wall. She felt jolts of lightning and tightened her inner muscles. As she climaxed, she felt Duncan's forceful ejaculation. She cried his name and he cried hers. Their breaths came in ragged gasps. He let her slide over his sweat-slicked skin until her feet touched the floor. He covered her face with kisses.

Duncan staggered to the steps and sank onto one. Astrid walked to him. "I love you."

He pulled her onto his lap. "I love you. Marry me."

She leaned against his chest. "When?"

"Soon. We'll fill this house with children the way it was meant to be."

She looked up at him. "What about my career? I'm starting a Master's as a nurse practitioner."

He touched her lips with his fingers. "Work. Stay at home. Your choice. I'll hire a nanny or a dozen if you want."

"Maybe three." She pressed her lips to his throat. "Don't you think we'd better see what's happening at Antiquities?"

He winked. "I'd like to shower and change clothes first. I was attacked by a wild woman." He kissed her lightly.

"Wild woman loves wild man." She leaned into the kiss. Joy erupted. She was with the man she'd loved and lost time and again. This time he was hers forever.

THE END

Don't miss out on collecting these exciting Harmony™
titles for your collection:

Clone Wars: Armageddon by Kaitlyn O'Connor (Futuristic
Romance) Trade Paper 1-58608-775-4
*Living in a world devastated by one disaster after another,
it's natural for people to look for a target to blame for their
woes, and Lena thinks little of it when new rumors begin to
circulate about a government conspiracy. She soon
discovers, though, that the government may or may not be
conspiring against its citizens, but someone certainly is.
Morris, her adoptive father, isn't Morris anymore, and the
mirror image of herself that comes to kill her most
definitely isn't a long lost identical twin.*

The Devil's Concubine by Jaide Fox (Fantasy Romance)
Trade Paper 1-58608-776-2
*A great contest was announced to decide who would win
the hand of Princess Aliya, accounted the most fair young
maiden in the land. The ruler of every kingdom was invited-
-every kingdom that is save those of the unnaturals. When
King Talin, ruler of the tribe of Golden Falcons learned of
the slight, he was enraged. He had no desire to take a mere
man child as his bride, but he would allow the insult to go
unchallenged.*

Zhang Dynasty: Seduction of the Phoenix by Michelle M.
Pillow (Futuristic Romance) Trade Paper 1-58608-777-0
*A prince raised in honor and tradition, a woman raised
with nothing at all. She wants to steal their most sacred
treasure. He'll do anything to protect it, even if it means
marrying a thief.*

Warriors of the Darkness by Mandy M. Roth (Paranormal Romance) Trade Paper 1-58608-778-9
In place where time and space have no boundaries, ancient enemies would like nothing more than to eradicate them both, just when they've found each other.

COMING in APRIL:

Labyrinth of the Beast by Desiree Acuna (Erotic Fantasy Romance) Trade Paper 1-58608-782-7

Conclave of Shadows by Julia Keaton (Historical Romance) Trade Paper 1-58608-780-0